S0-AIB-210

Antiques From Hell

Antiques From Hell

by

P. L. Hartman

Strategic Book Publishing and Rights Co.

Copyright © 2020 P. L. Hartman. All rights reserved.

No part of this book may be reproduced or transmitted in any form
or by any means, graphic, electronic, or mechanical, including
photocopying, recording, taping, or by any information storage
retrieval system, without the permission, in writing, of the publisher.
For more information, send an email to support@sbpra.net,
Attention Subsidiary Rights Department.

This is a work of fiction. Names, characters, places and incidents
are products of the author's imagination or are used fictitiously
and are not to be construed as real. Any resemblance to actual
events, locales, organizations or persons, living or dead, is entirely
coincidental.

Strategic Book Publishing and Rights Co., LLC
USA | Singapore
www.sbpra.net

For information about special discounts for bulk purchases, please
contact Strategic Book Publishing and Rights Co. Special Sales, at
bookorder@sbpra.net.

ISBN: 978-1-952269-61-5

Book Design: Suzanne Kelly
Cover Art: Jim O'Brien

My thanks to a couple of school superintendents: Sel, who gave me inspiration, and Z, who gave me the lowdown. And to a couple of business managers, Tim and Bob who, along with the guys and gals in PASBO, clued me in on the fiscal goings-on of school districts. Thanks to my friends and fellow dealers at Apple Hill Antiques, whose enthusiasm for "old stuff" never quits. Always, my gratitude to Bill, invaluable source of knowledge and assistance, and to Tod, who forever encourages me.

Abandon All Hope, Ye Who Enter Here
Inscription on the Gateway to Hell from Dante's *Inferno*

...I hope the land will heal.
Jamie Hodges, *Driller's Lament*

Prologue

In the early morning hours on the third of February, while a swirling snowstorm descended on the hills and hollows of Cross County, the Elk Creek elementary school burned to the ground.

The school's location, at the end of a rural lane with playground and playing fields on either side and a wooded slope rising behind, was undoubtedly isolated. Still, there were a handful of houses in the vicinity and a mobile home park only a short walk away, where many of the children who attended the school lived. It would be expected that some of the neighbors might have noticed dark smoke mingling with the blowing snow or smelled the acrid odor of burning insulation or even, had anyone been up in the middle of the night and looked in that direction, seen a red flickering glow. Or heard a crash when the roof fell in.

But it was a weeknight, so most people had turned in early and, because television reception was affected by the weather, no one was staying up to watch TV. Windows were shut against the storm and the wind was making a racket all night. And, since many households were heated with wood stoves, a smoke pall hanging over the neighborhood in winter was a common occurrence.

It would have been the residents of the closest house who could not have failed to notice. However, quite unexpectedly, they were off in Florida for a month's vacation, a surprise gift from a distant relative. The result of this series of circumstances was that the fire did not get reported until the next morning.

By 7:00 AM, snow was still coming down and when the volunteer fire company arrived, there was little they could do. The fire had mostly burned itself out, while snow continued to pile up. The firefighters put yellow tape around the site and left, postponing an investigation until the snow subsided.

As was the usual winter storm procedure, the Colton Area School District's business manager, who subscribed to a service providing advanced, detailed weather information, had called a snow day the previous afternoon and all classes in the district had been cancelled. When he was alerted by the fire company, he immediately set about trying to reach the district's superintendent, who had been out of town, although due to return the evening before. But he was not able to make contact by phone, text or email. After leaving several messages, he turned his attention to finding space in other schools for the children displaced by the fire. This logistical task was made easier by the fact that he had already been studying enrollment demographics, since the school board had begun to look at closing one of the district's elementary schools.

It wasn't until the following day that the fire investigators were able to get into the burned-out school. There they found empty gasoline cans, several disposable lighters and charred, disfigured remains, identified as the superintendent of the Colton Area School District.

Chapter 1

The skinny guy in the battered black pickup had been waiting in the parking lot for nearly an hour. For a time, he wandered around his truck, sipping coffee from a foam cup and scrutinizing the many dents and rust patches on the truck's body. Once he walked over to where the orchard began at the edge of the parking lot. He came back zipping up his pants, then stood leaning against the side of the pickup, facing east into the slanting sunlight of a morning in early October. There was heavy dew and it was still chilly, not yet 9:30, but even though the shop didn't open until 10:00, he was in no mood to mind. He was content to wait, waiting being something he was accustomed to, and because he was very sure that what he had on the passenger seat, wrapped in an old blanket, would be bought and for an extremely good price. He knew about antiques dealers and he also knew that he would not have to answer, truthfully at least, any questions.

Elaine, first to arrive, came driving in at 9:40 and viewed the beat-up truck with a mixture of interest and disgust. Interest because, in spite of it being unlikely that here was a customer with money for antiques purchases, she was sure this was a person who had something to sell and she had experience with treasures lurking in unprepossessing vehicles. Disgust because, even though parked a tolerable distance from the wrought-iron post with its pretty gold-bordered *Cider Run Antiques* sign, and parked as if the owner were indeed conscious of the pickup's disreputable appearance, to Elaine's finely-honed sensibility the truck was a blot on the landscape. Dressed impeccably in a linen suit with her trademark strand of pearls, a bouquet of Michaelmas daisies in hand, she emerged from her new model SUV with a sigh and muttered disdainfully to herself, "Cross County."

Nevertheless, she gave him a smile and paused to see if he would approach her with an offer, an offer that, over the thirty-plus years she'd been dealing in antiques, she'd heard how many times? Hundreds, probably. She couldn't even begin to remember how often she'd bought antiques from people who needed money or more space or help with a relative's out-of-control clutter. She'd certainly bought from people like this pickup driver, ones who came in rusted-out cars and dented trucks, where the offer, usually accompanied by downcast eyes, was delivered with an apologetic air: "Have a look at something I got, it's out in the parking lot, not much but maybe you'd be interested or can someone else come see?"

Quite often she did buy and both parties went away satisfied, because Elaine was honest about what the items would fetch and fair in her prices. But the skinny guy just gave her a little nod by way of acknowledgement and didn't shift his position, and Elaine walked on to the shop, unlocking the door and locking it again behind her.

No, he said to himself, this swell lady isn't who I want. He'd driven up to Marten County, to the antiques co-op that had over a dozen dealers to see one person in particular, one who dealt in what he'd come to sell. He'd wait and maybe have a look around the shop, to get an idea of what things sold for in case he decided to bring more stuff in. Yep, he'd wait.

It was Hal, in his company's truck with *Thompson Engineering* tastefully printed on the doors, a newly refinished chestnut dining table secured in the bed, who came next. He eyed the pickup and its driver with a wrinkled brow but getting out said cheerily, "Good morning!" and, being an all-around genial sort and a stalwart member of the Presbyterian church, went over to shake his hand and extend a greeting. "Are you here to see one of our dealers?" Hal asked pleasantly, knowing unequivocally why he was hanging around the parking lot. Hal also noted that the bottoms of his pants were wet, figured he'd been in the tall grass of the orchard and for what purpose, and with the accuracy borne of long familiarity with that part of Pennsylvania, thought to himself, "Cross County."

The skinny guy straightened up slightly and, with a jerk of his chin in the direction of the shop, said somewhat warily, "You the guy that does firearms?"

Of course, thought Hal, I might have known, with that cap he's got on, *Sure-Shot Taxidermy*. "No, you'll want Keith Mackinnon. He'll be here any minute. Do you mind waiting outside? We're not open yet, but will be at 10:00."

The skinny guy gave a nod, mumbled, "No problem," and Hal went into the shop.

It wasn't Keith driving up next but Owen, riding his bicycle, because it was a Saturday and he didn't have to commute forty-five minutes by car from Martensdale to his job. He was winded, he was sweating, but he was happy, looking forward to being at the shop among friends, among antiques: no stress, no tension. He didn't even notice the figure by the pickup or even the truck itself, but unbuckled his bike helmet and, swinging it carelessly by the strap, walked his bike quickly in the door.

The skinny guy saw him, though, and did a double take. He rubbed his chin, squinted and lowered the cap over his eyes. No doubt about it. It was Mr. Griffith, the vice-principal at the high school. What the hell was he doing here? Was he one of them antiques dealers? Must be. Gotta watch my step, he thought.

Then Keith's car pulled in and he got out. The skinny guy detached himself from his truck, walked over to Keith and asked, "You Mr. Mackinnon?"

"Right," Keith said. "You've come to see me?"

"Got somethin' in the truck there I thought you might be interested in." Hastily revising his strategy, he added, "I'm sort of in a hurry, so could you have a look at it out here?"

"Glad to," Keith answered amiably.

I'm no different than a hunting dog with its blood up, Keith thought about himself. It's like a scent, the scent of opportunity, of something scarce. You don't hesitate, you can never tell what might be on offer. You just go right for the goods, even when they're brought in by someone, obviously, from Cross County.

Chapter 2

Marten County, and especially the college town of Martensdale, had long enjoyed an existence both prosperous and cultured. With its favorable geography spanning several ridges and valleys of the Appalachians of central Pennsylvania, Marten County had the combined wealth of iron ore in its timbered hills and fertile farm land in its wide valleys. The iron ore brought industry and commerce, created rich, civic-minded businessmen and quite a few governors of the Commonwealth. The farms fed, clothed and sent their products to people across the area, the Prohibition years being no exception, as corn went to stills instead of mills. In Martensdale a major university grew up, attracting scholars from all over the country and around the world. The town was a cosmopolitan mixture with excellent schools, art, music and cultural events.

Cross County, on the other hand, was an area of less auspicious circumstances. Settlers found the mountains more daunting, the valleys narrower, rocky, prone to flooding. There were more hollows, deeper forests and heavier snows in winter. In time, jobs came with the coal mines, but the owners lived elsewhere and most of the real wealth went to Pittsburgh. The towns that grew up with the coal boom began to die during the Great Depression of the Thirties, and decayed further when the mines closed in the Seventies. Red brick buildings, once proudly housing stores and banks, theaters, hotels and Ford garages, gradually fell vacant. In Cross County, rural electrification was slow to come and the outdoor privy remained an acceptable alternative.

Even the origin of its name was indicative of the county's humble nature. Colonel Marcus Parmalee Tyler, writing in 1888, left no doubt about the infelicitous impression this mostly vertical region had on the first would-be settlers. In his acclaimed reference work, *The History of Cross & Marten Counties, Pennsylvania*, he states that "not only did the wagons find rough passage, but the soil had little to recommend itself to those who were set on tillage as their livelihood." He goes on to comment, "In attempting to traverse this inhospitable territory numerous unfortunate accidents occurred, including grievous damage to many a wagon's undercarriage." Instead of giving up then and there, settlers chose to continue their journey as soon as possible "after making what repairs they could effect." The rugged terrain was a powerful deterrent to settling, and the whole area was seen as an impediment merely to be crossed on the way to more propitious places for homesteading.

And yet, there were those who stayed. They did so because they appreciated the intense beauty of wildness, the intimacy with nature possible in such a setting. Its topography gave the place a remoteness which resonated with those living there. Mountain folk: that's how they thought of themselves, and proud to be. This semi-isolated existence, not totally isolated, as there was the railroad, and city people built hunting camps and resorts and managed the mines, had two distinctive results. One was the trait of staunch self-sufficiency among the inhabitants, certainly a laudable characteristic in the early days, although possibly taking some unhealthy turns in later years.

The second result, a consequence of the understandable need to hang onto things, had an unforeseen and benign outcome: a quantity of indigenous, oft-times unique, and absolutely genuine antiques. And even though of late the stream had turned into a trickle as the amount diminished, every year a few surprising finds were made. In the back of barns, hidden in cupboards, moldering in basements, languishing in attics, decaying beneath blackberry brambles, or underneath piles of junk in garages, they had slowly come to light, to be sold to antiques dealers and their lucky customers. Some, that is, not all. Since many mountain people had the habit of mistrust, goods were often stowed away in secret places. A self-defeating tactic; assets could be lost over time, never surfacing or, surfacing by accident, raising unsettling questions about ownership.

But now, because Cross County sat atop the rich natural gas deposits of the Marcellus Shale, changes were occurring, most of them obvious but some much subtler, which had the ability to set off a whole chain reaction of unanticipated effects.

Saturday morning at the shop: Elaine behind the front counter, getting the computer and cash drawer ready for sales, Hal back in the kitchen brewing a pot of coffee, and Owen turning on lights in dealers' areas. Keith came in the door and, since it was nearly 10:00, did not relock it behind him. As he passed by the long oak church pew that defined one side of the entrance and came abreast of the front counter, Elaine raised an eyebrow and gave him a quizzical look. "Hal said there was a guy out there waiting for you. So, what did he have?" she asked.

"Several teeth missing," Keith said smartly, lingering, ready to get a rise out of Elaine.

Elaine snorted at the evasion. "Come on, give. What did you buy? I know you bought something. You have that cat-who-ate-the-cream expression. It's written all over you."

Having seen Keith arrive, Owen hurried up to the front counter. He had caught only the tail-end of the conversation, but leapt right in. "It's that new mustache of his, Elaine. A man with a mustache can get away with anything because you can't tell what's going on underneath it."

Keith, taller by a head than the athletic, excitable Owen, reached over and tousled his hair. "You've got bike helmet hair, little buddy. I'm going to call Lynn and tell her to come and comb it for you."

Owen swatted Keith's hand away. "Aw, cut that out!" he protested.

Elaine said, "Keith is very full of himself because he has just bought some major antique out in the parking lot off of a guy from Cross County. I'm right, aren't I, Keith? He was from Cross County, wasn't he?"

"What guy?" Owen asked. "I didn't see any guy."

"Parked near the orchard," Elaine explained. "He was here when I pulled in. Skinny guy. Wearing a cap advertising a taxidermist. Driving a truck that must have had a very bad winter, several very bad winters."

"And you think he was from down in Cross County?"

"There's no question," Elaine stated emphatically.

"How so?"

Keith answered for Elaine, "The diagnostic gaps in his smile. Not that he ever really smiled. Hey, Owen," Keith went on encouragingly, "now that you're the Principal-in-charge-of-Vice at the Colton Area High School, we've been wondering, you still brushing your teeth?"

All three of them would have been happy to keep going, having just warmed up, but before they went any further the door opened and the first customers of the day came in. Instantly the group at the front counter underwent a transformation, becoming professional, helpful dealers, ready and eager to share their knowledge of and passion for antiques.

The stone building that housed Cider Run Antiques was older than the antiques it contained. Dating from

1789, it was an original settler's cabin, built with limestone cleared off the hillside in order that an apple orchard could be planted. From cabin to farmhouse to inn with a second floor, to tavern with the second floor removed, and then to restaurant, speakeasy, and more restaurants, it was enlarged over the years and finally repurposed to become an antiques shop, refitted, rewired, air-conditioned, heated and ventilated, per Hal's engineering firm. It retained its age-darkened wood-beamed ceiling and handsome stone fireplace, both of which contributed to its ambience and enhanced the display of antiques. Located at the top of a hill, it had a sweeping view of Appalachian ridges. These features and its interesting history had given Cider Run the reputation of a destination not to be missed and, with fourteen dealers' areas, a treasure trove for antiques lovers.

Hal, making coffee in the kitchen, the large former restaurant kitchen, was justifiably proud of the shop. One of the founding partners, he had helped buy the place. Now having begun its fourth year, the shop and its dealers were thriving, enjoying success and becoming well-known for the variety and quality of their antiques. Of course, there was that rough time, Hal reflected, when a homicide had occurred in the shop. But they got through it and everyone became all the closer for it, redoubling their efforts to make Cider Run the best antiques shop around. People like Keith and Owen, best friends...

Keith and Owen! He just remembered the dining table sitting in the back of his truck. Sylvie, his wife and the family furniture expert, had transformed the tired wood and given it a softly gleaming finish. It needed to be brought into the shop, posthaste, so he'd better have a quick cup of coffee and get one of them to help him unload it before the day got busy. And what was that guy from Cross County selling anyway?

Chapter 3

What the skinny guy was selling was something Keith had heard about but had only seen a few times, one of the most sought-after of all American hunting pieces: a Parker double-barreled shotgun, circa early 1900s. Keith, who on weekdays was assistant director of housing and food services at the university, happily spent weekends in the role of antiques dealer. For years he had been buying antique firearms and military paraphernalia, a legacy from his stint in the army, and he also collected and sold antique sports equipment and hunting and fishing gear, as well as old coins. Keith and his wife had been friends with the Thompsons and, when Cider Run opened, he easily went from collector to dealer. Going to public sales, doing research and talking with people at the shop had made him more knowledgeable, made him even more appreciative of the rare and old things. But what was on offer this morning was way over the top. He couldn't wait to tell Owen.

Owen and his wife had also been collecting antiques for years. Owen's specialty was antique toys. Electric trains had first got him hooked, soon followed by all manner of railroad accessories: scenery, buildings, bridges, signs and stations, colorful snap-together Plasticville houses. Next in this logical progression came games, holiday items, toy cars and trucks and, at Lynn's urging, dollhouses and doll furnishings, all at least 50 years old—fun to buy and fun to sell.

Owen and Keith found it enjoyable to go to auctions together. Because they didn't compete in their merchandise, they could be supportive of each other's finds. Not unlike a self-improvement group was Cider Run, Owen had often thought. We all aid and abet and encourage each other because we understand this love and regard for antiques. And sometimes, he admitted, we do so because it makes our own impetuous purchases seem less extravagant.

That it wasn't their day job was a factor too. This was an avocation for the dealers at Cider Run. Some were retired, some had income-producing spouses, and others were working at jobs that gave them time, weekends at least, to indulge their passion. They were not killer dealers. They could afford to be laid back and they were. But that didn't mean that they weren't passionate about what they liked.

How passionate? Keith pondered this from time to time during the day. Was he passionate enough to buy something from an unknown source, something possibly illegally obtained, and most certainly bound to raise some uncomfortable questions in the "where did it come from" department? Never mind the cost which, to Keith familiar with prices for antique shotguns, was probably reasonable, even though astronomical in relation to most other things, never mind that. Well, maybe he'd better think about that, ethics aside.

On this Saturday, as most Saturdays, the shop was busy. Elaine had arranged for several people to come in, as she had recently scored an assortment of miniature oil paintings from an estate in the Poconos, signed, dated from 1920 through 1936. It was a find and they were going to go fast. Elaine hoped she could sell them to her regular, loyal customers before dealers from out of the area wandered in.

People were looking for furniture too, as the start of the school year at the university had brought new faculty to town, many still in the throes of furnishing their homes. It didn't seem to make a difference whether their houses were new or old. Antique furniture, from country to Victorian to Craftsman to Mid-century, whether left as original or refinished, imparted a defining character. Hal and Keith had agreed to deliver one marble-topped walnut chest of drawers after closing and when Hal had, not too surprisingly, sold Sylvie's just-finished dining table, it would be delivered as well.

The shop looked particularly attractive. Customers were greeted by the bouquet of daisies Elaine had brought in and arranged in the old wooden cider press by the front counter, and many of the dealers had autumnal touches in their areas. Stoneware crocks held cattails and copper bowls were filled with gourds. Globe-trotting Emmy, who never came back from her travels empty-handed, had put her British charity shop finds on a small mahogany table—interesting English silver fish knives and forks, set off by a natural linen runner and a dark green majolica pitcher containing dried flowers in russet hues. Sally Ann's stock of exuberantly colorful 1930s through 1960s housewares had a harvest motif. Wheat sheaves, apples, pears and grapes brightened tablecloths and dish towels, plates and juice glasses.

Someone had gone around the shop scattering autumn decorations here and there. "The decorating fairy" was how Keith described the person responsible, who always had supplies of seasonal embellishments to bestow indiscriminately. He figured it was probably one of the dealers who had taught elementary school, of which there were three, not counting Owen, who was a teacher at the high school before finishing his degree and making the switch to administrator. The decorating fairy has been at it again, Keith thought to himself, and has a sense of humor, because even stout iron farm implements were not spared, and little paper pumpkins had been artistically taped onto a manure spreader.

It was a good day of sales and it wasn't until nearly 5:00, while downing a soda in the kitchen, that Keith and Owen had a quiet moment.

"Owen," Keith began, "what do you know about Parker shotguns? There was a guy this morning selling..."

"A Parker?" Owen said excitedly, suddenly alert. "You bought a Parker? How much did it cost? Are you going to tell June and the kids? Where is it? Can I see it?"

Keith started to laugh at Owen's unfailing enthusiasm.

Owen went on, "Which kind is it? My grandfather on my mother's side had one. It got passed down to an uncle, not my mom. It wasn't the fancy kind with engraved scenes carved into it. I only saw it once. But it was a legend in the family, I mean, that we had a Parker at all, and my dad a shopkeeper in a coal town."

"Well, old pal," said Keith, "this is the engraved scenes kind and the carved stock kind and the interchangeable barrels kind and made, as far as I could tell, before 1920."

"Wow!" exclaimed Owen amazed by this astounding information. "Theodore Roosevelt had a Parker."

Keith nodded. "He even talked about it in his hunting books. Yes, this one has everything."

"And you paid how much?"

"Well, that's just it. I haven't bought it yet. I think I ought to check a few things out about it first. Like where it came from and who it has belonged to—the history of the piece."

"You took a picture of it, didn't you?"

"No. Guy wouldn't let me. So I need to find out more about it."

"Like if it's hot?"

"Yes, that too."

"How you gonna do that?" asked Owen doubtfully.

"That's where you come in, my friend," Keith grinned.

"Me? Why me?" Owen said frowning. "Oh, wait. Cross County. But I'm still pretty new in my job there; it's only been since last spring. I don't know that many people yet." Owen took a big gulp of his drink. "There's an antiques shop in town, but it's more of a second hand store and I've seen everything they have." Then he continued with rising excitement in his voice, "But it would be fun to snoop around. I'd get a chance at some really nifty antiques, I bet." He finished with a grin that matched Keith's. As had happened before with the two of them, there was a meeting of the minds, the mark of their friendship.

Keith said, "The engraving might give us some clues, since it was usually a custom job. I could describe it and see what the gun collectors' association can tell me. But what it was doing in Cross County, if that's where it came from: that's what we want to find out."

"Got it! Guy didn't realize who he was dealing with, someone who knows about forensic accounting and is a finance officer at the university. You don't look a whole lot like a big muckety-muck, but we know better." Owen relished the rare moment to get a dig in at Keith, who was a mere graduate student when they first met.

Keith was not about to let that pass. "Mr. Vice-Principal has had quite a meteoric rise himself. I remember him arranging 10th Grade science projects on a folding table in a back hallway in Martensdale High School, and getting beaned by fly balls during the baseball team's batting practice. Although, I guess, you did coach them to a few wins back then," he added.

"At least I've learned to duck faster."

"A skill one might need in Cross County," Keith advised.

The door to the kitchen swung open and Elaine came in. "Is Keith still gloating over his buy?" she asked Owen.

"I haven't bought it yet, Elaine," Keith admitted. "Owen's going to do a background check."

Owen assured her jauntily, "I may find out all sorts of things; I may also *find* all sorts of things. I'll see just what they've got down there."

"Apparently," Elaine said dryly, "a dearth of dentists."

Hal poked his head in. "Lynn's here for you, Owen. She doesn't want you riding your bike when it's almost dusk. Keith, we've got some deliveries, as soon as we can close up the shop."

As Owen and Keith left the kitchen, Owen asked, "How much does he want for it?"

"Twelve grand," replied Keith.

"Holy shit," Owen said respectfully.

Chapter 4

Owen had been hired by the Colton Area School District in April, the ink on his just-completed principal's certificate barely dry. Colton Area was the largest school district of the three in the county, Colton being the county seat and the only town of any size. There were no cities in Cross County; until now there had been but one traffic light in the whole county. The school district never had to go very far for their staff, since enough sons and daughters went away to college and returned to become teachers and a few, eventually, administrators.

But lately there had been changes occurring at the district, and the school board had reacted with some unprecedented hires. The year before Owen became assistant principal, there had been a series of crises. It began in the summer, when the business manager accepted a position in another part of the state. Then, with the population influx due to gas drilling, the high school principal's need for a second-in-command became acute. Next, the teacher who doubled as coach for the baseball team got injured and was told by his physician that his coaching days were over. And in February there was the tragic, accidental death of the superintendent.

In this sequence of events, the first necessity was to get a business manager installed, as the multitude of procedures for operating the district's financial affairs had to be continued without delay. The district's budget clerk was very competent, but hadn't finished her accountancy training yet, so the school board set about hiring a replacement early in the fall. There were few candidates, however, and in this narrow field the board had little choice but to go out of the local area. It eventually settled on an experienced business manager from eastern Pennsylvania, who was extremely qualified, with a doctorate in education, as well as being a CPA, and although the salary and benefits package was high, it was felt that his presence would help counteract the district's down-at-the-heels Appalachia image.

Then, after the terrible occurrence in February, a superintendent had to be found. The board conducted a hasty search, but no one interviewed was deemed acceptable to the majority of board members. To end the stalemate, one of the board members appealed to a professor of education at the university in Martensdale. The upshot was that an educator, well-respected and innovative, who had retired from the superintendency of a school district in New England, agreed to take the job as acting superintendent for a year. Owen was hired soon after, during this time when the board was willing to cast its net farther than Cross County.

No doubt the school board was pleased with itself, having brought in both a high-profile superintendent and business manager, and being able to fill the position of assistant principal and baseball coach with one hire. The board president, in particular, was more relaxed than she had been in the past. People saw a distinct brightening of her attitude, even a smartening up of her appearance. Optimism, so long absent, was cautiously beginning to emerge.

Owen's idea of how to find out about the skinny guy centered, as he told Lynn after the children had been settled for the night, on the Sure-Shot Taxidermy cap although, he had to allow, half the kids in the high school wore similar headgear. The place was in Colton; he'd passed it several times. "It can't be all that difficult. I go there, give the description of the guy, and see if they know who he is."

"Among the throng of skinny men with missing teeth," Lynn had answered. "Aren't hunting and shooting the main recreational activities down there? Hunting as in animals, shooting as in feuds."

Lynn had not been altogether happy that Owen's first administrative job was in Cross County. Of course, it was a step up for him and, if a position opened in Marten County later, he'd have experience under his belt. But Cross County had a reputation and Owen's asking questions could be construed as meddling. She went on, "Why would they give out information to someone wearing khakis and a tie? OK, you'd take off the tie. But still, you don't know how inquiries might be perceived. Would it be threatening, do you suppose?"

"I could bring in Grandpa Charlie's old deer head, say I'm thinking about having it remounted," Owen proposed.

"Oh, Owen!" Lynn exclaimed. "You'd be the joke of the high school when they hear about that moth-eaten relic and, in a place the size of Colton, everyone is bound to hear and pass it on. 'Hey, have you seen Mr. Griffith's trophy?' The kids would never let you forget it. They probably bag a buck every season themselves."

Owen looked temporarily set back, then rallied. "Keith got the license plate number off the guy's truck, if worse comes to worse."

"Much more sensible," said Lynn. She paused and thoughtfully added, "And then what?"

"Then what, what?"

"Say you can trace him that way, which may not even be possible. But say the motor vehicle registration people give you information. You get some directions, go up to a rotting cabin deep in the woods, isolated place by the way, knock on the door and say...what?"

"Where did you get the Parker? Is it stolen?"

"Oh, Owen!"

What he would say and do, Owen mused, was not clear yet, but the idea of being out in the country, where the goods presumably were, was far less a menacing prospect to him than it was an appealing one. Well, maybe there wasn't much in the way of toys and games to find in a derelict cabin, but then again there might be stuff. Keith was right. He knows me, thought Owen. Keith knew a quest like this, an excuse to hunt out antiques in a place like Cross County, would be irresistible to Owen. Lynn just hoped a school administrator would be treated with respect.

Respect, though, was not lacking in Owen's case. It wasn't only being vice-principal at the high school. It was also that Owen had managed to coach the baseball team to many more wins than losses in the spring, a feat that had not happened in most people's memories. His stock was especially high, as he was viewed as being responsible for helping a group of previously dispirited boys obtain a real feeling of accomplishment and, concomitantly, boosting the whole school's morale. Being not at all a self-regarding sort, Owen was pretty much unaware of his popularity, was only happy for the kids, and this further endeared him to the school community, an achievement in and of itself and of which he was more or less oblivious.

As he drove to work Monday morning, Owen was, rather, thinking excitedly about his mission, what he might run into. Over the weekend, he and Keith had discussed it some more, Keith giving as much information as he could, but warning Owen not to take any chances.

"Chances?" Owen had responded. "What do you mean, chances?"

By way of answer, Keith said, "Do you remember that conversation we had, oh, it must have been a couple of years ago now, when we were out in the woods together for the first time?"

"You mean when we found the CCC hunting camp?"

It had been a day when the auction they had set out for had not materialized and instead they went to see some property for sale in the mountains nearby, and stumbled onto a piece of Depression era history.

"Yes, that day. Did I mention my uncle, the one who had been in the Civilian Conservation Corps as a teenager in the Thirties?"

Owen nodded, "I remember." Then he gave Keith an inquiring look. "Wasn't it in Cross County, where you said he'd been in the Corps? And that he'd taken you somewhere down there when you were a kid?"

"That's right, decades after his CCC days, of course. Some of the places had gone to ruin, but one or two were still operating as camps and the stonework was as good as new. Beautiful stone walls, bridges, cabins, even a couple of lodges. He was very proud of his work, learning to be a stonemason. But what sticks in my mind was the feeling of isolation being in those hills, where it was wild and lonely, the sun getting low behind the trees and my uncle telling us we'd best get going before dark. I knew, instinctively I guess, that he wasn't just trying to spook us, my brother and me; that he had reasons which went beyond losing the daylight."

Owen, thoroughly fascinated, opened his eyes wide. "Like what?" he asked breathlessly.

Keith laughed. "Hey, I didn't mean to give you the heebie-jeebies!"

"But what did he say, your uncle?" Owen persisted.

"He didn't have to say anything. As we were walking down the road away from the camp, we ran into a guy sitting on a boulder, shotgun over his knees. He squints at us, nods and says, 'Good evening' and we say, 'Good evening,' and he watches us all the way back to the car."

"I see," said Owen thoughtfully. "But maybe it was one of the men from the hunting camp?"

"No. No one was at the camp. It was deserted and this guy, well, he was grubby and downright dangerous-looking, but at the same time, strangely civil. Anyway, the point I want to make, my friend, is take care."

Which is exactly what Lynn had said, Owen reflected, turning into the parking lot at the high school. But it didn't dampen his enthusiasm one jot.

Chapter 5

Jerome Strauss was intrigued by the possibilities in Cross County. His old colleague Eric Arden, who was chair of the educational administration program at the university in Martensdale, had been candid when, in late February, they discussed the position.

"You may not want to touch this one," he said during the course of their conversation, "but it is a reemerging place and needs all the expertise it can get to guide it in the right direction. I think the people there are malleable. They've been poor for so long and now, with the gas drilling giving a boost to the overall economy, they are not opposed to upping their standards and seeking more highly qualified administrative staff and educators."

That Jerry had been superintendent of one of the wealthiest districts in Massachusetts was an advantage, as he'd been able to initiate many innovative programs and make changes benefiting educational outcomes for preschool through 12th grade. He'd had experience with success and knew what worked. His challenge there had been mostly limited to convincing the school board and townspeople to move in new directions. Cross County was a different sort of challenge. The district had not been able to do much for years and was ready to upgrade in all sorts of areas. It was hard to resist, and as an acting superintendent he could make bold moves without worry about a contract being renewed.

"It does sound interesting," he told Eric, "and as you know, I'm at loose ends right now since the divorce..." Here he sort of trailed off, as the subject was slightly distasteful, not only to himself but, he realized, probably even more so to the colleague who had known him for over three decades and was not ignorant about his past entanglements.

However, Eric didn't follow that line, as he had something more important to impart to Jerry. "A note of caution, though," he began. "What were you told about the last superintendent?"

"You mean, how he died? Trying to put out the school fire is what they said," Jerry replied. "Is there something else I should know?"

"You heard the fire was arson?"

"Yes, and they haven't found who started it."

"Right. Well, it's only speculation at this point, but there are several rumors. You may hear them, so I think you should be forewarned. Before the school was burned down, the board had been discussing the possibility of consolidating the three elementary schools into two to save money. There was widespread protest among parents and townspeople over the idea of closing a school."

"There often is. A superintendent's vision does not always coincide with the community's. But, yes, I'd heard that. What is being said?"

Eric, whose long association with Jerry was both professional and personal, thought how he still had an arrogant air about him. But in spite of that, Eric was well aware that Jerry was sharp as a tack and, always an asset for a public figure like a superintendent, unconscionably good-looking. He went on, "One version has it that he burned it down himself and didn't get away in time."

"Unthinkable!" Jerry protested.

"Or, alternatively, he was deliberately lured there because of his unpopular stance."

"Hmm. And they have no leads, no possible suspects?"

"None at all. One gets the impression they are not really trying. That's the disquieting part. That's what I wanted to warn you about. It's a strange environment down there."

"Sounds like they need a dose of civilization."

Eric thought, I certainly hope he won't go making statements like that in Cross County or he'll be roundly disliked. Aloud he said, "Anyway, let me know what you decide." He really didn't think the sophisticated, urbane Dr. Strauss would want the job once he'd visited Colton. But if Jerry did land there, it could provide an excellent venue for some of Eric's graduate students doing school district research.

In early March, Jerry drove down to Cross County for an interview with the school board. His route took him southwest, following the curve of the Appalachians. For part of the time he traveled the Allegheny Plateau, where wide vistas revealed rows of giant wind turbines high up on the ridgeline silhouetted against the sky, their blades turning steadily. When he got farther south the landscape changed, the broad valleys and vistas diminished and the countryside became tighter, as if it were closing in on itself. Side roads leading away from the main highway disappeared down into hollows or, by the side of tumbling creeks swollen with snow melt, climbed up into timbered hills. Agriculture in this area, Jerry considered, looked like it had always been a difficult go.

As he got closer to Colton, he was aware that trucks were the main vehicles on the highway: pickups, utility trucks, big tankers carrying waste water from the hydraulic fracturing process, semis hauling heavy equipment. Many bore the names of power companies and most had license plates from Texas or Oklahoma. Even though Jerry had been reading up on gas drilling in Pennsylvania, he was impressed by all the activity.

Dotting the countryside were the gas wells—round black steel enclosures with what looked like a stove pipe on top to funnel the burned-off excess gas. Clustered along the highway were new multi-unit residences and motels. Shopping plazas with mini-marts, fast food establishments, movie theaters and automotive services had been plunked down in strip-mall fashion. There were several car dealerships, all featuring trucks. This place, Jerry thought, is providing absolutely golden opportunities for business enterprises.

He saw signs placed to catch the notice of drivers: *Paying $ for Oil and Gas Rights* and *Now Seeking Leases for Gas Drilling*, with energy companies' phone numbers. Jerry was beginning to enjoy himself. "Lease your land; let us dig; get rich. What a seductive proposition!" he couldn't resist exclaiming to the scene he was witnessing.

He passed a large, well-designed and expensive billboard. It proclaimed: *Wind Dies. Sun Sets. Rely On Natural Gas.*

All right, he thought more seriously, I've got the picture. He pulled into Colton, his interest excited by this Marcellus Shale phenomenon. Here wasn't just some small ho-hum school district in a depressed community. Things were buzzing, and Jerry realized he also had a golden opportunity: to be an influential force for using the buzz to help guide and improve education.

The school board in Colton met on Tuesday night. Monday night was when borough council meetings were held, Wednesday evening was by long-standing tradition dedicated to choir practice for the Methodists and the Catholics, and Thursday was reserved for the county boards and commissions. Friday, of course, was when high school sports events took place. So on Tuesday, when Jerry arrived unannounced, he slipped into a seat in the back of the meeting room to get a preview of the public workings of the Colton Area School District.

He had dressed casually, sweater and cords, in order to be less likely to stand out, although the cords had a crease and the pullover was cashmere. There was elegance about him, but not wanting to attract attention, he donned a pair of reading glasses and scanned a copy of the agenda he had picked up from a stack by the door. Then, over the top of the page, he observed his potential environment.

The district offices, located close to the center of town, occupied the building that had once been the old high school. It had been constructed in the Twenties and served the youth of Colton until the early Fifties, when a new high school was built farther out. A former classroom served as the board room. Folding chairs were arranged in rows for the attendees, and the nine members of the board sat on similar chairs at a long table in front, with the administrative staff at a table perpendicular to it on the right side. No raised dais, no fancy upholstered chairs, no brushed stainless steel carafes: not what Jerry was used to, but then he would have been very surprised if Colton had exhibited the trappings of wealthy districts' board rooms. He had seen too many instances of boards purposefully creating a separation between themselves and the public, as if they were on some higher plane, literally and figuratively. The audience, after all, consisted of the people whose tax dollars supported the schools and for whose children the schools existed. So far so good, he thought.

The room was crowded and quite a few media people were there, since the school fire was still news. He saw two TV crews setting up and recognized the reporters by their dress—coat and tie for the men, business attire for the women. He'd spent most of his professional life attending school board meetings and had gotten familiar with the press. They stood out from the rest of the people here, who wore the heavy work clothes, sweatshirts and blue jeans of small towns and rural regions, many not bothering to take off jackets or remove caps. They might look like hicks, but did it matter? They came because they were interested in the running of their schools and they wanted to be informed and, when allowed, speak their mind. As it should be, thought Jerry. Apathy was not constructive. He had, moreover, always enjoyed the challenge of swaying the public to his way of thinking. Then he had a look at the board members.

At this moment his attention was arrested by the woman who had just come in and gracefully took her seat in the center, the president of the board. So this is the Pat Foster who called me, he thought. Svelte, composed, and attractive. She was unlike her fellow members on the board, who were solid-looking, rumpled and country. He had a moment of self-amusement: do we have Snow White, in this case a honey blond, and eight dwarfs? He watched her bestow a smile on her fellow board members and on the assembled crowd, then saw her glance in the direction of the administrators sitting off to the side and at one person in particular, at whom she smiled more subtlety. Jerry followed her look and saw the object of this special attention. Ah, he said to himself, this must be the Prince, and wearing a three-piece suit. Who would have thought there'd be a three-piece suit here? Wait, I have it. It's the business manager. He'd been told they had gone outside the area to find him. Very Philadelphia, very smug-looking too. The suit just screams, "I'm in a different class than the rest of you," Jerry thought. Was this a strategy to command respect?

But the meeting was starting. Pat called them to order, the Pledge of Allegiance recited, roll call taken and the president welcomed all those in attendance, particularly the ladies and gentlemen of the media. A few routine matters were approved and then the public comment part of the meeting was announced. A dozen hands went up and it began.

After giving her name and address, the first speaker led off, "I want to know what you are going to do about Elk

Creek School. Is it going to get rebuilt or what? My kids used to walk to school; took 'em five minutes. Now they have to leave early for the school bus and ride for almost an hour. An' it's so crowded they hardly have time for lunch."

At the end of this recital there was a chorus of agreement and more hands went up. The president explained that while she understood parents' concerns on this matter, no decision would be made until the new superintendent was brought in. This was greeted with groans from the audience and then the next speaker stood up.

"I'm sure we all feel bad about the fire and what happened and most of us here went to the memorial service, but just because that charter school opened, that don't mean we want to only have two grade schools for the rest of us. Is this new Super going to start on that again or will you see it don't happen?"

Here the chorus of agreement was even louder. Four or five others addressed the board, all in a similar vein. Pat was either unwilling or unable to stem the flow of very sincere questions about Elk Creek School from the parents whose children were displaced.

As he listened Jerry became aware of a singular and slightly eerie omission, namely that in the references to the fire, not once was there any mention or speculation about those responsible. He could think of several possible explanations, all of which were disturbing, all of which might be applicable. Either everyone already had a pretty good idea of who had set fire to the school or, secondly, no one wanted to know, as it could likely be any of their friends, neighbors or relatives. Or thirdly, arson had been, historically, an appropriate form of expressing opposition, so there was no point discussing it, particularly in front of the media, and risking a more aggressive investigation than what he heard had been carried out. This is no ordinary school district, Jerry thought.

There were several other items that people wanted to weigh in on. Jerry listened to remarks about after school activities, test scores and amount of homework, topics which were familiar, as he'd dealt with them many times in his experience. But then there was a new one.

"What are you going to do about the roads? Ours has gotten so bad that last week the school bus couldn't get up it at all and the kids had to walk down to the highway. Sometimes it's all night long with them trucks." Fallout from the gas drilling, thought Jerry. How does she handle these questions?

Jerry noticed that Pat nodded in the direction of the business manager. He addressed the speaker in a rather, it seemed to Jerry, nonchalant fashion.

"There's not much we can do when it comes to anything that halts the progress of gas drilling. They have leased land up your way which, as you know, has brought tidy sums to a couple of your neighbors. I can call the company and have a load of gravel put down, but that's about it."

This response brought head shaking and murmuring from the audience and the last speaker said accusingly, "There's a lot more you could do. I've heard tell from the wife's relations in Allegheny that the Super there threatened to call the Oklahoma City headquarters if they didn't patch up the road so's the kids could get to school. Next day there were crews out."

"Well, then," said the business manager, "we'll just let the new superintendent deal with it."

And I can't wait, Jerry said to himself.

Chapter 6

Pat had not been unaware of the handsome, distinguished-looking man sitting in the back row. She had tried to catch another glimpse of him as the meeting broke up, but wasn't successful. He had disappeared during the melee that often followed board meetings, when people pressed forward to make their points. The discussion had begun with the new superintendent and the school closure issue.

"When is this new guy coming anyway?"

"I think you should make it clear to him that closing schools isn't an option around here."

"Yeh. This has got to be nipped in the bud."

"We need a new school on Elk Creek Road as soon as possible. The playgrounds are still all right."

"Hey, we got money enough, now with the drilling."

Pat had to clarify the last statement. "Gas drilling doesn't automatically benefit the district, you know, Mr. Hodges. It helps landowners who have leased gas rights and it has created jobs, but property taxes are what pays for schools. At least in Pennsylvania. At least for now."

"What about that there charter school, Miz Foster? Seems the drillers support that, leastways it was them had it built. That's a bunch of kids we don't have to pay for."

"Unfortunately," Pat clarified, "the school district has to foot the bill for charter school tuition. That's the state law."

"How much do we have to pay for them kids to go to their fancy new school?"

Pat would rather not have had to answer that question, but this was information in the public domain and, more importantly, these were her people and she was not going to be cagey with them. "Costs run about $10,000 per student, almost double that if they have special education needs," she said. "And we have to provide transportation."

There was, Pat thought, an almost shocked silence for a few seconds at this discouraging piece of intelligence.

"The law oughta be changed."

"So, who did you vote for, Jamie? The same Rep? He won't never change a damn thing, 'cept to make it worse."

"Who else is there to vote for? Left-wing crazies don't do no good, Carl."

"How about all that development, Ma'am, the new shopping malls and the housing going up? That's property, ain't it?" someone asked.

"And I jes' heard the old mobile home park out by Elk Creek is gonna be sold. They're plannin' to tear everything out and build a dozen McMansions," another put in.

"They're what?!" Carl exploded. "I got most my family livin' in that trailer park! How come I din't hear nothin' about this?"

Pat interjected with, "But it will be revenue-producing for the school district, Mr. Morgan."

"Cold comfort, Mrs. Foster," said Carl, turning away.

She had hoped to talk to Elliot after the meeting, but she hadn't seen him and the BMW wasn't in the parking lot. As Pat got into her car, she felt let down. There had been more than the usual complaints from the public tonight. She could understand their frustration and unhappiness, but there was little the president of a school board could do except listen and try to make good policy decisions. She would have liked to relax a little after a meeting like that, to hash it over with Elliot in his office. Maybe he was at her house, stirring up a cocktail right now. She pulled down the mirror and had a look at her face. It was tough enough to be in your mid-fifties, and then to have your husband announce he was leaving you for someone younger. At least he'd been a decent father, and their boy was in the military and advancing. Not one to stay down for long, this thought cheered her up. I guess, she said to herself, things turned out for the best, especially since last fall and Elliot. With the hope of seeing him tonight, she made a few repairs to her makeup, then backed the car out and headed home.

Elliot. How her life had changed since he came. He had brought an aura of glamour to Colton, no doubt about it. And he'd been attentive to her right from the start, even before she'd gotten her hair a better color and lost those extra pounds. Such an impetus to self-improvement, she thought, smiling. A new wardrobe and a man to appreciate her. What could be better for giving you a lift, something to look forward to?

Even though, she thought, after almost six months I know so little about him. I mean, I do, but only on the surface. He won't ever talk about himself, what he does when he isn't at the office, or his past at all. I can't help thinking he's keeping me at a distance for some reason. But why? So he won't get too involved with me? Maybe that's it.

Then he continually worries about being careful enough in a town this size, since he is employed by the school district and, in a way, I am his employer. So we never get to go out together or anything.

But still, didn't he look stunning tonight, the way he always does, she thought. Like a banker, like a stockbroker, like nothing you ever see in Cross County.

Except...tonight. There was that man in the back row, striking, with an air of quiet sophistication. It was almost too much to hope for, but could he be tomorrow's interview for acting superintendent?

Elliot Lucas, MBA, Ed.D., was not at Pat's house waiting to comfort and console her. Elliot was at a bar, a dim and smoky bar. Colton's no smoking ordinance made exceptions for certain establishments and this was one of them. As the very tall Texan said when he addressed the borough council, "Y'all ain't gonna make them boys go outside in the cold for a simple leetle cigareet, now are you? They're used to warm weather. Cold might have the effect of makin' 'em ornery and mean." How could the borough not make exceptions, with all the business that had come to their doorstep? From the beginning they realized things would go much better if concessions were made to keep the drillers happy. The council even had a recently-elected member from the gas industry, a chemical engineer who had bought a large home in the older section of town, although he also had a ranch outside of Austin. Money, for so long dwindling, draining away and practically non-existent in this run-down area, had made a comeback.

Elliot was at The Pit. That was the name given to it by the locals when Prohibition started. In 1920 there was a fortuitous find: an abandoned mine tunnel was determined to be accessible from a lower level and, therefore, ideal in which to store various illegal beverages. One had only to climb down a stairway to procure liquid refreshment. Although the entrance was boarded up when Prohibition ended, the name stuck because over the years the place never quite relinquished its dark and slightly squalid feel.

Elliot was there to meet someone, someone from the gas industry. He had parked his BMW around back and, in the recesses of a booth in the farthest corner, was engaged in conversation.

"Cut 'em off at the pass did you?" the man from Texas said with a grin. "I heard how you handled it." He was on his third whiskey, the first two of which he had polished off while waiting.

Elliot sipped a martini. "I referred it to the new superintendent. That seemed to mollify them."

"Well, we can spread some more gravel. As long as they understand the trucks are going to keep using those roads."

"The issue isn't a handful of residents understanding. It's will the new Super understand? We're interviewing him tomorrow and my guess is he'll be hired. Good credentials and a track record of making changes. He's older, though. Retired. I don't think he's the type to come in swinging randomly, poking his nose into everything. He's more likely to focus his energies on upgrading the curriculum."

"And you'll see to it that he does."

"There's plenty to busy him along those lines. Don't worry."

"Well, keep me informed. We have a lot at stake, you know."

Elliot gave a perfunctory laugh. "And more than trucks hauling frack water." He paused and took a sip of his drink. "I don't foresee any problems."

"No problems at all, given what you've got goin' with the boss lady, huh?"

Elliot raised his glass. "I'll drink to that," he said coolly.

Two other people had met at The Pit and were having a conversation over a couple of beers. Their mood wasn't as sanguine, their interaction not as upbeat.

"You gave him the information he wanted?"

"Yep."

"How about the Doc?"

"Yep, him too."

"How come you keep doin' this, Carl? It ain't safe, dealin' with them both."

"I tol' you. I need the money."

"You can't need it that bad, to do..."

"To do what?"

"I dunno."

"Spit it out, Jamie."

"Not for money you wouldn't. You know."

"I don't do stuff like that. Hell, my sister's kids was goin' there."

They drank their beers mutely for a while.

"Lots of jobs in the gas business," Jamie ventured. "Why don't you drive truck? That's a bunch of dough if you can get the license. Shouldn't be hard with the people you know."

"Not gonna work for that outta-state drilling company."

"Carl, you don't make no sense at all! You're already helpin' one of them Texas guys find out things."

"Well, I still don't see how *you* can work for them," he said accusingly. "Chrissake, Jamie, they're ruining our roads and our air and poisoning our water, not to mention throwin' their weight around. It's them coal barons all over again."

"Pay good money, though. Child support's been killin' me. You only got one year of that left with your boy."

"Won't stop there. He thinks he's goin' to college. I tol' him 'Great, but how do you 'spect to pay for it?' He said he'd find a way." Carl had another gulp of his beer, then pointed his chin in the direction of the corner booth. "Look at 'em over there. Don't have a care in the world. Now I gotta think how to help pay for a new place for my folks to live. Rents are sky high since them drillers are here. I'd like to find out who it is buyin' the trailer park."

"Won't it show up in the *Clarion*?"

"Not likely. I reckon it'll be kept quiet. Lots of people gonna be riled." He stared off in space for a bit, then said in a softer voice, "Them trees there've grown up so nice and shady-like."

The two considered their beers in gloomy silence.

"How 'bout the school district?" Jamie proposed. "I hear they need a custodian at the middle school. That ol' Uncle Burton of mine has wandered off again. I don't know why they put up with him for so long. I s'pose it's the competition." Janitorial jobs, being what they were, had become even less appealing since the gas industry began to hire, although in this case the custodian in question had a history of notable unreliability and not just during hunting season.

"Yep, I bin thinkin' about that," Carl allowed. "Maybe I'll go see Mrs. Foster and try to get her on my side before this new hot-shot Super gets here and thinks I ain't good enough." And I also better get Pappy's stuff out of the trailer and find a safe place to store it, he thought. Some of it is damned valuable.

Jamie finished his beer and stood up. "Shift starts in an hour. I guess your cousin isn't workin' tonight?" he asked, looking around hopefully.

"I don't keep track of her," Carl answered into his beer. He'd seen her, all right, earlier. Mel had brought drinks to the corner booth and the Doc that taken the opportunity to give her a pat on the bottom. Carl had seen him do that before too. Mel never looked happy about it.

"Did I tell you I'm writing a song for her?" Jamie had a country music group; he was lead guitar and banjo, and he and Mel both did vocals. "She's gonna love it. Well, see ya', Carl. I gotta go."

He's crazy about her, thought Carl after Jamie left. He'd go nuts if he knew what the Doc was up to with her. Carl took a last swig. Guess I'll go line me up a job tomorrow, he decided.

Chapter 7

Not surprisingly, Dr. Strauss was overwhelmingly approved by the school board to become Acting Superintendent of Colton Area School District. His technique of addressing people with an almost hesitant thoughtfulness, of looking them directly in the eye, and giving the impression that theirs was, indeed, an important question, worth pondering and answering with deliberation, made up for his not being "one of us." Also, he was supremely articulate without resorting to academic jargon. They could understand him when he talked about the curriculum and new teaching patterns. He came across as slightly reticent rather than glibly know-it-all. This strategy of Jerry's was intentionally chosen because he was on their turf and it was prudent to acknowledge that they were in the driver's seat. He knew his tactics would be successful and he was right.

His other aim was to put the business manager at ease, since he would be working closely with him and didn't want friction from the start. He had sensed that Elliot could easily view him as a threat, was probably already seeing him as a competitor, stealing his thunder. When the subject of district revenues and expenditures came up, Jerry deferred to Elliot, even though it was apparent that he had full knowledge of the fiscal operations of school districts.

"A superintendent functions most effectively when he's on the same page as the district's business manager," Jerry had said, nodding in the direction of Elliot. "You have an exceedingly well-qualified individual in Dr. Lucas, and I would certainly feel comfortable relying on his expertise."

What a bunch of smoke, Jerry thought to himself. I know little about this guy, except that he's overdressed and has something going with the lovely Mrs. Foster.

Elliot, Jerry noted, gave a brief smile at his last remark. He thinks I'm some old out-to-pasture type, just here to kill time in my retirement, thought Jerry. Yes, this will be fun.

"You do understand," Pat had said, wanting Jerry to have a realistic picture of the district, "that although we are experiencing a boom economy in Colton, its impact on education is not direct. With the new construction, revenues from property taxes are starting to improve, but we are like the suitor who has 'prospects.' Great expectations, but not for a while. The package we can offer you may be less than you had anticipated."

Jerry smiled at Pat. "I'm sure we can work something out."

Wasting no time, Jerry hit the ground running. His days were full, getting to know the staff, visiting schools, holding meetings to learn what parents and teachers wanted for their children. One of the first things he did was to hire an assistant principal at the high school. Again Eric Arden was helpful and promised to send his best graduate student, who had just gotten his principal's certificate. "His name is Owen Griffith. He's likable and unassuming and coached Martensdale High's baseball team to a winning season last year. And incidentally, he's also one of the dealers at Cider Run." Since Eric and Jerry shared a love of antiques, it was a shame, Eric thought, but understandable, that Jerry had yet to visit the Martensdale antiques shop.

"Owen sounds like a good fit," Jerry had answered. The right hires were crucial to a superintendent's effectiveness, arrows in his quiver, as Jerry visualized it, which could be relied on when needed. Another person who understood antiques, well, that was just icing on the cake.

"By the way," Eric asked, "have you learned anything more about the fire that killed their former superintendent?"

"They don't talk about it. It's as if there's a tacit agreement not to speculate; there's just silence, almost a conspiratorial silence. But it does enter the room like an uneasy presence from time to time: What happened? Who is responsible?"

"And," Eric added, "could the same thing occur again?"

Jerry chuckled. "I've got a well-developed instinct of self-preservation. As you know, old friend."

Colton, or Deems Mill as it was called in its early days, was settled at the beginning of the 19th century in a valley running roughly north and south between a jumble of hills. Elk Creek provided the water power for the mill, coming down out of the hills from the east and running to the west. Since the creek only crossed the north end of the valley, the effects of spring flooding were limited. This meant that shops, businesses and houses could be built in the relatively flat area of the valley, a larger flat area than anywhere else in Cross County.

With the beginning of coal mining in the latter 1800s, prosperity arrived in the form of two hotels, a theater, many eating and drinking establishments, and a handsome Second Empire county courthouse with a gilded dome, and the citizens adopted Colton as a more fitting name.

As the town grew, homes were built on the hillsides. The prosperous residents, professional and business leaders, built on the southwest facing slope. These were grand and sometimes ornate places meant to show wealth and taste, with ambitious landscaping wrested from the rocky soil and ever-encroaching woods. When, in the 1970s, coal mining had given its last gasp, many of these houses were boarded up and deteriorating, or turned into apartments. The gardens were swallowed by native trees and Virginia creeper, and stone pillars marking driveway entrances tumbled on their sides. A few hardy plant species survived and propagated, to dot the April hillside with flowers, while in June escaped roses put forth their blooms in scented profusion, a living testimony to what had once been Colton's pride.

But with the economic recovery, crews had been busy restoring many of the older homes, and this historic residential area was again seen as a desirable location. Downtown Colton, where crumbling curbs and broken sidewalks had been the norm for years, had also been given attention by merchants and business owners whose trade was picking up. No longer were there cracks in the concrete and weeds growing rampant. New businesses were moving into and renovating old buildings. Street trees were planted, bushes and shrubs trimmed. Repairs, repaving and repainting were bringing Colton a new image. Hard cash was coming into the town and civic improvements followed.

Jerry was fond of older homes and was able to rent the carriage house of one of the renovated mansions, belonging now to a gas industry executive and his family. Living so close to town meant he was able to walk to the school district office, and each day he met and exchanged ideas with people, showing interest in them, hearing their views on the schools. And, as importantly, they learned about him.

"That new Super don't hold hisself off. He wants to know what we think about stuff."

"He really cares about kids. You can tell that."

"He asted me about Lizzie. Can you believe it? He remembered her from when he visited the school."

"He'll stand up to them drillers tearin' up our roads!"

"Not when his landlord is one of 'em."

Jerry mingled, he observed, he asked pertinent questions, he paid attention to what people told him. When he was invited to address professional and business groups, he introduced some of his thoughts for improving the schools. People found him consistently pleasant and interesting, quite, in fact, charming. He was gathering data, winning support. Moves would come soon, but not until he felt the town's confidence in him. In the meantime, he particularly kept an emotional distance from Pat.

He knew, well he knew, she was attracted to him. She had made a few tentative suggestions: that they have dinner together and talk about New England schools, or that they meet for lunch so she could introduce him to her favorite restaurants. He smiled and said he'd love to, then somehow it never could be worked out. Each time it came across as if he were holding himself back from temptation and, actually, that wasn't so far from the truth. Each time he was more certain their getting together was inevitable. But the minute he began with Pat, he knew he'd have to reckon with Elliot, if only in the sense of her having any leftover feelings for him. So he held off, let the anticipation build, and continued educating himself about the Colton Area School District.

Pat spent the first two months of spring in a state of semi-excitement. Jerry was proving to be an outstanding choice; people were telling her what a good decision the board had made in hiring him. He listened, he had fresh ideas and he made friends among the townspeople. That she could never get him alone was, she felt, only temporary. He was obviously a gentleman and would not rush her into a situation prematurely.

Pat was still seeing Elliot, but was becoming increasingly impatient with the shallowness of their relationship. Trying to figure out what was going on, she attempted to start a dialogue with him. He was unwilling.

"Pat, you know a man doesn't like to talk about relationships," he had objected.

"Some men do," she countered and then, seeing the deprecating smile her last words had brought, hastily went on in what she hoped was a more conciliatory vein, "It's communication I'm after, not true confession."

"With you, I communicate best in bed," was his reply, delivered with a seductive narrowing of the eyes.

And that's the way he'll always be, she had decided. Take it or leave it. They rarely had anything like a substantive conversation, except at the district office and that about school business.

"Too much water under the bridge with us," he had told her early on. "We're better off without that baggage—your ex, my ex."

Is that why he left Philadelphia? Or was it mid-life crisis in general?

And then there was his almost obsessive fastidiousness which, at first, she found refreshing. Over the months, however, it had become clear that fastidiousness imbued his whole personality. Perhaps, she thought, this was what accountants were like and one laughed it off as a quirky, but endearing, idiosyncrasy of the occupation.

But, no, it went farther than that. Feelings of insecurity on her part had arisen from it. She worried about her appearance, her hair, her clothes. How about the house? Were there unwashed dishes in the sink? Was the place tidy enough; scrupulously clean was more like it. She had taken to reading his face, seeing the disdainful looks with which he regarded things that didn't meet with his approval.

He had once said to her, after she apologized for a pile of books and papers he'd had to move, "I'm a Virgo. Virgos aren't happy with anything short of perfection."

He did deliver this statement with a laugh at least, but a dismissive laugh, as though she ought to be amused by this uncustomary lack of sophistication on his part. But at the same time, Pat thought, expect her to have no qualms about viewing it as an acceptable explanation for a very complex pattern of behavior. She wondered again why she had never been invited to his home, one of the brand-new condos or so she understood. Not that it mattered. Or did it? He kept his distance from her; he kept his life apart from her.

What she missed was intellectual intimacy in their relationship. She began more and more to let herself think about Jerry.

Chapter 8

On one of the side streets downtown, there was an old storefront housing an antiques shop. In keeping with the current practice of sprucing up, the windows were tolerably clean, there was decent lighting, and the merchandise was displayed so that it could be seen. Jerry had been brought up with family antiques and, once he had discovered the place, he dropped in regularly. Even though these were not the kind he was used to in the antiques mecca of New England, he had found several things of interest. He had bought a 19th century hand-made oak rocking chair, a theater broadside from the 1930s advertising the latest Noel Coward offering at the Colton Playhouse, a well-used, mellowed wooden batter bowl to hold fruit and a white ironstone pitcher with only a tiny chip. He had plans for the pitcher. He also ran into Owen there and the two talked antiques continually while roaming the aisles.

"You getting that piece of ironstone?" Owen asked when Jerry held up the pitcher for Owen to see. "Nice! What's it got on the bottom?"

Jerry turned it over. "It has the raised diamond. So it's from England, but before 1891, since it isn't marked with the country of origin."

"Hey, you know your china. There's a dealer in our shop who specializes in ironstone. She'd love that baby. Only the one small chip? She could pinpoint the date for you."

"I bet she could," murmured Jerry.

"I can't believe you haven't been to Cider Run yet. Let me know when you're up in Martensdale and I'll show you around."

There was a reason Jerry felt he should stay away from Cider Run Antiques. Owen was likely to know sooner or later. Make it later, thought Jerry. He had nothing to reproach himself about, but didn't want to cause any awkwardness. It had happened years ago and he had more than lived up to his end of the bargain. Right now let's see what we can do for Colton, he thought.

June had only a few more weeks to go before school was out. Things had gone well. The annual high school musical came off to enthusiastic applause, even though the initial choice, *Phantom of the Opera*, which had already started rehearsals, was scrapped owing to its being deemed unsuitable after the tragedy in February, and *Pajama Game* was substituted. Graduation was held under cloudless skies and baseball season, wildly successful for Colton, was over. Jerry decided to give his vice-principal some special assignments before Owen went on vacation.

On a bright June morning, Jerry and Owen met at Jerry's office, then set out walking towards the center of town to have lunch there. It was a pleasant stroll and lent itself to conversation.

"Owen, I want to tell you again what a boost you've given to the boys on the baseball team. To the whole school. I've been getting compliments on hiring you, but the compliments should go to you," Jerry started off.

"It's the kids!" Owen replied with fervor. "They were terrific. No one ever missed a practice. They didn't even complain when it rained."

"Did you identify any outstanding players, juniors who'll be on the team next year?"

"Yeh, definitely. At least three. Seth Morgan, for sure. His dad is custodian at the middle school. What do you have in mind?"

"Scholarships. If you could research what's available, we'll get the process in motion to help kids apply for college scholarships."

Owen stopped in his tracks. "I'm on it!" he exclaimed with a wide grin.

Jerry, caught off guard, threw his head back and laughed. Owen's grin was infectious. Jerry let go of a lot of superintendent's stiffness in that moment. Could there be, he asked himself, some happy intersection of time and place that's having this effect on me? Has Cross County, far from being merely a hopeless embarrassment as outsiders have assumed, opened my eyes to the possibilities inherent in change? And that includes me as well? he thought, slightly amazed.

They broadened on the theme of seeking financial aid for graduates, a topic that met with enthusiasm on both their parts. "Starting in the fall, I'd like to have a series of meetings with parents and townspeople," Jerry proposed, "to discuss after-graduation options."

"Options other than driving trucks for the gas industry?" suggested Owen.

Jerry nodded. "Precisely. Apparently, the school board has never funded a high school counselor. I don't want to wait for the new fiscal year. I want to get the ball rolling now. It's such a temptation to graduate and find you're able to make what must seem a fortune when you're only 18. Like the kids in Pittsburgh who followed their fathers into the steel mills the minute they left school."

"And look what happened to the steel factories. Shut down and put half of western Pennsylvania out of work," Owen added.

"Anything we can do to inspire them to look a little farther into their future would be infinitely worthwhile."

Owen related a little about his own background. He would never have gone to college, he said, if he hadn't been motivated by his teachers in high school. "Coal miners' kids; well, in my case, the grandson of a coal miner. My parents had the local hardware store. But the mines were on their way out in eastern Pennsylvania, and things were looking pretty down. Like here but, really, Colton's not a bad town now. It's more livable than I'd been led to think. And just because you get a higher education doesn't mean you can't come back."

"And make it a better place," Jerry affirmed. "That would be the theme of our meetings: investing in kids to reinvest in the future of Cross County."

"I like it," Owen agreed. "It would help with the loyalty conflict that can come up when kids want to go away to school."

"From what I can tell, not too many kids have had that option. We'll introduce some college prep classes into the curriculum. There's no reason our kids can't have accelerated placement courses too."

They had come to the building that housed the *Colton Clarion*. Jerry slowed down and regarded it thoughtfully. "Owen," he said, "there's something else I'd like you to do when you get a chance." It had been on his mind for months and he needed to try, at least, to sort it out. "What have you heard concerning the fire?"

"You know, it's funny. If I bring it up, people change the subject or kind of dance around it. 'Oh, it was a really old school,' they say, or 'Yep, that was sad all right,' or they just shrug. Not that I've asked a lot. I got the feeling it was taboo. Makes you wonder."

Jerry nodded. "Off limits. That's been my take on it too. It almost seems as if it's a breach of good manners to talk about it. I'm also wondering if there is more I should know, being as how I'm in his shoes now."

Owen followed Jerry's glance in the direction of the newspaper office. "You could read the back issues, what was reported when it happened. But maybe you oughtn't be seen sitting around there doing that. You want me to check it out? I can do it. I've done research there and in the Colton Public Library about the county. I didn't know what the kids were referring to when they'd talk about state game lands, or where the railroad used to go, or which mine was operating in which place. Give me a day; I'll see what I can learn."

They slid into a booth at the Colton Diner and continued their conversation about new programs and directions for the high school.

A good head on this lad, thought Jerry about Owen.

Boy, have I landed on my feet having such a great Supe, thought Owen.

Chapter 9

The third area Jerry wanted to deal with was the Power Learners Charter School, a name he had almost choked over when he first heard it. But there were things that concerned him about the charter school. One was the amount of money it was costing the district. Should it be so much? The other was that it was pulling in not only children of the energy company people, but some of the brighter kids from the district. He could, he supposed, talk to the family from whom he rented his house and whose children went there, but first he should learn what he could from the district angle. As was the case for many other school district aspects, it was the business manager who had data on charter schools.

Jerry and Elliot had been meeting regularly from the time Jerry was hired. It was Elliot who had gotten Jerry up to speed on the operational functions—transportation, building maintenance, food service, school accounting practices—everything, in fact, that went into the budget and they worked together on the budget itself. In his handling of the business side of the school district, Jerry found Elliot meticulous regarding detail and knowledgeable regarding Pennsylvania codes and practices. He felt well-instructed and let Elliot know he was doing an outstanding job.

But still he didn't like him. Was it Pat, he wondered, the old green-eyed monster lurking around in his mind? No, it was the guy himself. Something about him. He was so smooth, so cool, with a slightly superior smile. Well, haven't I been that way, Jerry asked himself? Didn't I have a reputation for arrogance, as someone told me once, before she left me for good? Being arrogant in an affluent suburb of Boston went with the territory. In this district it stuck out like a sore thumb. Maybe it wasn't arrogance he was reacting to with Elliot; maybe it was something else, but he couldn't put his finger on it. And perhaps he was being overly judgmental. Elliot was competent, he was smart, Jerry had to grant. But then why, said a voice in the back of his mind, would he make a mid-career move to a place like Colton?

Jerry didn't like having this attitude about Elliot. His former business managers had all been equally competent, yet they had an enjoyable sociability about them. While serious in regard to their work, they had been spirited, humorous, and fun to be around, as if aware of the necessity to counteract the dour stereotype associated with the profession of accountancy. With Elliot he felt an irksome tension and constraint, and it popped up whenever they were together. Nonetheless, he headed into the meeting, hopeful that he'd learn more from him.

"All we're doing," Elliot explained after Jerry had outlined his concerns, "is following the law. Parental choice." Elliot shrugged his shoulders. "That's what the legislature wanted. We have to go along with it."

Jerry said, "At least we only have one charter school here. If you will, Elliot, please give me what you have on Power Learners," he tried not to smile over the name, "before you go on vacation. The budget items pertaining to it, enrollments, transportation data: whatever will make me informed, so I can get a picture of how it is impacting the district."

Did Elliot, so responsive to all Jerry's requests for information in the past, hesitate for a second before answering? Jerry had that impression.

"Sure," said Elliot. "I can pull that together for you. It will be on your desk before I leave in July."

Jerry would have liked to see it the next morning, but he smiled and replied, "Thanks, Elliot. I knew I could depend on you."

It was time, it was past time, he met one-on-one with Pat. There had been meetings all spring at Jerry's office, but always with others in attendance—staff, administrators, teachers, other board members. They planned the agenda of the regularly scheduled school board meetings and work sessions at these times, and went over items Jerry wanted the board to be aware of. Now he felt he could finally justify getting her alone, to allow her to express her private thoughts on the charter school. Or anything else she wanted to bring up. And more? No, not more, not yet. He needed to put her at ease, no ulterior motives. Just let her talk. They were interested in the same thing: the improvement of Colton area schools. First things first.

He asked her to have dinner with him and, while it was put in a way that was work-related, it conveyed a sense of personal interest. "Pat," he said on the phone, "it's time we got together and talked about the district, and I don't mean at my office with all the formality it entails. I want to know what you think about several things. Off the record."

"I couldn't agree more, Jerry. It's a pretty structured environment there and I'm not always comfortable about speaking my mind," she answered, her heart beginning to race. Was it happening at last? "We can go to one of several restaurants I know; there are always tables where conversations aren't likely to be overheard."

"No, I'll cook. At my place. I'll pick you up, in case you don't want your car parked at my door." At least while Elliot is in town, he thought. "Friday? 7:00?"

"May I bring wine?"

"White," he said.

Owen had spent an afternoon combing through back issues of the *Clarion*. He wasn't able to do it unrecognized. Someone said, "Hey, Coach!" to him as he passed the newsroom and one of the secretaries looked up with a "Hi, Mr. Griffith!" as he went by. So much for doing this anonymously, he thought. Next time I wear glasses and a false beard. He took copious notes and the following day he and Jerry met behind the closed door of Jerry's office.

"It was ugly, all right," Owen began. "The photos were mostly of the ruined building with snow-covered fields in the background and the superintendent's car sitting there by what had been the back entrance. That was how they were able to identify him. His car and his keys near the, er, remains." Owen had experience with the aftermath of death by misdeed. This had brought it back to him and he was silent for a while.

Jerry let him take his time. He knew about the other death from Eric Arden and respected Owen's need to collect himself. He'd not seen Owen this somber; it was understandable that he would be affected by what he'd been reading.

Owen went on, "No one quoted in the paper hinted outright that the superintendent might have been responsible, but one of them suggested that the district had made the closing of an elementary school easy by hiring someone to burn this one down. Someone else opined that there was a grudge against the Super and he brought it on himself by his policies. Mrs. Foster was the voice of reason, stating that until they had a thorough investigation, it was not in their best interests to speculate, and the district would carry on as usual. Colton Area would mourn the death of a fine man and continue its commitment to quality education, as had been his most cherished goal. But Dr. Lucas," here Owen paused and looked up at Jerry, "he comes off as if he were totally unmoved by the whole thing. You could almost hear Mrs. Foster breaking down in the interview she gave but, sorry, Dr. Strauss, I just can't see how he could sound so unfeeling about what happened."

Jerry acknowledged this with a nod, not wanting to admit aloud that he shared Owen's opinion. But it was interesting to know he wasn't the only one who felt that way about Elliot.

"Dr. Lucas," Owen continued, "tells the reporter that as soon as he heard about the fire, he left phone messages for the superintendent. Then he goes on about how he started arranging classroom space and transportation for the displaced children. And that's all he says."

"Explanation why the fire went unnoticed for so long?" Jerry asked.

"The main reason was the weather, although if the people who lived in the house close by had not gone to Florida, it would have been discovered far earlier. This was mentioned briefly and not referred to again. I wondered about that because a Florida vacation seemed unusual for these folks. Their house was in one of the photos, and I've seen it when I was biking with some of the students. It's little more than, well, a shack."

"No follow-up interview with them?"

"None that I could find."

"I suppose we could try to view TV footage," Jerry suggested.

"I was recognized by two people at the *Clarion* office. I'm thinking that with the TV crews all over us when we won our last game..."

"And at the board meetings. We're going to have to be more circumspect than that."

Owen had a look at his notes. "A couple more things: the paper dug into the past and came out with all the related stories on arson as a form of protest in Cross County. There were more than a dozen reported grudge burnings in the last half of the 1900s alone. It was written with a sort of toss of the head, if you know what I mean."

"I do," Jerry affirmed. "Kind of a pride, would you say?"

"Yeh. A bizarre kind of pride."

"You said a 'couple' of things. What was the other?"

Owen put away his notes. "The other is a strange coincidence. They brought in an investigative team from Marten County when they couldn't go any farther in their own efforts. It was headed by someone I know, Detective Paul Willard. He and his team were down here for a week. They were supposed to be preparing a report, which was to go to the county sheriff. The sheriff said he never heard from them and, essentially, fired them. Now, this does not sound like the Paul Willard I know. He's excruciatingly thorough, honest, dedicated. I can't say enough good things about him. My immediate thought was that he was pulled off the case for some reason. The more I thought about it the more I smelled something fishy. Or," he said looking candidly at Jerry, "gassy."

"You may be on to something," Jerry said.

Before Jerry could ask, Owen volunteered, "While I'm on vacation, I'll have a talk with Paul and see what the story is."

"Owen, you shouldn't if you think that in any way it could have repercussions."

"Hell, no, Supe! This guy is a buddy of ours! He's one of our own! He collects antiques."

Chapter 10

The *Colton Clarion* was delivered around 6:30AM, a time when Jerry was usually fixing breakfast. Normally he would have a quick glance at the headline and then take it up to read when the coffee was ready. Friday morning, however, the headline got his full attention. *ELK CREEK MOBILE HOME PARK PROTEST,* it proclaimed in large type and beneath, a sub-heading, *Residents to Appeal to CASD.*

Elk Creek and its environs were not in the Borough of Colton, but in Deems Township, which covered a large, semi-rural area abutting Colton to the north. As such, it was not subject to the regulations of the borough, a fact which annoyed some residents who would have liked to see ordinances regulating trash burning and abandoned vehicles, for example, but which suited others who were in favor of no prohibitions against discharging firearms. The township was served by the Colton Area School District; parents of children residing there were often more likely than borough residents to attend school board meetings, as it was by way of being a social event for them.

Jerry read through the article with interest, the gist of which was that residents of the mobile home park planned to take their grievances to the school board, their request for a delay of eviction having been turned down by the township on legal grounds. Why the school board? What could that body possibly offer them? Jerry decided he needed to learn as much as he could about it in time for next week's board meeting. One more topic to discuss with Pat. Even if he had wanted to pursue another avenue of activity with her, given all the agenda items he was putting on the table, there wouldn't be an opportunity to create anything like a romantic mood. He smiled to himself. OK, Elliot, you're still safe, but not for long.

There wasn't enough time to call a meeting of representatives of the protest group, but he did get on to some of the staff of the Elk Creek Elementary School, now assigned to other schools, and to one of the bus drivers who had the trailer park children on her route. A few phone conversations convinced him that the trailer park had a real identity, that it was a community for its residents and functioned, when necessary, as a mutual aid society, particularly in regard to looking after children.

"How did the kids do in their new school? Were there adjustment complications?" Jerry asked the principal of the school that had taken children from the mobile home park after the fire.

"It seemed to go smoothly, even though we were overcrowded," he answered. "Actually, they did quite well, although they complained about the bus ride."

"Any talk among them about having to move?"

"Not that I heard. At the last-day picnic the children all played together, but the parents from the trailer park only socialized with each other. I spoke with them, of course, but not about the park closure. It was mostly to tell them how the kids were doing."

In his conversation with the school bus driver, Jerry inquired about any changes she saw in the four months she had this new group of children in her charge.

"They kinda stayed together at first, but after a month they would go sit with classmates or other kids. Some of 'em. 'Course we had a problem with the bullying."

Why had Jerry not heard about this? "Bullying?" he asked, concerned.

"Heckling. Name calling. 'Trailer trash.' You know. That sort of thing."

"What did you do about it?" Jerry expected that some action had been taken.

"Didn't know what to do. Some of them kids are bigger'n me."

So, no report. Why wasn't there a zero tolerance policy on bullying and procedures for staff to follow when it happened? Another issue he must tackle.

One of the teachers had heard a rumor that tensions were running high among the parents at the park, and that nobody wanted to move. Over the weekend, Jerry decided, he would visit the trailer park himself, talk to the people there and try to get a feel for what was going on. Someone from the district should go with him, so they could check perceptions afterwards. Only one other; he didn't want to inadvertently intimidate, to give the impression of authority figures bearing down on the residents. He'd have to think about who might be the best person to accompany him, although he was pretty sure who it would be.

Jerry left his office early on Friday afternoon. He'd already gotten groceries the day before and saw to it that the house looked as good as the weekly cleaning service could accomplish. He was picking Pat up at 7:00. There were a few more things to do.

It was one of those June days before the heat and humidity of summer settle in, when the sky seems higher and the air lighter, the sun not yet overbearing. Jerry took a pair of clippers and went outside, heading up the brushy, wooded slope behind the carriage house. All spring he had noticed non-native flowers growing here and there, garden plants from years ago thriving where there were no more gardens. In March the daffodils had pushed up through the brown and rotting leaves of autumn. In April there had been hyacinths. May had brought tulips, lilies-of-the-valley, and the opulent blooms of old lilac bushes. Now, there were roses. They were the old-fashioned kind, thorny, but wonderfully fragrant, as old rose varieties can be. Jerry cut a bouquet of floribunda branches, then paused for a moment looking at the view from this elevation.

Below, the newly leafed-out trees along Main Street gave Colton the appearance of a charming and picturesque little village. He could see the spire of the Catholic Church downtown and the 1879 County Courthouse with its gold dome. Farther to the west, the hills, green and softened at this distance, climbed benignly into a clear blue sky. There was no evidence of gas drilling from here, no noise of changing gears as trucks made their way from drill sites, only the muffled sound of a lawnmower off in the neighborhood somewhere. Around him birds darted and flitted among the oaks, their spring songs vying with one another for territorial preeminence like operatic counterpoint.

On a day like this, he thought, even this scruffy hillside is beautiful. On a day like this, he could well understand why people had chosen to live here. Was Pat from Cross County too, he wondered? She had gone away to college; that was apparent. Standing on the hillside gazing at the town and valley below, then across to the hills beyond, he suddenly felt a pang of nostalgia. Not nostalgia for New England, but for a time of emotional fulfillment he'd had in his life and then lost. What he had now was a temporary situation and abbreviated at that. Well, you never saw this as anything else, he reminded himself. You saw it as a challenge, an adventure. And, he supposed, Pat was part of it, the challenge and the adventure? Damn this perfect June day, he thought, it throws your perspective all askew. But he was aware that his perspective had altered since coming here, and he was receptive to the idea of entertaining more changes. Mutual changes. He was determined to do all he could for Colton Area School District.

Pat stood in front of the opened double doors of her closet, taking stock of her wardrobe. Everything, she thought, everything in here was chosen with Elliot in mind. All of these clothes are associated with him, are bound up with our relationship. Whatever that was, she amended. Not for the first time, she thought of it as slipping into the past.

Jerry would be here in less than an hour. Should she invite him in for a drink? She did not want to appear inhospitable, but he had mentioned not having her car parked at his door, and perhaps they shouldn't advertise his being at her house either. Elliot always insisted on parking several blocks away in a 24-hour shopping plaza. And at that thought, their affair, which had afforded her so much excitement and given her so much confidence, looked tawdry to her.

Pat refocused her energies on her wardrobe and chose a linen shirt and a pair of denim slacks. It could get chilly later; she reached for a twill jacket, then changed her mind. Jerry appeared to be familiar with understated luxury. She took out an ivory cashmere cardigan she'd bought last fall in Martensdale: too light a color to go with her winter wardrobe, but just right for now. Then she stood in front of her mirror to evaluate the effect.

Her honey blond hair, soft blue eyes and slim figure reflected back at her, as if trying to convince her that she'd look smashing in whatever she wore. But Elliot's face came into her mind and gave her a jab of guilt, as though she were betraying him. "I will not have this!" she told herself. What did she feel towards him? She wasn't in love with him.

She had never envisioned a future with him. She was, what? Pat felt a compelling need to persevere until she reached a better understanding of her mental state. She studied her reflection and, as she did, her thoughts went back to what her image was a year ago, before Elliot. Not a pretty picture, she remembered with a laugh. Hair dull, a lot of gray. Extra weight around the middle.

"Grateful." There it was. She said the word aloud and not without a sense of surprise at uncovering such a fundamental sentiment. I am grateful to him for coming into my life when I badly needed to pull myself up. I am grateful for the attention he showed me. Gratitude: a powerful and complicated emotion and so easy to misinterpret. With this revelation, she felt an unmistakable feeling of freedom pervading her whole being. I do believe I can move on now, she thought with something close to astonishment.

Carl, having finished the last lawn mowing job of the day, put the leaf blower into the bed of the battered pickup truck. Seth was already sitting behind the wheel, the 17-year-old eager to resume his role as driver. His dad grunted as he climbed in. At least the two of them were having time together; anything to get him away from that nag of a mother of his. How come she got custody was beyond Carl, but Seth would be old enough to move out soon. Then, since it was summer, they had income from their lawn jobs and most of that the kid was saving for college. Not nearly enough, though. He'd have to think of how to come up with more. Carl stared morosely out the window as they drove down the winding streets of the hillside, past the newly restored homes of the people with money. He saw the Super's car stopping in front of that little place of his. Then he noticed the passenger side door opening. "Huh?" said Carl, squinting thoughtfully, as Mrs. Foster got out carrying a bottle of wine.

Chapter 11

The carriage house Jerry was renting was initially built in the late 1890s and modernized in the 1920s, when it was expanded to accommodate the new motor cars. His living quarters covered most of the whole span above a three-car garage. A private entrance in the front opened on a small area with the stairs to his apartment, plus washer and dryer and a few other amenities tucked behind. When the rehab was done the previous year, no expense had been spared on both house and garage, and the carriage house had been given up-to-date plumbing and insulation, heating and air-conditioning, new windows and a small but state-of-the-art kitchen. A narrow deck with an outside stairway had been added onto the back.

There was no doubt in his mind that Jerry regarded the evening with Pat as a date, even though he was not planning to press it to a date's normally preferred conclusion, however much that might be desired. What he intended was to create an atmosphere which would allow her to feel unselfconscious, be able to express herself freely, and bring out whatever facets of her personality she wished to share with him. Keep it light, friendly and open would be his approach.

Jerry got out in front of Pat's split-level ranch, trying not to let his expression indicate the distaste he felt for its ungainly aspect, and then saw Pat closing her door and coming down the walk with a smile for him. The house receded into the background. He was enchanted by the sight of her. Away from the district office her attraction seemed to double.

"Madam President," Jerry said in the gravest possible tones but with a clearly discernable twinkle in his eyes, "you do me an honor to ride in my painfully utilitarian conveyance."

She laughed as he opened the door for her. This was a side of his personality she hadn't seen before from the always pleasant, but unfailingly business-like Dr. Strauss of her experience.

"I've never been in a Land Rover," Pat began the conversation as they got underway.

Jerry admitted, "Neither had I, but someone suggested I might need a vehicle that could withstand the many hazardous conditions encountered in the wilderness of Cross County."

"Anticipating the worst, were you?" she asked brightly.

"High water, bridges out: the usual," he answered matter-of-factly.

"What bridges? We ford our streams around here, Mister."

Beautiful and a sense of humor! It must be totally wasted on Elliot. "During which, I suppose, one would invariably meet up with a hungry bear?"

"Bears," Pat corrected him. "In Cross County they travel in packs, along with the wolves. For protection from the panthers."

Jerry laughed in appreciation. A side of her he hadn't anticipated.

Pat went on, "You know, seriously, Jerry, if you'd been to Colton only a few years ago, the chief hazard was potholes in Main Street. We've come a long way. In Colton, at least."

"Not Deems Township, I take it?"

"Still primitive."

"A throwback to an earlier age?"

"Like the rest of the county."

Pat was happily letting herself be charmed by Jerry. His wit and lightheartedness brought out a similar reaction in her. How long was it since she'd known someone like him? Not since she'd come back to Cross County, over twenty-five years ago. Jerry was becoming more engaging every moment, and the sense of freedom she had begun to experience earlier was reinforced by being with him.

They were starting up the road in the hillside neighborhood where Jerry lived and Pat looked with interest at her surroundings. "Gosh!" she said. "How this area has changed! When I was last here it was so sad and run-down. It's anything but sad now."

They had turned into a driveway, heading toward a grand Edwardian stone house about which, as they came closer, Pat said, "The Mitchell Mansion," in a hushed voice.

"Not anymore, though," Jerry responded. "It's a family from Texas."

Jerry drove on up the driveway to where the bays of the garage faced the side of the main house and parked in front of the last one. "This is my humble living space, Ma'am," he said when they got out. "Well, not the garage," he clarified. "We go upstairs."

He took the proffered bottle of wine and they walked around to the deck stairway. The landing step was a single piece of limestone with plantings on either side. Jerry said, "The old carriage block," then noticed that Pat had paused, staring contemplatively at it.

"I remember..." she started to say, looked away and didn't finish her thought, but took hold of the handrail and headed up the steps.

The sun had moved around to the northwest and the deck was bathed in the clear glow of late afternoon. They stood at the railing, taking in the view of the hills beyond and what Jerry called "my vertical backyard."

Pat said, "It's beautiful here, just beautiful. I had no idea. Well, maybe I should have guessed."

"Guessed?" he asked, tilting his head to look at her. "Do I have 'garage' writ large all over me?"

"No," she said laughing. "It was when you picked me up. I could see you were regarding my house with something less than unconditional approval."

"Did it show so much? I'm terribly sorry..." he began, but she interrupted, shaking her head.

"I wouldn't have expected anything else, truly, Jerry. The house was built by my ex-husband's construction company and when he cut out, with the young secretary, by the way, I got it and enough assets to be financially secure. The only reason I've kept it is for John, who grew up there and wants his mom to be where he's always known her. Plus, he's got a hundred cubic feet of stuff stowed in the place. Frankly, it's inertia or I'd sell, but the side effect is that it makes me seem more on a par with many of my fellow Cross Countians."

Jerry digested all this, glad to have the most acceptable explanation, glad she felt like telling him, and so easily. "I wondered, Pat. You are so damned classy; it just didn't compute. Sorry again!" he apologized. "How dare I judge?"

"Judge away," she answered. "I'd rather you gave me the benefit of your perceptions. They mean a lot to me."

"Come. Let's go in and you can have a shot at my domestic arrangements." He opened a French door and stepped back to let her go through.

The room she entered seemed the ideal living space to Pat. With windows front and back it had the feeling of light and spaciousness. On the left was a compact, well-endowed galley kitchen and on the right doors to the bedroom and bathroom. Oriental rugs in bright hues covered the wooden floor. Instead of the traditional sofa there were window seats with moss green cushions, but Pat also saw a sturdy old rocking chair. "That looks like vintage Cross County," she said, turning to Jerry for corroboration.

"It is," he affirmed. "Stress-reducing and very comfortable, when there isn't a stack of books on the seat." He took them off and put them on the floor. "I couldn't find a place for bookcases," he explained, "so I've learned to ignore the problem."

A late 19th century oak desk held file folders and computer, and there was a round oak dining table of the same era, set for two, in the middle of which was a white pitcher filled with a luxuriance of roses. Pat flew over to the table, stroking the glossy white ironstone and inhaling the roses' incomparable fragrance. She sighed and Jerry smiled. "I hoped you'd like them," he said.

"I like everything! But where in the world did you find roses like these?"

"Rose bushes, escapees, I imagine, have propagated all up the hillside. Given their variety, I'm guessing they must have been planted over a hundred years ago, about the same time the pitcher was potted. They're what my gardener calls heirloom roses."

Pat looked up. "Your gardener?" she asked uncertainly.

"I should have said ex-gardener. As in ex-wife, as in ex-wife's home and garden."

"Oh, I'm sorry," said Pat, "I didn't mean to pry."

"Not a bit!" Jerry exclaimed. "You were not in any conceivable way prying. Let me just say that no longer having a gardener is a small price to pay for freedom."

"I can understand that without any difficulty," Pat replied with a nod.

Jerry had marinated chicken earlier, which he now grilled out on the deck. With fresh vegetables and bread from the farmers' market, they ate at the table in a lively yet unhurried manner, both in surprised awareness that it all, somehow, seemed so natural.

Pat complimented him lavishly. "Everything you've fixed is delicious and, what's more, goes together perfectly. No mean feat. Likes antiques *and* cooks. What a find you are! You enjoy cooking, I can tell."

Jerry smiled, glad that he'd pleased her with so little effort. "I do, yes. It's both relaxing and challenging. I was surprised to see the extent of produce on offer at the growers' market here. I hadn't been expecting such an abundance of resources locally."

"You can thank the out-of-towners for that. The energy companies underwrote the cost of farmers' high tunnels to extend the growing season and paid for advertising and rental space for the market. Things like that were done deliberately, to help compensate for the difficulties caused by their presence, mainly the large number of drillers, sometimes unruly, who came with them."

"Pluses and minuses," Jerry said, "a bit of a revelation to me. I think this calls for dessert."

They had local strawberries which Jerry had sliced ahead of time and sprinkled with brown sugar. These went over frozen yogurt, "from Lancaster County, PA," he announced.

"You *are* settling in nicely," she said. "And you whip up one tasty meal." She gave him an odd little amused look after this remark.

"What?" he asked her. "What have I done to cause that look?"

"Nothing you have done or are ever likely to do. I take it you haven't heard of Cross County Cuisine?"

"No, but I can guess. It involves hunting?"

"Hunting, trapping, scavenging on the highway. The smaller animals mostly: squirrel, possum, muskrat. I won't go on. You have just given me a scrumptious dinner and here I am talking about the unmentionable. Please forget I told you about Cross County's embarrassing culinary secret."

"One of many secrets? And are they all as unappetizing?"

"More so, I should think," Pat admitted. "Cross County has a reputation for keeping its secrets, but now and then the public has to be warned."

"Well, that's a comfort. I'll try to stay alert." Then he made a stab at returning to his agenda. "But I asked you here to let you talk about whatever is on your mind, district-wise. I still want your opinion on a few things. Are you up to doing that? Or am I being a bore about it? We don't have to."

"I'm completely at your disposal. We've wined and dined, as goes the old refrain..."

Jerry uttered a brief cry of dismay. "Oh, darn, I'd meant to put on some music! I'll clear up and make a pot of coffee if you pick out what you'd like to hear," he said, indicating the modest system set up on an old maple school desk.

Pat looked through a collection of CDs, mostly classical, opera and choral music, but also an impressive group of jazz: Miles Davis. Billie Holiday. Brubeck, Desmond, Getz. *That* brought back memories. She started a disc and sat, hugging her knees, on a cushion on the floor. Bossa Nova: bars in Seattle, fog coming in.

"Pat?" Jerry was standing close to her, holding a tray with two cups, a coffee pot and a bottle of cognac.

"Lord, Jerry, I'm back at U Dub," she said, uncurling herself and getting up. "It's as if thirty plus years have just been erased."

"Well, I can see you're no good for all practical purposes now," he responded pleasantly. "We'll head for the outdoors. Fresh air and the last of the sunset to buck you up." University of Washington? More and more unexpected.

They seated themselves at the small table on the deck. Almost the summer solstice, the sky still held a trembling luminosity at 9:00. Nearby, hidden amid branches, a robin was tirelessly chirping its two-note end-of-the-day song. Jerry served the coffee and added cognac to the cups.

"You are probably wondering," Pat began, "what I was doing wallowing in the past."

"I'm wondering about a lot of things," Jerry admitted and, confident they were moving to a new and closer phase in their relationship, went on. "About the way you said 'The Mitchell Mansion' in such hallowed tones. About the aborted phrase 'I remember' when I pointed out the stepping stone. About the fact that you are fully conversant with the culture of Cross County and yet are so much more cosmopolitan. Your vocabulary. Your inflections. I've been trying to puzzle it out. Your accent is not really Eastern Seaboard. Certainly not Appalachian. I had placed it as West Coast, but that was pretty much a guess based on the process of elimination. Pat, please, tell me: who are you?" he implored.

She said simply, "My maiden name was Mitchell."

Chapter 12

The light had faded and in the dusk of the June night they sat talking.

"I didn't start out with the purpose of unloading my life history on you," Pat said. "Everyone around here knows anyway. Then we came up the driveway and I wanted, unconsciously I guess, for you to see this place through my eyes. Strange, do you think?"

"It's where we are, what memories the place has evoked," he ventured. "They want communicating."

"More than that. It's you, Jerry. You being so receptive to me. And you're very observant. You seem to be reading my mind, although I assume you're just picking up on behavioral clues. Oh, crap, I sound like a damned sociologist. Well, I was, you know. A social worker."

"Ah," said Jerry.

"Ah?"

"It's what I've sensed. That you are compassionate; you sincerely try to understand others' viewpoints."

"See? There you are: observing."

"Sorry," he said contritely.

"No! I like it! It's one of the many reasons I like you so much." Oh, what am I saying, she thought wildly? He'll wonder what I'm up to.

"Pat," Jerry said, making a sudden decision, "may I kiss you now or do I have to wait until the evening is over?" He reached across and put his hand under her chin, lightly lifting it towards him, gave her the gentlest kiss he could manage, and leaned back again.

For a little while there was an unaccustomed loss of speech on both their parts. It was not an awkward pause, but rather a moment to savor the new, welcome intimacy they had experienced. Pat let the softness of his kiss wash over her, Jerry was concentrating on how her lips felt on his. He poured cognac into their empty cups and they drank in a kind of blissful silence.

With an effort, Jerry pulled himself together and lighted the citronella candle on the table. "For the mosquitos," he said in what he hoped was a normal voice. "I assume it keeps them away, because I haven't been bothered."

"It also has to do, I think, with the limestone soil around here," Pat managed, amazed at her ability to muster an ordinary-sounding statement when her thoughts were flying around in an extraordinary fashion. Reassured by her ability to function, she went on, "The drainage is such that there isn't enough standing water for them to breed,"

"Another well-kept secret of Cross County?"

"Mmm," she answered dreamily, her mind going back to his kiss.

"Lovely, lovely, Patricia Mitchell," he said softly. "Won't you continue your story?"

"Oh, dear," she said, "I wasn't what anyone would call lovely back then, back when I was a skinny little kid, and my brother and I would sneak over here to play, even though it was strictly forbidden for us to go anywhere near the old Mitchell place."

"But you did," he encouraged.

"Wild horses couldn't have kept us away."

The big stone house had been bought in the 1920s by Pat's grandfather, a physician from Baltimore. He had been asked to help start a hospital in Colton when the mines were in full swing. He came and settled in Cross County, knowing his medical expertise was desperately needed in this out-of-the-way locale. Dr. Mitchell and his wife were civic minded, sociable and supportive of the growing town. He became an influential member of the community, serving on the borough council, while Pat's grandmother organized a ladies' book circle, started a local historical society and founded the hospital auxiliary. A leading family, they endowed the fledgling library, entertained frequently and hosted charitable events. They had one son.

Pat's father was expected to follow in the footsteps of his successful parent, and he duly went to medical school, coming back to join his father in practice at the hospital. After several years, it was clear that bad habits he had picked up while away at school, namely drinking and gambling, had not been left behind. The elder doctor was increasingly exasperated with him, even though young Dr. Mitchell had skill and popularity. His parents decided that the answer was to find him a suitable wife, who would straighten him out. The daughter of old family friends in Baltimore was sent for and, although she was quite a bit younger and of a different religion, she was beautiful and willing. The marriage seemed to be what was hoped for. They had a boy, then a girl.

In the 1970s what mines were left in the county were shutting down. Pat's grandparents had died and the young Mitchells could not keep up the stately house. It was closed and they moved to a smaller home near the hospital. Colton started to take on more and more the feel of a depressed area. There were always people in need of medical attention, but patients had difficulty paying their bills and Dr. Mitchell forgave many fees. The hospital itself was struggling and the staff was reduced. The big house was sold, bought by someone who was hoping to turn it into apartments. For several years it stood vacant, its handsome leaded-glass windows boarded up.

The neighborhood with its once-proud homes held an irresistible attraction for the two children. In the tangle of overgrown, ruined gardens, they found marbles, lead soldiers, and shards of delicately painted pottery; sometimes there were coins, a silver fork or spoon. All these they kept hidden from their parents, a windfall of riches to be taken out privately and viewed with wonder again and again. They played games they imagined children played long ago: a form of tag with a crumbling stone pillar as home base, and Indian hide-and-seek, where the rule was to make no noise whatsoever, almost impossible in the rustling undergrowth.

"Sometimes we pretended to be owners of the house," Pat told Jerry. "It was vacant by then, although a caretaker was supposed to be living on the premises, probably up here. We never saw him, so were quite bold, going up on the porch, then walking down the steps in a lordly fashion. My favorite game was horse-and-carriage."

"Ah, ha!" Jerry exclaimed.

"Yes, we had discovered the carriage block. Tim knew what it was, probably from books he'd read. I was the fine lady who stepped up on it preparatory to entering my carriage, while Tim was footman and coachman, holding the door for me." Pat laughed lightly. "Sometimes, though, I was the restless horse, pawing impatiently at the ground, eager to be off."

Jerry smiled at the quite-believable image of Pat as a prancing steed. "And now, all grown up," he said, "you have trod upon that same mounting stone. Yes, it must have been strange."

"Strange and familiar. So many memories. Well, that phase came to an end when workers arrived to knock out interior walls and convert it into an apartment house. I never came here again. Until tonight."

She was quiet for a moment and Jerry let her collect her thoughts. "I'm going to finish in a minute, Jerry. It gets painful, so please bear with me."

"Pat, you don't need to go on."

"No, I do. Five years later—I had just turned twelve—my father was killed." She paused, then went on, "He had started to drink again and, I guess, gamble. One night he didn't come home. There was a train trestle a little way out of town..."

It was a high trestle over a deep gully. The trains no longer ran, but the tracks were still there. Why he had decided to go walking on the railroad tracks was a mystery. The newspaper reported that someone recalled they'd heard a man singing "Maryland, My Maryland." His body was found the next day in dense brush near the trestle.

Pat continued, "The accident was more than my mother could bear. A few months later she called her sister in Spokane to come get us for a 'vacation,' wrote two letters, one to Tim and one to me, and after we'd left, took an overdose of pills she'd been hoarding."

"Oh, Pat," said Jerry, and reached out and took her hand.

She gave him a smile. "Well, now you know," she said, feeling the firmness of his hand lending her strength.

Then she went on, "Funny, but at the time, it wasn't as bad as it should have been, seen now in retrospect. I was so young, our aunt and uncle were wonderful to us, we had cousins to be with, new schools and new friends. The West was an exciting place. In the summer there were hot, dry pine forests and cold, clear lakes; in the winter we went skiing. Then Seattle, university and graduate school. But after I got my MSW and was doing social work, I began to think more and more about coming back again. Much of the rural area north of Spokane and east into Idaho has a version of Cross County's wild, forlorn beauty and, among the inhabitants, the same combination of poverty and obstinacy. It reminded me of home."

They were quiet for a moment, reflecting, each of them. He still held her hand. They had only begun to learn about each other. Her freely-disclosed past, his readily-given support.

Jerry spoke first. "Thank you, Pat, for telling me. I am, for probably only the second time in my life, humbled."

"No, it's you I should thank, for listening. For letting me unburden."

"And in doing so you have given me a gift. You've unabashedly handed me your past. It's saying you trust me; it's a statement about your belief in my compassion and understanding. Not too many people have done that before," he confessed.

"I don't see why not. You are eminently approachable," she said earnestly.

"I've been accused of insufferable arrogance in the past." She began to protest and he shook his head, saying, "I think it was a sort of armor. I must have felt the need for it."

"And now? I don't see a trace of arrogance about you."

He responded with a smile, "It has dissipated under the natural goodness of Cross County."

"And what has replaced it?" she asked. "How do you protect yourself now?"

His answer was to the point: "From you? Strength of will." He saw the slight widening of her eyes at the implication. "But it's only a matter of time before you'll break through. Or perhaps I'll give up the struggle first. It's only a matter of time for us."

The candle flickered and beyond, in the dark, an owl hooted. The deep, haunting sound, solitary and compelling, brought near the lonely, untamed nature of Cross County. Pat shivered.

Jerry got up, releasing her hand. "Hey, none of that! Let me get your sweater." He was back in a minute and put the cashmere cardigan around her shoulders.

"Thanks, Jerry. We can go in if you'd rather, although it's heaven out here and I'm not a bit melancholy, really."

"Then will you tell me one more thing? Are you glad, all in all, that you came back to Cross County?"

"Yes, very glad, even though the man I married turned out to be a mistake. He was a good father though, and John is doing well in the army. They feel he's officer material, so they're sending him to college. My brother, however, never wanted to set foot in Cross County again. And yet he followed family precedent and went to med school. He's a pediatrician in California, close to where John is stationed, so Johnny gets to see his Uncle Tim and family often. That's where I'm heading at the end of July." She looked pensive and then said, "I knew from the start why I wanted to come back here. Maybe it was the social worker in me or maybe it was some intangible legacy from my grandparents, but there is so much good about this area, and I felt a strong need to do what I could to help the people of Cross County." Her eyes rested on Jerry in the candlelight. She thought she detected a wistful look on his face. "Jerry," she asked, "Have I made you sad? I didn't mean to."

"No, not sad, just turning over in my mind this feeling of affinity with you that I have, a sense of connection."

"Then you must tell me about yourself. I want to know you better."

"I will, I promise. But it's too long and far too lugubrious to begin now. However," he said in a lighter tone, "what are you doing on Sunday?"

"This Sunday? No plans. What do you need, Supe?" she asked brightly.

"An accomplice to go on a fact-finding mission with me."

"Elk Creek Mobile Home Park?"

"How did you know?"

"I saw today's *Clarion* too."

"How does that sound? Shall we pay a visit to them?"

"An excellent idea. I should think by 4:00 in the afternoon any of them who went to The Pit the night before will have recovered."

He took her home and they continued talking about the trailer park closure. When they got to her house, she opened the car door and turned to him, saying, "Thank you for this evening, Jerry. I can't tell you how much it has meant. But I'll try to, next time."

He looked at her fondly, knowing it probably showed in his face. "It has been delightful, Pat, being with you. Thank you for wanting me to be part of your life. I'm glad there will be a next time."

They smiled at each other and then she leaned over and, in a swift movement, took his hand, pressed it to her lips for a second, and got out.

Chapter 13

That night, Pat lay thinking about Jerry and how much she liked the man she was beginning to know. His humor, his receptiveness; she'd had no idea he'd be this way. Amazing, too, that he was living in the one place which brought a reawakening of her past, and then being able to share it with him. Most of all, she relived his kiss, a kiss so politely requested, gentle though by no means shy, and holding a promise for the future. I wonder, she thought drowsily, if it seemed odd to him that I kissed his hand before I got out of the car. She had wanted to give him a sign of the affection she felt towards him, and that was the hand he'd reached out to hold hers. She was starting to fall asleep. Words and phrases came back to her. Just a matter of time, he had said. A small price to pay for freedom, he had said. Some relationships, she thought, are hampering and some are liberating. I must remember to get my house key back from Elliot.

Jerry drove home, parked and went up the back stairway to the deck. The waning moon had just risen through the trees and gave the night sky a presence, a completeness. He stood at the railing, taking it in and experiencing a sense of ebullience tinged with wonder, thinking: this evening did not turn out entirely as I'd planned. Let her talk, yes. But he certainly hadn't any intention of giving her that kiss. Premature? Yet at that moment it just seemed right. And then, in parting, she had kissed his hand. What a charming gesture. Don't you dare think about it, he told himself, whether she'd ever kissed

Elliot's hand. Madam, I kiss your hand. What was its origin? It was a form of tribute, wasn't it? An acknowledgement, a sign of appreciation. Sometimes of submission.

What had impressed him was her unaffected candor. No theatrics, and it was quite a recital, that tale of three generations, accidental death, suicide, starting anew. He was in awe of her resilience and even more so of her composure. She's too good for Cross County, he started to think, then immediately checked the thought. This is where she wants to be. She is fully conscious of herself as a bridge to a better future and I applaud her. One could worship that woman, he thought. There are worse religions.

He looked at his watch. After 11:00. He still had work to do, reading, answering emails. He had a final look at the night sky, then turned in the direction of Pat's house. "Goodnight, Miss Mitchell," he whispered. "It's only a matter of time."

On Saturdays Jerry played golf with a floating foursome, the membership of which varied with who was in town and free. The course had been carved out of rocky, hilly country west of Colton and underwritten by the gas industry. A small clubhouse had been built and it had attentive staff, a well-appointed dining facility and a first-rate chef. The staff were trained; they came with the gas companies.

The country club was semi-private; one needed an invitation to play there and only those with relatively prestigious positions in the community were invited. The people who made up Jerry's foursomes were mostly members of the Rotary Club, which he had joined when he first came to town. It was a social outing and, for Jerry, a chance to take the pulse of the elite of Cross County.

Rotarians are a gregarious bunch, Jerry had always thought, an attribute he found useful. After a round, there would be lunch at the clubhouse, where lively conversations were the rule, springing up, not only among the foursome, but with whomever else happened to be drawn in. While he was content to be a listener, he also answered questions about the school district and was often asked to elaborate on policy.

On this Saturday they were serving on the veranda, where the tables overlooked a view of fairways in the foreground, hills in the background. A gentle breeze rippled the flags on the greens. Players were in no hurry to leave this idyllic setting, and iced tea had been refilled for some, whiskey for others. A couple of gas industry executives were present and one of them had put forth the general question asked of school superintendents, "How are things going education-wise?"

Jerry decided to see if he could broker a deal in this relaxed ambience. "We're looking to put some courses in place for college-bound kids or those who might be interested in going on. But just as important, we'd like to have options for careers that don't initially depend on higher education. There's no vo-tech school here, as you probably know. I want to begin with some programs in the fall."

The executive looked interested. "Are you thinking about the kind of training for entry level jobs in the energy industry?" he asked.

"Definitely. Kids are seeing it as a real opportunity for them. It would teach skills they could use in a variety of places. That's the point: options."

"Sounds like a very good idea. Have you sketched out some areas for these vo-tech offerings?"

"Well, we've got the hospital committed for the medical technology angle and one of the restaurants has agreed to partner with us. But we would absolutely need your input to map out other courses. I'm afraid we'll have to start modestly, as our finances are limited due to the expenditures we're experiencing with our obligations to the charter school," and here he fixed a pleasant but serious look on his listeners, "particularly if it goes ahead and adds grades."

The executive turned to one of his fellows. "You have kids at the school, don't you?" he asked him.

"My son is there, but my daughter started at the high school last year and I want you to know," he said to Jerry, "that she loves it. She's on the rifle team. That little gal is a regular Annie Oakley. She couldn't be more tickled. I tell you, the boy is so jealous, he wants to leave Power Learners, but his mom won't hear of it." He gestured to a man sitting apart who had just been served another glass of bourbon. "Hey, Clarence, you're on the board of the school. You could answer the superintendent's questions about what it's gonna cost."

Clarence frowned. "I don't have that kind of information," he said with annoyance in his voice. "We contract that part out to a corporation."

"Oh, that's right, I forgot. Star Learners is it? Or Learning Star? Or maybe Star Power?" And he laughed.

Clarence's answer was inaudible.

"What say," the executive proposed to Jerry, "you write me up a list of what you'd like to be able to offer kids and shoot it to us. I'll see what we can do from our end. I think this could turn into a very beneficial collaborative effort."

And that, thought Jerry, is why I play golf.

Owen tried to put in a day at the shop at least every other Saturday. Cider Run was a stimulating place to be on weekends, with a busy stream of customers. During lulls he and Keith could have a chance to catch up, and Owen looked forward to seeing the other Cider Run dealers he'd gotten close to over the last few years. Today they were working with Emmy, always an interesting, if exhaustive, source of information and Sally Ann, a sweetie if there ever was one. Sally Ann, whose wardrobe typically reflected one of the four decades of her merchandise, was togged out in a Sixties get-up—linen sleeveless sheath in an avocado and burnt orange abstract print, avocado high heeled pointed-toe pumps and plastic clip-on earrings, the look completed by a platinum blond bouffant hairdo. Emmy was dressed in black, as usual.

Between waiting on customers, dealers often congregated at the front counter where they chatted, gossiped, told stories and traded quips and insults. This enjoyable activity was sporadically disrupted by customers coming in, so conversations were often abruptly terminated or disjointed at best.

Owen had started by saying that he had the greatest Supe. Keith was asking what kind of soup was that?

Sally Ann said, "Honey, when I lived in Cross County, that was all we had. You didn't want to ask what the meat was in it."

Emmy entered in with a nod at Sally Ann. "In China it's the same way. On our last trip I could swear that it was dog..."

"How could you swear to that, Emmy? Have you tasted dog?" Keith challenged.

"Not S-O-U-P," Owen shouted, "S-U-P-E, as in Superintendent!"

"Why didn't you say so?" Keith rejoined quietly.

"The food was barely edible," Sally Ann persevered, "but we were so poor I was just thankful that my mother-in-law fed us. I know it wasn't only because she felt bad about her son running off and leaving me before Rosie was a week old. Yes, I owed Rosie's Grandma Hodges the world and she died before I could repay her." A few tears welled up in her blue eyes.

This brought a moment of sobering silence on everyone's part.

Sally Ann brightened, "But I did take Rosie to see her a few times and that made her happy."

"When was the last time you were there?" Owen asked.

"Oh, years and years ago. Rosie couldn't have been more than five. It was sad to visit, because Colton was so shabby and worn." Once again, her face registered downheartedness.

"Well, you wouldn't know the place now, Sally Ann," Owen said. "They have fixed up everything, repaired the streets, planted trees—you name it. There are all sorts of new businesses and housing developments going up."

"Food any better?" Keith asked laconically.

"Hey, they even have a farmers' market with local produce, breads and all. Lynn always has me stop on Thursdays before I come home."

"In England they don't only have food," Emmy, whose son was finishing up an advanced degree there, needlessly explained. "The outdoor market in Cambridge runs every day and you could furnish your whole flat from the stalls. When we were visiting Noel last spring..."

It was a shop practice to interrupt Emmy. "By the way, Emmy," Owen cut in, "I'm looking for information on scholarships, and since you teach piano I thought you might know about music stipends and such."

Emmy nodded enthusiastically. "I had a pupil from Cross County; she was exceedingly talented. We got her a grant to spend her summers at the music camp at Interlochen in Michigan. When she graduated from Colton High she had offers from all over. She's at Julliard now."

The door opened and several customers came in. Emmy went off to be helpful, while Keith took his turn at the computer. Owen said to Sally Ann, "Is Paul home? I need to talk with him."

Sally Ann shook her head. "He's in Harrisburg for the Homicide Investigators conference this weekend. Can I do anything?"

"Thanks, Sally Ann, I'll see him next time."

Pat had gotten in the habit of reserving Saturday evenings for Elliot, even though he didn't always spend them with her. This Saturday, however, she made other plans and, instead of staying home, went up to Martensdale for a night out with some girlfriends.

And Carl decided that tomorrow he'd better start thinking about where to store his family's stuff from their trailer.

Chapter 14

On Sunday morning when Jerry went out on his deck with the coffee and newspaper, he was aware that the weather was starting to turn. While the forecast hadn't called for rain, there was more humidity in the air and the view towards town was not as clear. The sky was a paler blue, giving the impression that it wasn't as high as before and would soon lower itself even more until, white and opaque, it rested upon the hilltops of Cross County. Rather than being upset at the ending of perfect June days, Jerry looked forward to his next experiences in this new locale of his or, as they say in Pennsylvania, "What is Coming Down the Pike." This optimistic feeling was due in no small part to Pat.

The beginning of a love affair, he reflected, is always like this. There is a state of heightened awareness, of excited hopefulness, even of self-congratulation, because one has unfolding pleasures to anticipate. To postpone making love is in itself a luxury, prolonging the sweet agony of desire. Since Jerry's ego was well-developed, he had no doubt that when he was ready she would be ready. But he had also learned a few things about her over the months he'd known her: that she was forthright and not reticent when it came to taking the initiative. And that might be even more fun. A challenge and an adventure. He was quite equal to all the challenges. Now for the adventure.

Jerry gave Pat a call to arrange their visit to the mobile home park. "I can pick you up if you'd like, unless you'd rather take your own car," he offered. "However, I don't see why we can't arrive together."

"No reason at all. But since I live farther away, why don't I come and get you? About 4:00? And do I mount by way of the carriage block?"

In accordance with his plan to keep temptation to a minimum, but maintain the frisson of Friday evening, he answered, "Would we make it to the park at all if you were to appear on my threshold? I'll come down. See you at 4:00."

When they arrived at the trailer park in Pat's older model sedan, they had been talking about the district's responsibility to these about-to-be evicted families. Both had agreed that because of the school fire and the dislocation it caused, there was a basis on which to argue that the children needed more time to adjust before having to make another move.

"It wouldn't be right to displace them again, and this time an even more traumatic disruption," Pat had said.

Jerry put in, "Although, when I asked the principal if he thought they had experienced difficulties in their new school, he replied that they had done very well."

"He would. He's the principal," was Pat's terse response.

"Oh, ho!" Jerry exclaimed. "Do I detect a modicum of doubt about his veracity? Or perhaps his powers of perception?"

"Both. It's why Owen Griffith was hired as vice-principal at the high school, instead of this guy. Don't get me wrong, Jerry. It's not that he's being intentionally dishonest. He's typical. You know: first of the year letter to parents, 'We're off to a great start!' when things are in complete disarray and half the kids are still out in the woods hunting rabbits."

"You do understand your target audience."

"I was one of 'em once."

Pat pulled into the entranceway, a gravel drive over which arched a delicate wrought iron structure, anchored on either side by stone pillars. A sign affixed to the span read *Welcome to Elk Creek Mobile Home Park.*

"The pillars and ironwork came from an estate in your neighborhood that was torn down in the 1970s," Pat said, seeing Jerry's interested look as they drove beneath it.

"Touch of class," he remarked. "Unusual to say the least."

"Adaptive reuse, a timeless tradition," she said, as she parked in a gravel area underneath mature maple trees, their spreading branches shading two trailers.

The park had been laid out on a south facing hillside. Maples were planted between many of the concrete pads on which the trailers sat and, in this late afternoon, the sun was a softly filtered light beneath mature, full-leafed trees. The sound of children's voices at play could be heard and they began to walk up the road.

While the homes were modest, they were in decent repair. Jerry noticed that several had small gardens in which vegetables were growing, and there were planters and pots of flowers by many of the doorways. Pat knew Jerry was making a mental note of these evidences of civilized domestication. "It's not your usual trailer park," she explained. "Some of these families have made their homes here for over thirty years."

"I was told it was a real community; it certainly seems there's community pride in operation."

They had begun to be noticed. A few curtains moved behind windows. A woman came out on her stoop and said, "Afternoon, Miz Foster, Dr. Strauss."

More people started to appear, most of whom Pat spoke to by name. The residents were friendly but guarded. To be expected, thought Jerry. No one asked why they had come nor did they have any questions for the pair, but several followed in their wake up the hill.

The playground was a small, flat area equipped with swings, a slide, a climbing structure and sandbox, and children were using them all, bouncing around everywhere, uninhibited. Not bad, Jerry thought. Unlike many new housing developments, where everyone is assumed to have their own play equipment, so why bother with a communal effort? Because then kids can play together. Like they are here, learning socialization skills. More points for the park.

A few parents and grandparents were sitting with toddlers on what looked like newly-installed benches. Jerry was ready to begin a conversation, outside of nods and greetings, but he was letting Pat take the lead in this, and she was waiting for the residents to feel comfortable with their presence. She had begun with some small talk about the weather and the high school baseball team, and soon a dialogue emerged.

"What a terrific play area this is!" she had said. "And I see you have put in benches."

"They do give a nice sit-down, Miz Foster," chirped a mother of two who was expecting her third in the very near future.

"How did that oldest one do in her new school? It must have been different, going all the way into Colton."

"Oh, she din't mind, 'cause the other kids went with, on the bus, you know."

A second mother got into the conversation, demurring, "That bus was some gettin' used to."

"Well," said the first speaker, "it toughens 'em up, to be called names."

Jerry put in. "I heard about that. Name calling isn't right. No kind of bullying is right."

A group had been forming around Pat and Jerry, and at this exchange someone thrust his head in and demanded,

"What can *you* do about it? *You* ain't gonna ride the bus with them kids."

Jerry looked at him, a frank and friendly look, and said, "We want to put a stop to bullying in the bus and everywhere else it happens. But I am wondering: you know your kids. What would you suggest? What might work?"

This brought a number of people weighing in on the subject and Jerry, in the middle, listened. Offers came fast and furiously. Many had to do with firearms, the carrying and displaying of same, but there were more constructive suggestions as well, such as rewarding kids for not bullying and having alternate forms of transportation available. Jerry responded, learned their thoughts, gave examples of what had worked in other schools, got some fresh ideas and thanked them.

Pat was beaming at him by this time. He's doing his magic, she thought. She let him take over.

"But why we came to see you today was to learn more about the park closure. We are very involved in what happens here. These kids are our kids. They go to our schools." He paused for a second to let this point sink in, then went on, "The younger ones have had a big disruption in their lives because of the fire just a few months ago. How will they cope if they have another, even greater, disruption? That's what concerns us."

One member of the group separated himself out, apparently by agreement of the others, to act as spokesman. "Well, we was gonna go to school board meetin' come Tuesday night an' say jes that."

Was going to? Pat and Jerry looked at each other. "Have you changed your mind, Mr. Duncan?" Pat sounded disappointed.

The speaker turned to Pat. "We was told wouldn't do no good, Mrs. Foster. Not to waste our time."

"Who told you that?" Jerry asked, irritation in his voice. "We were anxious to have your views on this whole situation."

"One of folks said he'd heard it. Said he was told to pass it along. Didn't say who 'zactly."

"Certainly not someone from the school district. Must have been the township. Or the buyers. Do we know who they are?" Jerry asked Pat.

Pat answered, "We don't. That was one of the things we were hoping we'd learn today."

"Oh, them buyers wouldn't talk to us. Anyway, it's some corporation. I kept the notify letter. Most folks threw 'em away, bein' so disgusted."

"I'd like to see what your notice says, Mr. Duncan, if I may," Jerry requested courteously.

"I'll go find it if you'uns want to drop by on way out."

Pat asked, "So you think the township people discouraged you from meeting with us?"

"Naw. Wouldn't be township. They said they'd put 'em off eviction as long as they could. We got good people on township. Yep. Thems the ones tol' us to go meet with the school board, hopin' it'd help. We reckon someone else."

"No one from the schools would do that," Pat said frowning.

"Not you, Mrs. Foster. Nor ain't Dr. Strauss here. T'other guy most likely."

"Other guy?" Pat asked.

"That there other Doc."

Pat's face blanched. "Dr. Lucas?" She almost whispered it.

"Dunno for sure. Just a guess. Said he wanted to spare us the bother an' all. What we heard."

"You don't say," Jerry murmured.

Chapter 15

The floodgates having been opened, a torrent of suppressed comments was released by those clustered around. Jerry noticed that Pat had gone ashen. It looked like she might need a little time to regain her composure, so he made replies and fielded remarks.

"We tried to buy the park, you know."

"Yeh. We bin tryin' to buy this place fer couple o' years. They weren't never interested in sellin' afore."

"Why, do you suppose," Jerry asked, "did they decide to sell this year?"

"Money."

"A lot of money."

"Could be gas," someone suggested.

"Naw. I heard there ain't no gas under this slope."

"Could frack. If they frack, they kin go out under anywheres for the gas."

"Wanted to build houses they said. Liked the idea of our hill for sites."

Jerry took them back to the first comment. "How did you propose to buy the park, when you tried before?"

"Same as now. We formed a resident 'sociation. There's over a hunert of us, most working. It'd be worth it. But by the time we heard, we were tol' it was a done deal. Don't know how much was paid. No one's sayin'."

"Had a lawyer an' everything."

By this time Pat had recovered from her shock and they were slowly making their way down the road. She said, "I wonder how done a deal."

"Do you still have your lawyer?" Jerry asked.

"Yep." A name was mentioned that Pat knew.

"Please ask him to call us," she said.

"Will do, Ma'am. You got some ideas?"

"I want to look into the legal aspects, see when the sale was finalized. If it is finalized. Who the parties were. I think the school district has a legitimate interest in this."

"The welfare of the children," Jerry underscored, "has not been considered. That's our role."

They had come to the mobile home where Mr. Duncan was waiting, paper in hand. "Here's yer letter. You kin keep it far as I'm concerned."

Jerry took it, thanking him and said, "I'll make a copy and get this one back to you." He folded it and put it in his pocket, not wishing to look at it right away. He wanted more than a quick glance, to reflect on what he might find if, that is, there were anything to find.

Pat was walking on, talking with some of the parents. They were passing a large trailer, one that had a garden. As she came abreast of it, she heard a dry, high-pitched voice say, "Pat Mitchell. They tol' me you was come." Sitting in a wheelchair in the doorway was a man who looked to be in his nineties, his face wreathed in smiles. "I'd of known you anywheres."

Pat stopped and smiled at him. She couldn't for the life of her identify this person from her past, but said sweetly, "And isn't it a fine afternoon for being out here?"

Jerry had caught up and joined her, listening with interest.

"She's Mrs. Foster now, Dad. Or was." A man who appeared from behind the wheelchair, himself close to seventy, nodded at Pat. "Afternoon, Ma'am" he said.

"Good afternoon, Mr. Morgan. I didn't realize your father lived here with you. I don't think we'd ever met before."

The old man cackled with glee at this. "Hee, hee! You don't know me 'cause you never seen me. But I seen you, you and brother Timmy, playin' games all around the house. I seen you from up top of garage. Kept my eye on you, made sure you was all right."

"Oh, Mr. Morgan!" Pat exclaimed. "You were the caretaker!"

"Yep. An' it was some job makin' sure you'uns din't come into no predicament. Jumpin' off things an' all like you did."

Jerry couldn't resist. "Playing runaway carriage?"

"Yep. That's right. You was a tomboy then. But I kin see you ain't no more."

The group of residents who had been around Pat and Jerry quietly melted away, no doubt uncomfortably aware that they had drifted into the murky waters of sentimentality and were in danger of drowning.

Jerry looked at Pat and saw tears shining in her eyes. He wanted to put his arms around her, kiss her eyes, kiss her mouth.

Pat held out her hand to old Mr. Morgan who took it in one gnarled hand of his. "I am so happy to have met you at last," she said with genuine sincerity. "Thank you for looking after Tim and me when we were little."

"You was worth it," he answered, a tear rolling down his face.

After several more tender reminiscences, Pat and Jerry made their goodbyes and walked down towards Pat's car.

Talking together about the coincidence of meeting a former tenant of the carriage house, they failed to notice the battered pickup truck parked behind the trailer or see Carl Morgan standing off to one side.

"Aw, hell," swore Carl softly. "Aw, hell. I forgot Pappy knowed her from when she was a young 'un. Now I can't do nothin' 'bout what I seen t'other day. Aw, hell."

They had gotten into the car, but Pat didn't start it right away. She took out a tissue and wiped her eyes. "Oh, Jerry," she said, "what a remarkable experience. What a lovely old gentleman. I think I'm going to cry again."

"If you do, beware," he cautioned, "you are impossible to resist with tears in your eyes."

At that she smiled. "I'm glad you're here with me. I'm feeling more and more that we're confidants."

"And we can, I hope, talk about anything." She was silent and he went on, "Are you ready to talk about it yet?"

She looked at him and bit her lip. "Not quite yet," she answered, starting the car. She backed out, then turned onto the gravel drive and headed out under the archway to the main road.

Jerry said, "There is somewhere I'd like to go, since we're in this vicinity. I have yet to see the Elk Creek School, what's left of it. I'd like to get the lay of the land. If you don't mind."

Pat nodded and took the next road to the left. They drove by a line of small homes on either side for a short distance. Then there was mostly underbrush and woods for a stretch, until a house came into view on the right, what Owen had called a shack and, Jerry thought, it was certainly that. Ahead of them loomed a high chain-link fence topped with barbed wire. They came to a stop by one of the many signs that said *KEEP OUT.* Jerry opened the door. "Pat, I'll only be a minute if you'd rather stay in the car."

"Maybe I will. No, on second thought," she said, getting out, "I'd like to remember Hank."

They stood silently looking into the desolate, blackened foundation of the school. Weeds and grass had begun to grow in, nature reclaiming its domain. They walked around to the back where the playgrounds, bereft of equipment, stood vacant and forlorn. Off to the left was the path that led to the trailer park, partially visible through the trees.

"It seems a shame that children can no longer walk to school," said Pat with a sigh.

"We must face the problem of what to do with this property sometime soon, I suppose. We can't let it go on just sitting here much longer."

"We had offers in the weeks right after the fire, did you know that? Gas industry, so I understood. We were enjoined not to do anything, since the investigation wasn't complete. But we had to demolish what was left standing, as it was too dangerous. I guess this all took place before you came."

Jerry nodded. "The questions are: do we need another elementary school and is this the best place for it?"

"And can the district afford to build? Lots of questions, Jerry."

He looked at the hill rising up behind the property, a slope of green—oaks and maples with an understory of mountain laurel catching the evening sunlight. "It's a beautiful setting here, though."

They started back to the car. Pointing to the run-down house, he asked, "What do you know about these people, the ones who lived here but were gone when the school burned down?"

"It was an elderly couple who had only occupied it for a short time. I can see why. It's in terrible shape. They moved away shortly after the fire; I don't know where. I heard the place is vacant now."

So much for that lead, thought Jerry. He looked closely at the house as they drove back down the road. Tire marks showed in the long grass. Vacant? Maybe not. Someone had parked there recently. Pat followed his glance.

"Not too surprising," she allowed. "This is Cross County after all."

Jerry raised his eyebrows at this remark.

She explained, "Places that are tolerably habitable are inhabited."

"Like things that are tolerably edible..."

"Are eaten." She finished the sentence for him with a laugh. "I guess you've got us down pretty well now."

As they drove, they resumed their discussion about the residents of the trailer park. Pat had learned that most of them owned their homes, but moving them to another site was very expensive and the nearest mobile home park was over sixty miles away. "Worse, it's not in the county."

Jerry said glumly, "Housing anywhere close by, I was told, is out of the question for most of the families. The downside to the economic boost. Local folks can no longer pay the price to live here. If this park is sold, what will happen is the breaking up and dispersal of an entire community, like they did decades ago in the urban renewal projects. But here there's nowhere for the people to go, and children require stability."

"I'll be interested in what their lawyer has to say. There are foundations to help homeowners and even renters." Pat tapped the side of her head. "Mindset from being a social worker: always on the lookout for alternative sources of assistance."

"Keen thinking like that deserves dinner. What do you say?"

"I'm all for it and I know just the place." She executed a neat U-turn and they drove in the opposite direction, away from Colton.

"Is anything open Sunday evenings?" Jerry asked her. "I'd have thought the Methodists would still be enforcing blue laws."

"A lot of things changed when the drillers got here. Many work night shifts and they like barbecue. There was a small place in Deems Township that had been there for years. Its business was modest until the gas people discovered it. Now it's going great guns. Oh, and yes, they have guns and a lot of other things. I think you'll like it."

Pat took a side road leading into a hollow. In the distance, Jerry could see a column of smoke rising. "They do their cooking outside," Pat said. "The whole area is absolutely redolent."

She parked in a nearly-full parking lot, and when they got out of the car, a tantalizing barbecue aroma engulfed them. "Ah," said Jerry. "We've come to the right place."

The restaurant was a long, low wooden bungalow that had been added to many times. They climbed a short flight of steps to a porch, where a row of rocking chairs, similar to Jerry's, had been placed. Quite a few were occupied by toothpick-chewing diners.

Jerry looked with interest at the chairs. "Well, Mrs. Foster," he said, "so this is how you knew about my find."

"Wait till we get inside," she said encouragingly.

As they walked in, Jerry could see that the walls were hung, seemingly every inch of them, with antiques. "Where have you brought me?" he exclaimed.

There were buck saws and train lanterns, tin advertising signs and lunch pails, fuse boxes and miners' lamps and, of course, hunting knives, traps and rifles of every description. On the floor were stoneware crocks, butter churns and iron pots. The room was crowded with diners, so Jerry was trying to be inconspicuous in his rubbernecking. "How will I be able to concentrate on food when there's all this around?" he said, indicating the wealth of artifacts.

She laughed. "So you won't be completely distracted, we'll order in here and then go outside where they'll serve us. It's much quieter and we can talk."

They went to the bar to scan the menu and order. "Wine or beer?" Pat asked Jerry. "I'm thinking lager."

"Exactly right."

They took their drinks out to where rustic tables were sitting under the trees. The fragrant wood smoke reminded them they were hungry, and when the ribs and sliced beef brisket came, complete with barbecue beans, coleslaw and roasted potatoes, they happily gave themselves over to an appreciation of all things Deems. As the light left the hollow, their server brought candles to the table, along with mugs of coffee. And because it was June, a slice to share of strawberry-rhubarb pie, which they hadn't been able to resist ordering.

In the glow of candlelight, and the afterglow of a splendid meal, Pat smiled at Jerry. She was relaxed, she was sated, and she was with someone she knew she could trust. "I'm ready to talk about it now," she said.

Chapter 16

He waited, he did not prompt. She took a tack he never would have expected.

"I'm falling in love with you, Dr. Strauss," she said, looking evenly into his eyes. She hadn't meant to spring it on him like this, but it was happening and he may as well know. But with the briefest of pauses, she went on, "And that is why I can tell you what's on my mind."

Jerry was awestruck. Rarely having been in the position of being taken so completely by surprise as he was now, he could only wordlessly reach for her hand. She smiled and left her hand in his.

"Loving, for me, means trusting and I already know I can trust you. Friday night…"

Jerry found his voice at last. "You trusted me with your past."

She gave him an appreciative look. "And you gave me such kindness in return. You were so warm, so open to me."

"Why ever not? Couldn't you see I was falling in love with you?" What did he just say?! How extraordinary to make such a statement, without any preamble. *Was* he falling in love with her? This wasn't what he'd imagined. But now, being with her, he wondered if it might not be an accurate description of his feelings about this exceptionally compatible relationship.

"Ah, Jerry," she started to say, then remembered the topic waiting to be covered. "Elliot," she began, a serious note in her voice, and she withdrew her hand, as if not wanting to soil their newly-discovered affection while this distasteful subject was being discussed.

"Yes. Elliot," Jerry echoed.

"Elliot and I were having an affair. I want you to know that first off."

"Pat, I figured that out the first board meeting I went to, before I was hired. It was pretty obvious."

"Probably," she responded. "I didn't think it mattered, but Elliot was always worried." She had another thought, "Will you and I be talked about now do you suppose? And do I care?"

"I don't," said Jerry truthfully. "People will always talk."

Pat smiled at him and went on, "I was never in love with Elliot. I'd been divorced after a marriage of twenty-five years that ended badly. My self-image had gone to pot. Johnny wasn't even there to keep me company. When a man actually showed me some attention, I responded, gratefully. That's the key word. Gratitude. Someone to shape up for, get a new hair color and wardrobe for. All the things women do and that, by itself, does not guarantee any sort of a real relationship."

"So there was no depth?"

She shook her head. "I learned after a while not to expect it. In fact, we never talked about anything in depth except school district business. There were times when I tried to talk about our relationship, but he was not willing. I knew, I still know, very little about him, and he did not appear to be interested in knowing me either. It was more than shallow. I kept seeing him because, well, because it had become a habit." She stopped, gave Jerry a candid smile and said, "It's over."

He wanted to take her hand again at this welcome confession, but the chilling effect of the subject matter held him off. He asked, "Does Elliot know?"

"Not yet. I hadn't put it that succinctly to myself before, although I was ready to end it months ago." She told Jerry she had been more and more convinced that Elliot had what she called a secret life. "He never invited me to his place, never spoke about what he did when he wasn't at the office. I wondered why, but it got shrugged off when I asked." Someone had told her that they saw him at The Pit talking with one of the gas industry people.

"The Pit?" Jerry asked. "That's not a place I'd associate with Elliot in his three-piece suits. Oh, sorry, Pat, I didn't mean to be catty."

"A real paradox, isn't it? I thought the same thing. It didn't sound right. I also have been told that he has informants. Why should he? So, when Clem Duncan said what he did this afternoon about who he thought had discouraged the residents, something clicked into place. I don't know why and I don't know what, but it reinforced my decision to end things."

"I guess I have no right to ask," Jerry ventured, "but I wonder how he'll take it when you tell him."

"You have every right to ask, to ask anything you want." She stopped and pondered his comment. "I have no idea how he'll take it. Nor do I know when I'll see him again outside of the district office, and I certainly can't tell him there." She looked worried, then went on, "I don't believe he's dishonest or anything. But he is extremely guarded. Tell me, what is your take on Elliot?"

Jerry, trying to be fair, said, "He's been very helpful to me. He's competent, smart, efficient, knowledgeable," and I hate the bastard, he thought to himself, but that's because he's been sleeping with Pat. He finished the sentence, "and, yet, I don't like him."

Encouraged by Pat's understanding nod in response, he went on, "I've always sensed an annoying tension when I'm with him, as if he's wary of me, and I can't think of any reason for it. He comes across as cold and aloof. Why? I don't treat him in a less than friendly fashion. I think he's very sensitive to anything he perceives as a threat, so I intend to keep on acting the part of the curriculum-focused superintendent relying absolutely on my business manager for anything fiscal." Jerry sighed, "Here we are sitting in candlelight again, but what are we talking about?"

"It doesn't matter what we talk about. Just that we are talking together."

And, with the smile she gave him, Jerry thought, whatever has happened to me, I am not going to fight it.

Most of the tables were deserted by this time. "I think they want to clear up," Pat said. "Shall we arm wrestle to see who pays or will you let me, in return for Friday's dinner?"

While Pat paid the bill at the bar, Jerry had another look around at the intriguing display of antiques. These artifacts right here, he thought with growing respect, silently and eloquently tell the history of Cross County, and he made a promise to himself to come back often.

"A culinary and social oasis," he remarked approvingly to Pat on their way out.

"Deems Barbecue is an institution around the whole county," she affirmed.

As they drove back to town, Pat began talking about the upcoming week. "It looks like we're going to need a strategy to get the trailer park residents to the board meeting. I'll do a little groundwork. This is my area, Jerry, so you don't need to get involved yet."

"I will, happily, if you want me."

Pat glanced at him, then back to the road. With an effort, she resisted the urge to say "I want you." Too soon? she asked herself. Yes, probably, darn it.

When they got to Jerry's she turned off the engine but didn't unbuckle her seat belt. "I don't think I should come in, Jerry. If you were to ask me, that is. This thing about Elliot has me more disturbed than I realized. He's leaving at the end of the week, and I must tell him before he goes. Also, I haven't got my house key back from him yet. I could change the lock, but Johnny shows up at unexpected times, when he gets leave and a chance flight."

"You could move in with me," Jerry offered gallantly.

"Will you do the cooking?"

"Absolutely."

"Do you snore?"

"Hardly at all."

"Who gets to park in the garage?"

"We'll flip for it."

"Jerry, you are a dear."

"Only one problem though. Very little closet space."

"Oh? Well, then, sorry. Deal's off."

The next remark in this sequence, he thought, is "Not that you'll need many clothes," but this line wasn't at all right for the type of wit they had going. More what he imagined Elliot would say to her. Damn Elliot anyway, he thought to himself. To Pat he said, "The offer still stands. I'll even let you have the garage." He started to open the door then turned to her again. "You kissed my hand. I could hardly drive after that. Even so..." And he gently drew her face to his and kissed her with the greatest of delicacy. Softly he said, "Thank you, Pat. Drive safely." He got out, then leaned back in. "Offer stands," he reiterated.

Best offer I've ever had, thought Pat, as she drove home.

Chapter 17

Jerry took the letter out of his pocket and tossed it on the dining table. He got a bottle of Merlot from the kitchen, poured himself a glass and sat down. Before he read the letter, he wanted to go over in his mind what had given rise to this latest unease about Elliot. And all the while, he reminded himself, keeping his feelings for Pat strictly out of the equation.

In reverse chronological order then, starting with today: There had been the distinct indication that Elliot was responsible for discouraging the trailer park residents from attending the board meeting. Why? What reason would he have to not want them there, expressing their concerns and seeking ways to forestall eviction?

Secondly, who was the carrier of this message? One of his "informants," as Pat called them? And how was this person connected with the trailer park?

Going back a bit, why had he sensed a reluctance on Elliot's part when he'd asked for charter school data? And why should it take over two weeks to pull the data together? For that matter, what was this corporation that had been contracted to handle the charter school's business? "Star" something or other. Someone by the name of Clarence at the golf course acted annoyed when ribbed about it.

Then, who in the gas industry was Elliot meeting with at The Pit and why there? It didn't seem quite the place for Elliot.

And finally, Jerry thought, staring at the letter in front of him, am I going to find something to link Elliot to the eviction, as Clem Duncan hinted? And even if so, it isn't illegal, in and of itself, to purchase property. The school district isn't part of this potential real estate transaction. Although, he thought, just around the corner is a prime piece of real estate belonging to the school district.

Jerry put his glass down and unfolded the letter. He read quickly over the transfer of property legalese and the logistical details, looking for clues as to the buyers. It wasn't until the end of the notification of intent to occupy that he got to something about "per agreement between seller and buyer," with the buyer listed as Star Partnership, LLC.

Jerry sat back. It was only one word, a very commonplace word. It was a word that figured in thousands, tens of thousands, of names. Lone Star. North Star. Lucky Star. So ordinary as to be eminently forgettable but, to Jerry, it smacked of the charter school's business end. What connection could he make? Nothing, but he knew he had to look into it further.

He poured himself another glass of wine. On the table was the ironstone pitcher filled with the roses he'd picked for Pat, roses still as fresh and fragrant as Friday, when they'd had dinner. Jerry took his thoughts back to that evening. Had he been falling in love with her then? When he told her tonight that he had, he did not feel it was an exaggeration. He was, he admitted, wooing her. There was a time in his past when confessing love was all very momentous and implied lifetime commitments, familial and social obligations, ties that were assumed to be immutable. He didn't have that orientation now nor, he was quite sure, did Pat. So unlike his first, much-too-young marriage, so different than the compunction he felt going into the second marriage. It was only because of the interlude between the two, a relationship which had stretched for several years, that he'd realized what it was to love and he had, essentially, thrown it away. Had he a choice? At the time, he felt he hadn't.

A week and Elliot would be gone. He had already told people he'd be traveling, not available by phone or email, for the last three weeks of July. Pat said she wouldn't be going to California until the end of the month. Jerry, too, was going to spend some time at his family's place on Candlewood Lake for the first two weeks in August. When Pat got home, he would be back; in fact, he'd make damn sure he was, so she would not be alone and at Elliot's mercy.

Pat, not usually one to have second thoughts, was wondering briefly if she should have been so forward in her frank disclosure this evening. "I am falling in love with you," she had said with such self-assurance. His initial reaction, she had noticed, was speechlessness. But he had reached for her hand and she had sensed no reservation on his part. I guess I've always just boldly gone forth, she thought, when I've felt it's worth it.

She returned to the book she'd been reading, a book that had just been released and was recommended by the state school boards association. It covered the topic of ethics in school business management, and was written by Professor Eric Arden. In it were a dozen case studies on ethical dilemmas faced by business managers at the district level. Money, temptation, ease of concealment: all the elements were in place to make fraud possible. I wonder if Jerry has read it, Pat thought. If not, I'll give it to him when I finish.

On Owen's last day before he went on vacation for six weeks he and Jerry got together in Jerry's office. Owen came lugging a tote bag and after he sat down, flashed Jerry that irrepressible grin he had. "Bingo!" he exclaimed and gleefully took out a large stack of papers which he put on Jerry's desk.

Jerry couldn't help returning the grin as he surveyed the impressive pile Owen had brought. Owen was exultant. "You can't believe all that's out there! Scholarships and summer programs and camps for every conceivable sport. Look at this. There are even sharpshooter scholarships. Kids on our rifle team are going to go ape. I got a whole bunch for the arts too: music, writing, fine arts, you name it!"

"Owen, this is perfect. We'll send out a letter to parents telling them what's available and we'll keep a library of references for them to look at. Terrific job. Thank you!"

"And I probably just skimmed the surface. I'll keep the list updated. I've already signed up for a service." He grinned again, sat back and said, "OK, Supe, what's next?"

Jerry regarded this exceptionally capable and disarming administrator of his. "Next is you go on vacation and have a relaxing break at that antiques shop of yours."

"Hey, I can handle a special assignment while I'm at it. The school fire. I'm planning to see Paul Willard on that just as soon as I can. Do you want me to send you what I learn instead of waiting until I get back in August?"

Jerry thought a moment. "Yes, do, although I will be gone for a few weeks myself the first part of August. You can always call or email me. I can come to Martensdale to meet with him."

Owen said eagerly, "Good plan! Then you get to see the shop!"

Can't put it off forever, Jerry thought.

Owen went on, "You've got friends in Martensdale, haven't you? Dr. Arden? What a brilliant guy. Do you know his sister Ruth? One of our dealers. She's our resident redhead, specializes in ironstone and glassware and items New England."

"Yes, I know Ruth," Jerry answered. Oh, yes, he was thinking, I know Ruth. I know what she feels like, smells like, tastes like, at least I did, and for a long time there wasn't a day I didn't think of her and regret. Well, it's got to be faced and with Owen on the scene things might not be as difficult. Get the subject back to the fire, thought Jerry and he said, "I went to see what was left of Elk Creek School. You've been out there you said."

"I brought my bike down a couple of times so I could ride the new rail-trail with some of the kids. What a dismal scene. An ugly hole in the ground and those playing fields just sitting there. What will the district do about the site? Sell it?"

"That depends on whether there's a need for another elementary school, but even if there is, Elk Creek may no longer be the best location. By the way, did you see any signs of life around that run-down house, the one you insightfully called a shack? I was told that the people who'd lived there moved away shortly after the fire."

"Someone was there, doing stuff in the yard. I thought it could be the owner."

"I'm still hopeful there might be a lead associated with it about the fire. We also paid a visit to the Elk Creek Mobile Home Park, Pat Foster and I, last Sunday. You knew the park is being bought and the residents evicted?"

Owen nodded. "We took the path from the school. A couple of the kids live there. They didn't want to talk about it, having to move. I guess everyone is pretty upset." Owen gave Jerry a quizzical look. "You don't suppose the school district could help them out? I mean, there are lots of kids. Where can the families go? Rents in the Colton area are out of their reach."

"That's why Pat and I went there, to learn what we could. They were going to come to the school board meeting Tuesday night, but we heard on Sunday that someone had talked them out of it. Warned them off is what it sounded like."

"Who'd do that? The buyers probably," Owen said scowling.

Jerry sighed. "At any rate, we'll look for a loophole to slow this down, for a while anyway. In the meantime, see if you can set up something with the detective and let me know. And, Owen, when you get back I've got a treat for you. Can you stay down here an evening for supper? And do you like barbecue?"

On Friday morning when Jerry got to his office there was a large manila envelope sitting on his desk. "Dr. Lucas asked me to make sure you got it before he left," Jerry's secretary told him.

Jerry thanked her and put the envelope in his briefcase. I will deal with this later, he decided, and at home, where I can have a drink within arm's reach to mitigate the unpleasantness of the task.

Does this mean that Elliot is gone, he wondered? Do I now have leave to rush over to Pat's, lust in my heart, seduction in my eyes? Hardly, he thought. This weekend Elliot would doubtless be planning to see her. Would she be able to handle it all right? And what should his role be, besides feeling helpless over a situation in which he was on the sidelines? He found himself fretting about her the rest of the day.

Chapter 18

Pat figured that Elliot would most likely make contact with her over the weekend. She could avoid the confrontation by escaping again to Martensdale with her girlfriends, or she could hide out with Jerry in the carriage house. As tempting as the last option was, she wasn't a coward. Elliot had to be dealt with, the relationship officially ended and her key returned. It wasn't fair to anyone, Elliot, Jerry or herself, to postpone facing up to a decision she had made. She decided to be proactive, to try to reach him and set up a time for them to get together.

"Get together." Thinking about what it meant in terms of Elliot no longer held a thrill; she simply felt sorry for him now and, in doing so, she let herself have a brief cry. *I used him just as he used me. I tried to make things different, but couldn't get anywhere. Now I am going to dump him. For Jerry. No, not entirely. Because I want more in a relationship and it was never possible with Elliot.*

She called his office number and the secretary answered. "He's already left, Mrs. Foster. Do you want to talk with Francine? She'll be handling the accounts while he's away."

Pat knew that the budget clerk, herself a CPA now, was to be taking over in the interim. "Thanks, no, I won't bother her," Pat answered.

Fine, she thought, *I'll call his cell. When do I want to see him? I'm not going to let him make the decision this time. I am going to be the one to call the shots.*

"You have reached Dr. Lucas's cellular. Please leave a message."

"Elliot, before you go on vacation, I need to talk to you. It's important. I'll be home tonight." She ended the call, took a deep breath and phoned Jerry. He sounded relieved when he heard her voice, but it didn't shake his concern for her. "I applaud you, Pat, for your pluckiness in taking the initiative like that. You're very courageous, but that doesn't stop me worrying about how he'll react."

"And my being unable to control things? It could be tricky," she allowed.

"I'll be at home after a dinner meeting. Will you call me when you, um...."?

"When the deed is done? You're making me feel like Lady Macbeth," she said with a rueful laugh.

"I was thinking Shakespeare too, but more along the lines of Hamlet. Secreting myself *a la* Polonius behind the arras."

"If I had an arras, you'd be welcome to."

You have a very nice arras, Jerry didn't say. He substituted, "Tapestry hangings aren't quite the thing for split-level ranch houses."

"You think not?" she said, then, more serious, "Jerry, I will call you. You mustn't worry. Just talking with you gives me confidence."

At 8:00 in the far corner booth at The Pit, Elliot and Clarence were having a discussion.

"What's the plan for the next three weeks?" the Texan asked. As usual, he had a whiskey and soda nearby which had been refilled several times.

"Francine is doing the routine work, getting out the checks for salaries, paying bills. She's done it before."

"What if she sees something she doesn't understand? Will she run to the Super?"

"I've instructed her to take any questions to Pat." Elliot gave the briefest of smiles. "I can trust Pat to sit on it until I get back."

The Texan laughed at this observation. "You got some powerful hold on that lady. Wish I had your sex appeal. Gets them so they don't want to do anything but lie down and ask for it."

Elliot grunted an affirmative.

"Nice deal," Clarence said, "having it whenever you want it and keeping her from thinking that you are anything but pure as gold." He finished off his drink and motioned to the server for another.

Elliot frowned. "Some things are cropping up, though, that we need to talk about. The school district is starting to take an interest in the mobile home park sale. The Super was out there with Pat last week, talking to people and asking questions. I want the deal to go through, Clarence. We stand to make a fistful and I'm not going to let them stop us."

"Ramp up your charm on Mrs. Foster."

"Might take more than that."

Mel came over with Clarence's drink. "Something else for you, Dr. Lucas?" she asked.

"Yes, Mel," Elliot said. "There is something else and I'm sure you know just what it is."

Clarence gave a tipsy snicker, as Mel abruptly turned on her heel and walked away.

Elliot went on, "My concern is, with all the publicity about the trailer park and the fire, we may have to let it rest a while before we finalize this thing. Otherwise some do-gooders will be screaming about the poor kids being victimized. Also, I need to assemble or create figures showing we don't need another elementary school, and if that won't fly, that Elk Creek is not a viable site. And, of course, it's more understandable when there aren't all those kids living at the trailer park." He took a sip of his martini.

"Given the number of inquiries we've received, negative publicity hasn't hurt us one bit," Clarence put in. "Demand for what we can offer has only increased."

"And what we thought: out of state, out of the country, bowled over by the setting. Off-shore makes more and more sense."

"Which corporate name will we use for bidding on the school property? The one we came up with the week after the fire?" Clarence asked.

"That would be best. It was recognized as another energy company, which would seem logical." Elliot finished his drink and got up. "Pat says she wants to see me tonight, and that's just as well. I'd rather she thought I was leaving in the morning anyway. So I'll see you tomorrow night at the poker game."

"You got her begging for you. I don't know how you do it."

"Keep 'em guessing. That's how."

It had been a hot and humid day. By evening the air was oppressive and Pat planned to use it as a point of departure for the dialogue she was planning.

Elliot didn't call her back, but at 9:30 he showed up, unlocking the kitchen door. Pat was sitting lengthwise on the couch in the living room, shoes off, feet up, glass of wine in hand, reading. She'd finished Eric Arden's book and had carefully put it out of sight, and now had a detective novel on her lap. When Elliot walked in she smiled but did not get up, as she'd have done before, as he was used to.

"I would get you a drink," she said, "but would you mind helping yourself? I haven't the energy; it's been too hot today. And, Elliot," she held out her glass, "could you get me a refill on the chardonnay?"

She noted the slight hesitation at this out-of-the-ordinary request before he said, "Of course," and went into the kitchen. She rearranged herself to appear even more focused on the book.

"Here," he said, handing her the glass of wine. He sat on the loveseat with the coffee table between them, since she'd left no room for him on the sofa. He sipped his gin and tonic, looking around the room, not at her, as if the sight of her was displeasing. As if, Pat thought, she wasn't quite up to his standards in this attitude she'd adopted. Purposely adopted, so he was less likely to be aroused by her.

"You seem tired, Elliot," she began. "You must be looking forward to a few weeks away." I could ask where, but he'll be evasive. But I shall anyway. "Where are you going?"

"On a cruise, Pat. Everyone at the office knows that," he said in a bored voice.

"The Danube? With the scenery and the locks, it was fascinating," she said, in an encouraging tone. "I've yet to do the Rhine, though."

"Um," he nodded, busy with his drink.

She persevered. "Is there some reason you don't want me to know where you'll be cruising?" she asked innocently.

He looked up, a little startled by her question, but didn't answer.

"Or anywhere else you go? Or what you do when you're not at the school district or in bed with me?"

"What the hell is this?" he said in an affronted tone.

"It's called conversation," she answered. Sarcastic, yes, but she couldn't help it. "It's what I miss in our relationship."

"Pat," he said, and his voice conveyed annoyance, "this is ground we've gone over before. Living up to someone else's expectations is a fool's errand. It can never be done to the satisfaction of another."

"And yet, I have tried to, for you."

"Have you? You've met me halfway."

"And if I said I am no longer willing to? Meet you halfway?"

"What do you mean, Pat? Let's have it. It's Jerry, isn't it?"

His informants, she thought: the trailer park, the barbecue restaurant? "No, Elliot, it's you. I have been happy to sleep with you, to look forward to evenings of being with you, but I realized I needed more in a love affair. I need the closeness that comes with a sharing of the minds. Talk. Understanding. Histories. Ideas. Dreams. You keep yourself closed off and it perplexes and hurts me."

He shrugged. "You're sounding like my ex. I don't see the point."

"Look," she continued, "I'm not interested in marriage. But I am, no, I was, interested in you as a person. I have come to realize that you don't want me to know you, nor are you interested in knowing me. Our relationship is shallow, Elliot, and I don't want shallow."

"How about what I've given you? You told me I turned you on." He didn't say it particularly intimately; rather, he threw it out as a challenge.

"Yes, that's true."

"Then what's the problem?"

"Not enough for me. That's all." He was silent, and she went on, "We have a very good relationship at the school district and I don't want it to change, as we need to work together to reach our goals for education. I feel I can count on you and it's a good feeling."

"I can think of more exciting feelings," stated not in a seductive way but matter-of-factly.

Give it up, Elliot, she thought. "As I said, not enough for me. I'm grateful for what we have shared, I'm grateful for the attention you've shown me. But it's time for me to opt out."

She was surprised to hear him say, "I like what we have, Pat. I don't want to lose it."

"But I don't feel happy about it anymore, Elliot. It's not your fault; that's the way you are. And this is the way I am."

"We could continue this conversation in bed, Pat."

"No, we can't, Elliot."

He got up and came over to her. She straightened her back, put her feet on the floor. He was standing above her and she felt an inkling of fear. "I think we will, Pat," he said defiantly, taking the wineglass out of her hand and putting it on the coffee table.

It was time to deliver the *coup de grace*: "I have an infection," she boldly lied. He drew back sharply and she said, "These things happen to women my age."

"Sorry, Pat." He sat down on the loveseat again. It was the first time she'd heard anything like an apology from him.

"You know, Elliot, I cried this afternoon when I realized I'd have to tell you that our affair was over. I cried because for a while you were just what I needed."

"You still have what I need. We don't have to end it."

He's pleading with me, she thought, in his own fashion. "When are you leaving town?" she asked.

"Tomorrow morning. I had hoped one more night." He looked at his watch. "We'll continue this conversation when I get back next month."

"From wherever and with whomever you're going," she murmured as he walked out.

It took her a few minutes to calm herself. She was shaking at what could have been a very nasty scene. He had been menacing in that one moment and she had been made aware of her vulnerability. How much should she tell Jerry? All of it. She wanted him completely in her confidence. That was the basis for a real relationship; that was what brought the greatest rewards.

She rang his phone and when he answered, he began with, "Pat, I have been so worried I've been walking into walls. How could I have left you alone to face him? I must have been mad. A dozen times I almost drove over there, a dozen times I thought of worst-case scenarios. How are you? You don't have to tell me."

"Jerry, I'm all right. But there was a close call." She gave him a blow-by-blow of the evening and didn't mince words when it came to the frightening encounter. She told him what saved her, Elliot's fastidiousness that she used to her advantage. "He actually recoiled when I said it."

Jerry said, "I can't tell you how impressed I am at your ability to utilize timely mendacity. It's a gift."

"Oh, Jerry, I'm sorry I've put you through this."

"Pat! Not a bit of it! You are ten times worth it. Supper here tomorrow?" he asked.

"Wild horses couldn't keep me away from the old Mitchell place."

Only when she was almost asleep did she realize she hadn't gotten her key back.

Chapter 19

They had both forgotten that the next day, Saturday, was the Fourth of July. Months ago, Pat and her friends had planned to go to Martensdale for the annual fireworks show, and it was her turn to drive. When the phone rang and one of her girlfriends asked what time she would be picked up, Pat thought, darn! There goes supper with Jerry and the fireworks don't even start until 9:30. I won't get home before midnight.

Jerry, on his part, had volunteered to grill hot dogs and hamburgers at the Rotary picnic and help judge the children's contests. It was only during his golf round that someone mentioned the picnic and Jerry's heart fell. Maybe the picnic won't run too long, he thought, although there was to be a softball game for the adults too. Life in a small town and the Superintendent of Schools has obligations.

It was sultry and windless. From the veranda at the clubhouse Jerry could see cumulus clouds in the western sky. They'd had lunch, but people were not lingering, as most of them had Independence Day activities planned for the afternoon. Jerry had looked around for Clarence, thinking he could initiate a conversation and learn a little more about the charter school, but he didn't seem to be golfing today. Or he's avoiding me, Jerry thought. I do represent the "other side," after all. As he walked to his car, he heard the first far-off rumblings of thunder and hoped that it might cut the picnic short.

Both Pat and Jerry had left messages on each other's phones. Jerry had apologized for forgetting about the picnic.

"You take my mind off of everything else," he'd said, and that he'd call as soon as he could. Pat left a message while Jerry was getting a shower after golf. "No wonder I forgot about the fireworks. All I could think about was seeing you."

Carl and Seth were hurrying to finish their Saturday lawn mowing jobs before the rain started. They'd gotten delayed because Seth was at the Rotary picnic helping the little kids with the T-ball contest, and Carl was staking out Pat's house. When she backed her car out, he followed at a discreet distance as she went to various addresses, finally quitting when he realized she and her friends were taking the road to Martensdale. It ain't much money, he thought, but it's something. He reported in a text and then went to pick up Seth. The Super was there at the picnic, doing his thing, friendly with everyone. He reported that too.

There had been distant thunder sporadically. As they were driving, one particularly loud boom sounded very close by. Carl noticed that the dark clouds were still not upon them, as one would expect at so powerful a clap of thunder. Carl rubbed his chin. He'd heard that sound before, and out of a clear sky. Now, he thought to himself, they aren't working today, so it won't be one of them big trucks backfiring or some kind of blasting or anything like that. Hmm. I'll just have me a look around and see if it's what I think it might of bin. Later on after I take Seth home. Yep. I'll just have me a look.

In the municipal park downtown, people at the picnic had also heard the loud report like a thunderclap. Those few who were not running around also felt a jolt beneath them, but most took no notice of it.

The rain held off until after 8:30 when the picnic was over. Knowing that Pat would be gone until late, Jerry accepted an invitation for a cold beer with some of the Rotarians at one of their homes.

In Martensdale the fireworks were going off as scheduled; the storm hadn't begun there yet. It hit later and came with such a vengeance that Pat and her friends thought it best not to drive back until it abated. Not until 2:00 AM did she finally pull in and open her garage door, startling Carl, huddled in a slicker under a dripping rhododendron bush, into sodden consciousness. He duly texted this latest information and went home, muttering to himself, this is the last damn time I'm gonna do this, the last damn time, I swear.

The poker players were a disparate group made up of power company officials and locals including, among others, the business manager of the school district and the chief of police of the Borough of Colton. What they were doing wasn't illegal, so having the police department in on a friendly game was regarded as building good relationships between the borough and the gas industry. Not that it was advertised; in fact, the existence of the monthly poker game was supposed to be kept quiet by those involved. But secrecy would negate any advantages to be had in the way of status from being in this exclusive clique, so the phenomenon of card-playing Saturday nights was generally known.

All men, they met in a private backroom at The Pit, the establishment which tolerated what other places did not. Games ran into the wee hours, cigars were smoked, whiskey flowed, and amounts of money changed hands. It had the feel of something shady; consequently, the talk was often raunchy and profane. Politics of drilling and the problems engendered by it in the community and the Commonwealth did not enter into the conversation. Instead an attitude of acceptance for each other had developed over the months. Or rather, an attitude of agreeableness on the part of the townspeople to whatever the gas people wanted to do. So when someone brought up the loud boom that was heard earlier in the day, there was only the briefest of discussions.

"Was that thunder or something else we all heard before? Hit me again."

"Maybe a bit of shaking. I'll hold."

"Another leetle earthquake is all."

"Folks here said it felt like it was right underneath the kitchen. I'll take two."

Elliot got his texted report from Carl and smiled to himself. Clarence looked up as Elliot put his phone away. "Good news?" he asked.

"She'll be hungry for me when I get back," Elliot said complacently.

Pat slept in on Sunday morning, physically exhausted from the drive on rain-slicked, branch-strewn roads, and emotionally exhausted from the confrontation with Elliot the night before. She'd texted Jerry when she got in, only a quick "Whew! Made it home! Wake me if you want, but not before noon."

Jerry smiled when he read her text at 2:00 AM. He hadn't even attempted sleep earlier, knowing she was going to be driving down from Martensdale and having the storm to contend with. He had tried to read a journal article on school leadership, but his mind was wandering, partly on Pat, but also on several unresolved issues that had been plaguing him.

The charter school: he must start sorting out the data and see what he could make of it. The trailer park eviction: they had to find a way to prevent it from happening, at least so soon, and along with that, to learn what role Elliot was playing, if any. Elliot: what was he up to? How could their working relationship not be affected by the unease Jerry felt? While Elliot was gone, he intended to meet with the budget clerk. Francine seemed to be on top of things and just might be helpful. By exposing her boss? Fat chance. Then he thought about the school fire and that took him back to the conversation earlier in the evening with his fellow Rotarians. They had been talking about the storm.

"Lightning and thunder on the Fourth of July! Who needs Martensdale's fancy fireworks? We have pyrotechnics to spare."

"And what timing. Successful picnic and now we can sit around inside enjoying the show out there."

"Don't have to set off our own and risk burning something down."

Jerry had his segue. "You know, I can't get it off my mind that the last superintendent, well, that he could have been, well... I had a look at what was left of the school the other day and it made me, I don't mind telling you, scared." That performance, he said to himself, was worthy of an Oscar. Just the right amount of hesitancy and humility. People promptly chimed in with their comments.

"I can see how you might be scared. Don't like your Super? Lure him into a fire."

"You weren't here before the talk died down. But folks were wondering just what he was doing there anyway."

"Arson it was and arson we've had before, but trapping a man in it? That's something else."

In this atmosphere of peers, people were willing to speculate about it.

"How could he have been trying to put out the fire? How in the heck did he even come to notice the school is burning? No one else around there did."

"For gosh sakes, there was a blizzard going on."

"And he parks in the back. If you saw a building burning down, would you go around to park in the rear? I mean, wouldn't you just drive up and jump out of your car?"

"Maybe the fire was too wild out front. Maybe..."

"Maybe nothing. He was lured."

"Or he set it himself."

"That's crazy. Hank was a gentle soul."

The conversation halted in subdued reflection of the former superintendent.

Jerry broke the silence. "Is the investigation closed then? So many unanswered questions. It seems to me it shouldn't just be left hanging like this. I almost feel some responsibility..."

"Well, don't!" one of the Rotarians commanded severely. "Don't get yourself involved, Jerry. It's not safe. There are some strange folk among the population of our dearly loved county and they would not happily tolerate interference."

There were nods of assent.

"I see," Jerry had said thoughtfully.

So they're all frightened. Except me. Don't ask questions, they said. It's my job to ask questions. That's why I'm here. Guess the next steps are to see what Owen can learn, and identify the couple who lived close by, and find out who tried to buy the property in the weeks right after the fire, as Pat had indicated.

Pat. Had she gotten home yet? It was almost 1:30 and the storm was over. The CD she had chosen the other night was still in the player and he turned it on. Getz and Gilberto. Pat had known it from her college days in Seattle. Stan Getz's tenor sax gave the Brazilian genre the feel of West Coast jazz. Jerry gave up trying to read the journal article and let himself be lulled by the cool notes and warm lyrics and thought about Pat.

His contract as acting superintendent was for a year, unless they found a permanent replacement before then. And if they didn't? Would he stay for another year? There hadn't been any indication among the school board members about starting a search yet, although he'd mentioned it on occasion. Wait and see? How aggressive he might be in seeking a replacement hinged on whether he wanted to leave in a year or less. And that, he thought, hinged on Pat.

They were, without a doubt, on the brink of an affair, an affectionate, reciprocal and potentially serious affair. Would he be making another mistake by letting himself in for it again? What could go wrong? A dozen things. Her position on the school board could get in the way, make her feel used. Or she could get tired of him, tired of listening to his stories, his history, his views on education. A chance I guess I'll take, he decided.

The essential human need to give love: Jerry was at the point where he was happy just to have a woman to love. He was beginning to look at it as a coda to his life, and he told himself that he would, this time, remain conscious of its incalculable worth.

Chapter 20

In the morning, Jerry went out for a run while it was still relatively cool. Last night's rain sparkled on the leaves and recently mowed lawns in his neighborhood as he went up the hill. At the top, three roads met, and there was a grassy triangular parklet in the middle of the intersection. It had curbing on all sides and contained a few shrubs and an elderly willow tree, under which was a stone bench, well-mossed, facing the western view. There should be, Jerry said to himself, a plaque stating in whose memory this little park was dedicated or whose benevolence made the bench and up-keep possible. He sat down and regarded Colton below. A cardinal who had stopped its song at Jerry's invasion took courage and began again, hitting its stride with more and ever more repetitions. In the distance an answering cardinal attempted to outdo him. Jerry thought, once again, how charming this place was, how easy to think of it as holding a lasting perfection. He let the birdsong spill over him with an exuberance of sound, making a background to what was filling his mind.

He had every confidence that he would be making love with Pat tonight. It was his first thought on waking and he knew it would color his every thought all day long. Could he do anything constructive today or was he to be pulled about willy-nilly by this urgent desire, this insistent force that made birds sing their hearts out and normally intelligent men useless for any other endeavor? Jerry shook his head in disbelief that this was happening to him after so many years, this life-affirming, life-creating compulsion, dominating everything. Well, perhaps he was exaggerating things a little. What he was doing, he realized, was absolutely basking in it. But right now was the time to let himself. He'd worry about paying the piper later.

He heard a car approaching and roused himself. Finish the run, see if there are any flowers to bring in, get a shower, have breakfast and read the papers. Try to get a little work done. Then he'd call her.

When Pat woke up the day was well underway. 11:15. The afternoon to be with him, and the night? She hoped they'd have it together; they owed it to themselves. She would fix a chicken salad for their supper and take it to him. The beginning of a good, solid relationship all ready to be embarked upon. Once again, she thought, we throw ourselves in, forgetting how susceptible we are to heartbreak, not daring to look too far ahead. But we rush in because it is the only way we can find out what we are capable of, what love can bring into our lives.

Not too many homeowners wanted their grass mowed on the Sabbath, but Carl and Seth did have a few regular jobs, mostly businesses, on Sunday. These could usually be taken care of in the morning, so they had the afternoon free. On this Sunday Seth was eager to be done, as he'd promised his friends he would ride with them on the new bike trails.

"Coach asked us to scout them out for him. He said he was relying on us to show him where they are when he comes back in August."

Carl was glad that Seth liked to ride his bicycle and had friends to do it with. No way, he thought, could I afford a car for Seth. It's a good thing he doesn't nag at me for one. Let him nag his mother. She nags him enough. They stopped at a drive-thru for lunch and then Carl dropped Seth off at home. His mother's home, so Carl didn't stay, having no wish to see her. Carl had other things to do.

Somewhere close by there had been an earthquake yesterday. He hadn't been able to check on just where its impact may have been, as the storm hit and he had that damn stake-out for Dr. Lucas. He remembered his vow. I'm through doing stuff for him and that lush from Texas he's always meeting with. They can find someone else to do their dirty work. The money ain't that good. If I'm gonna spy on people, I'll do it for myself. Thus fortified with resolve, he turned his pickup in the direction he'd heard yesterday's boom, where things just may have been knocked around and destabilized.

The old two-lane highway in and out of Colton had been The Strip. It was where roadside establishments, serving the motoring public from the Thirties up to the Eighties, had thrived, until a faster, more direct route to the Turnpike rendered it obsolete. The old highway was, in fact, the remainder of even earlier times, being paved on top of the original wagon road which, in itself, followed a Native American trail winding its way through the valley. Now, its concrete surface crisscrossed by tar lines, the road still evoked the car-culture era amid a few vestiges from the years of its heyday. There was a small used car lot, a shade-tree mechanic, the Dairy Queen, the Sure-Shot Taxidermy. Intact, but closed for years, were the Blue Moon Motel and the root beer drive-in, with its upraised, defaced neon sign, and the boarded-up roller rink. Them musta bin good days, Carl thought as he drove.

Farther along, the roadbed narrowed, grass, weeds and debris claiming its verges. Here the highway led past disused areas gone to scrub and sumac, and to desolate patches of ruined land—black dirt—marking former coal mine operations.

Carl rounded a bend, woods began on the left, and he slowed down when a 40-foot high expanse of exposed limestone appeared on the right. The old road cut showed its age in crumbling, eroded, vine-covered stones, spindly trees growing out of its cracked face. Carl pulled off and parked in the gravel and stubble by the side of the cut. Somewheres here, he thought, it must of been. He got out and waded through tall weedy grass to the edge of a ravine.

What Carl was looking for were signs of the earthquake's effect. The Colton area substructure was honeycombed with old mining tunnels. They'd all been sealed up for decades. But you get a quake, Carl reasoned, and there's a pretty good chance one of 'em is gonna pop open. If I could find a way in, I'd have it made. I could stash stuff maybe, even wander around under Colton and, well, we'll just see.

He knew where one of the mine entrances had been, down in a gully, close to where the old train trestle had been before they pulled it down. That made him think of Mrs. Foster. I wonder why she even come back? It must be sorta sad for her around here. He shook his head at the thought and tramped on down into the ravine. The brush made it tough going, but the soil here was sandy and full of pebbles, grass growing sparsely. Riverbed once, it had the instability of continual spring and fall washes. Quake prone, Carl thought, as he methodically scanned the ground. Then he saw what looked like a newly formed depression. Carl squatted down and grinned. A caved-in area. It was here, all right. Get my spade. Got some diggin' to do. A whole lot of daylight left to do it in.

Seth and his friends had taken the old highway on their way to the bike trail. He noted his dad's pickup parked over by the side and wondered about that. Did he run out of gas? No, I just filled the tank for him.

"Wait up, guys," he called to his friends and walked in the direction the truck was facing. Then he saw his dad, down in the gully, doing something with a spade. Digging bait? It had rained hard yesterday. Probably that was it. He returned to his friends and they rode on.

After an hour Carl had a man-sized hole dug and had squeezed through and clambered down. He found he was standing on coal car tracks and when he shouted with laughter, it echoed for a long way. He was not equipped for exploring the tunnel, since he'd forgotten a flashlight, but there was plenty of time to do that. Yep. He'd be back. Can't wait to see where she goes. Once out he covered the opening with brush and laughed to himself all the way back to town.

Because it had become a habit to check up on people, Carl went by the Super's house. He noticed that Mrs. Foster's car was parked in front of the last garage bay. He also noted that it was still there when he drove by at 7:00 the next morning.

Chapter 21

Late Sunday afternoon Pat showed up at the screen door on Jerry's deck. She was wearing a longish crinkled cotton skirt in blue and a pale green top, and was carrying a covered dish and a hamper basket. Poking out of an oversized shoulder bag was a bottle of wine. Jerry was on the floor, cushions scattered around, using the window seats to lay out and put disorganized papers and files into order. He saw her and elation flooded through him. He scrambled to his feet and let her in, unburdening her of the heavy items.

"You *are* moving in with me then!" he exclaimed. "I'm delighted! Can I fetch the rest of your things?"

She thought how desirable he looked in track shorts, how relaxed he was in the easy comfort of his own surroundings. It was a thrilling prospect to be part of his private existence. "Thanks," she said, giving him a raffish look, "you can bring up the piano."

"I don't care if it's an elephant. As long as I have you."

He put the cold items in the refrigerator and turned to her. Quite suddenly, in spite of her elation, she felt inexplicably irresolute. It was as if some puzzling indecisiveness had her in its grip. It couldn't be because of him. No, it must be something else. Better clarify it, she thought, better try to understand it. "I fixed us some supper," she said in an earnest voice, stalling for time, not yet able to plunge into the crux of the matter.

"So I see and am looking forward to it immensely. It will be far better than the leftover hot dogs that were forced on me from the picnic yesterday." He held off doing what he would have liked, namely, to draw her close. He could tell that her normal composure had temporarily deserted her, and he didn't wish to add to the awkwardness he sensed she was feeling. She had come here to his house, to him, and perhaps needed a little while to settle herself before she confronted the actuality of what they were about to embark upon. Of what he fervently hoped they would embark upon.

She pulled a chair out and sat down at the table. He sat across from her, waiting. The ironstone pitcher in the center was filled with a variety of flowers he'd gleaned from the hillside: daisies, Queen Anne's lace, roses, clover blossoms. The aroma was sharp and sweet. Pat inhaled the summer fragrances and looked at Jerry, so patient, so considerate. "You are the most understanding man," she said, her eyes shining with appreciation for him.

He wondered if there would be a "but" attached to this statement. As none followed, he said, "Is that why you hired me four months ago?"

"I didn't know how exciting you were four months ago. I only knew I was drawn to you and wanted to learn more about you."

"And I've let you down."

"No, Jerry! Quite the opposite!"

"I mean, you haven't had much of a chance to learn my secrets. You spilled yours so willingly and made your request for mine so prettily and have gotten nothing for your pains."

"You did drop a few hints that whetted my appetite."

He got up and brought over two glasses and an opened bottle of white wine. "Shall we try to right this wrong? I'm only too happy to accommodate you, since you're moving in with me."

Pat's ambiguous state of mind began to sort itself out at his good spirits. How reassuring he is, she thought. He filled their glasses and she raised hers. "To you, Jerry," she toasted him.

"To us, Pat," he returned. "Now, what would the president of the Colton Area School Board like to know about her loyal and devoted superintendent?"

"Why you're so amenable for starts," she answered easily.

"Ah, love, all in the eye of the beholder. To some I am a constant irritation, handing out tasks and assignments and demanding deadlines."

"Not what I've heard. I've only heard how polite you are. They are falling over themselves to please you."

"Your sources have been bribed, obviously."

She thought, I want this man so much. Why am I holding back? To get my bearings? I wanted Elliot last fall. But that had a far different feel. It was about proving something to myself, that a man could be interested in me. Now it's a whole kaleidoscope of energizing and stimulating emotions. Now it's about knowing this one person, all of him. And I just sit here staring at him.

The sun had begun to slant in through the windows. Jerry got up and adjusted the blinds, letting Pat collect her thoughts. The room, now in shadow, lent an aura more conducive to intimacy. Whatever she wants, Jerry was thinking as he sat down again, we don't have to rush it.

He's giving me time, Pat thought. Do I need more time? No. She gave him a bemused little smile. "I think I've finally got a handle on what's bothering me," she confessed. "I want everything at once. It has me totally paralyzed."

"Everything? Cocktails? Dinner? Dessert? A stroll by the light of the moon?"

"At the very least. I want to, yes, drink with you, dine with you, walk with you, talk with you, look at you, feel you..." Here she faltered.

"And all at once?"

"If it's possible, yes."

"Right now?"

"Yes," she said, rising.

"Is there an order assigned to this list?" Jerry smiled up at her but his eyes were serious.

"Ladies' choice?"

"Ladies' choice," he affirmed and got up. He didn't have to ask what choice the lady would make. He knew.

Pat stood where she was, looking at him. "I want you, Jerry, and I don't think I can wait another minute." She said it evenly, with great control in her voice, but her heart was racing.

Jerry glanced at the bedroom door which seemed, at that moment, miles away. He kicked the scattered cushions together. "Come down with me," he said, taking her swiftly in his arms and lowering her with him onto the pillowed floor.

He brought her down on top of him and his kiss was not the token he'd bestowed before. This one had all the immediacy of desire no longer forestalled. They did not even take time for the niceties of undressing, simply pushing aside what was in the way, and yet, there was lingering in his caress, in their tightly wound embrace. He heard her quick intake of breath, felt her yielding. She was aware of his urgency and power and, afterward, when he exhaled in a sigh, his breath came in a gentle shudder.

She lay with his arms wrapped around her, her cheek against his chest in a cloud of contentment. He kissed the top of her head and whispered, "You are heaven."

"Mmm, this is heaven. With you."

"Pat, though," he said in an apologetic tone, "this was not what I meant for us the first time. But I needed you so terribly. I'm sorry I was in such haste. Next time..."

She interrupted, "I'm not sorry. I loved your haste. What better reason for wearing a skirt like this?"

He laughed and it was the warm, soft laugh of happiness.

Chapter 22

Since Monday was, as a consequence of decisions made by higher levels of government, an extension of the Independence Day holiday, Jerry and Pat were able to have the day to themselves. The weather was fine and they had breakfasted at the table on the deck, Jerry having sliced strawberries into glasses of orange juice, made coffee and fixed toast, while Pat scrambled eggs, adding some capers and pimento she discovered in the refrigerator. Her outfit for this summer morning consisted of one of Jerry's dress shirts and a pair of his boxer shorts. After they'd finished, they stayed at the table outside reading the newspaper.

"Like any old married couple," Pat commented.

"Not either of *my* ill-starred marriages. Too dull to enjoy even reading the paper together," Jerry remarked with a sour face.

"A speck of information!" she said brightly. "A teaser!"

"Details at 11:00," he announced in sepulchral tones.

"I'll be sure to tune in. Sounds very jolly."

Jerry looked at her sitting there, absolutely glowing. I guess I can take credit for that glow, he thought with satisfaction. But instead of inflating his ego, the thought gave him a sort of peace; it's going to be all right with us.

She put her section of the paper down to pour them both more coffee and saw the contented look on his face. Could life ever be as ideal as it is this morning, she wondered?

"What would you like to do today, Pat?" he asked. "Besides finding something else to wear," he added, indicating her unusual getup with a grin.

"You mean, what would people think if they happened to catch a glimpse of me out here dressed in your things? Not to worry. This is Cross County." She hoisted the paper up again, as she had started laughing at her own joke.

He batted the paper down so he could laugh with her. "You're beautiful and I love you," he said blithely. Are we going too fast? But why not?

She found herself momentarily tongue-tied. Yes, it followed. They did love each other. Did he expect she wouldn't respond in kind?

He held the paper with one hand, his coffee cup with the other, and was smiling impishly at her discomfiture. "Took you off guard, did I?" he asked. "It's about time I sprang one on you."

Pat rose to the bait. Taking advantage of his being encumbered, she reached over and deftly pulled off his reading glasses. "At my mercy now," she crowed, "you enchanting, generous, precipitate man: I love you."

Ah, wonderful, he was thinking with growing enjoyment, Romantic Comedy with all its fun and games, when his phone suddenly rang and he dropped the paper, splashing out his coffee, and said "Damn!" into the phone.

And then Pat heard him say, "No, not you, Mama. I spilled some coffee. No, just fine. Yes, a lovely day." He looked at Pat and rolled his eyes. She escaped to get dressed.

He went to find her, after he'd given his weekly assurances to his mother that he was not in any imminent danger in this remote and dubious outpost. Pat was washing up the breakfast things, wearing yesterday's skirt which, surprisingly, looked none the worse for its careless treatment the day before.

"My 84-year-old mama," he said, "is still not convinced it's safe for me to be here. She cannot know how unsafe it is, having given my heart to a *shiksa*."

Pat stopped what she was doing, dried her hands slowly and turned to look at him. "But I'm not," she said, "not technically."

"Miss Mitchell?"

"My grandmother's name was Somers. My mother's was Ash. Our families emigrated from Vienna to Baltimore in the 1800s." She paused. "Strauss. I didn't even think."

It was completely unforeseen. Jerry was astounded by this phenomenal information delivered, as she had done, with candor and sincerity. No wonder he had felt an affinity with her. He took both her hands. "This news is extremely dangerous," he said ominously.

"Why?" she responded. "Are we cousins?"

"In all likelihood."

"We're not going to be producing offspring," she pointed out.

"It's my mama. If she gets wind of this, our fate is sealed. She will not rest until we have tied the knot. She is, above all things, a Jewish mother."

Pat cocked an eye at him. "Even though ham on rye is one of my favorites?"

"Or even ham and Swiss. But she can overlook that."

"Oh, Jerry, why didn't we meet years ago?"

"Come, Pat," he proposed, "let's take a walk before the day gets too sultry. I want to show you a place up on the hill. There's a mystery about it that you might be able to shed some light on."

In the evening after Pat left, Jerry had the distinct impression that fate, in the embodiment of their combined ancestors, the Jakobs and Josefs, the Hermines and Lottes, had brought the two of them together and a delegation was hanging around to see what would happen next. He had a word with the representatives of this imposing assemblage. "Look," he told them, "back off. We must go at our own pace. Commitment may come, but we both have had some disillusioning experiences and need to resist the urge to jump prematurely into anything at all like permanency." But, my precious Pat, he said to her in his mind, after the last twenty-four hours with you, I would gladly be your slave.

Dreamland. That was what she and her brother had named the little parklet up on the hill. They had discovered it over 40 years ago, a special place, an enchanted place. "And the bench?" he asked her. "Was there a plaque?" They had searched for it today, but found only the holes where it had been bolted into the concrete.

"It was there, I'm sure. Some Cross County worthy, I think."

"Owen likes to do local research. He'll be bursting with curiosity if I tell him about Dreamland."

"I like Owen," Pat said. "He probably won't stay if something comes up for him in Martensdale, but in the few months he's been here, he's been such an asset."

"I think he has the same attitude about Cross County as you, wanting to get in there and do things to lift it up."

"I think you have that attitude too, Jerry."

He looked at her. "Perhaps because being here has made me happier than I've ever been before." And he thought, who would have guessed?

That night at home, Pat let herself luxuriate thinking about Jerry and their time together. They were so exceedingly compatible, she thought with quiet happiness. And then to discover they shared the same heritage. Not that she was brought up Jewish. The elder Mitchells had been Catholic, but when they first came to Colton, Catholicism was associated with coal miners and immigrants. It was more suitable for a doctor to be a member of the prevailing Protestant denomination. Pat's mother fell in line with this as well, so Pat and Tim had gone to Sunday School at the First Methodist. "And now, knowing you has made me aware of a whole world I'm part of," she said.

In the afternoon he had put on Strauss waltzes. He held out his arms to her. "May I have this dance, Madam?" he requested in his formal voice.

This was music she remembered from her childhood, old LPs her mother would play for them when she and her brother were young. She had never waltzed with a real partner before, but today to *Wiener Blut* her steps matched Jerry's. Viennese blood. They both had it, and it was activated by the music, like a race memory. The haunting melody of the waltz, with the past it evoked of vanished beauty and cultural grandeur, but also of great sorrow and horrendous loss, seemed to reinforce the bond they shared, what lay deep within them beneath the lightness of the present. Pat's eyes were full of tears and when they turned to each other, their love-making was colored by such profound emotion that it brought with it an undercurrent of mortality as if, by making love, they were paying tribute to those who had perished. For a few minutes afterwards they felt almost as though they'd had a brush with death. They were both shaken, and needed to talk about other things.

They discussed what they might do together in the next few weeks and what meetings they were involved in for the school district, which led inevitably to Elliot.

"Jerry, I am so sorry that he was ever part of my personal life," Pat confessed.

"There's no need to apologize," Jerry assured her. "It's done with and can't have any bearing on us, except that we must deal with him at the school district."

"In which environment, at least, things are not fraught with emotion," she allowed. "But that reminds me: Elliot specifically asked me to wait until he got back, if any financial problems arose or if Francine had any questions."

"Did he just?" Jerry observed thoughtfully.

Chapter 23

Having outfitted himself with a coal miner's helmet including working headlamp, two heavy duty flashlights and a miner's pick, Carl once again parked by the road cut on the old highway and walked down into the ravine. It was Monday morning but quiet, being a day off for most. He'd thought about taking Seth along on this venture. The kid would love it, he knew. But what would happen if his mother started pumping him for information on what he'd been doing with his dad? She had a way of coming at you like a fly buzzing around your head, Carl thought sourly, and you keep swatting at it and missing. She might get it out of him, where they'd been. Especially if he had coal dust all over him, like I had t'other day. Naw. Not a good idea.

He found his former excavation site and removed the obstacles he'd piled around it. Then he did a little more digging to accommodate all the gear he'd brought. When he judged it large enough, he got through, pulling a branch over the opening as he went. He slid the last few feet down, remembering that he'd had a bit of a scramble to get back up yesterday. Must bring me a ladder next time, he said to himself. He switched on the headlamp and one of his flashlights and, grinning with delight, had a look around.

He'd come in close to the front of the mine, as he'd thought. In one direction his light played over the concrete-sealed entrance. In the other direction the tunnel stretched out, tracks glinting at him, leading into the darkness. Carl was hugging himself, shivering with excitement and also with the cold that he'd forgotten about. Shoulda' brought a jacket, he thought. What was the temperature in most of them caves hereabouts? 52° year-round usually. But his enthusiasm overcame his discomfort and he began to follow the tracks.

He noticed that overhead and around him the rock walls glistened. Water was seeping down in several places. Not tight, he thought to himself. Good thing limestone leaks like a sieve. He'd been worried about black damp and methane, but not enough to give up this idea of his without making a try.

However, it did seem too wet a place for his plans. All Grandpap's things, he was thinking. Too bad they wouldn't keep down here. Gotta get a jump on the folks movin' outta the trailer park. Damn, he thought. What's Pappy gonna do? They'll have to put him in a Home. It'd kill him. I gotta take care of what he gave me. He 'spects it of me, the medals an' war stuff an' all.

After a couple of hundred feet, the tunnel branched. Carl stood thinking where the two branches might go. He knew the area and figured he was approaching the steep hill that rose up on one side of the ravine. Most likely the left branch goes straight into the hillside, he thought. That would be where a coal seam was. Keep that in mind till later. I'll take to the right. Might be more interestin' to see where I get to. Yep. I'll just keep on going.

Carl had been taken into the mines as a child, before they were closed and barricaded. His father had been a miner as a young man, and had finished his career with black lung disease. He had never spoken ill of coal mining, but Carl's distrust and animosity towards the coal bosses, the companies and the unions was formed early and only increased with time. That he was now contemplating using the abandoned mine for his own purposes tickled him no end. It was clear that his present appropriation of the tunnels was in no small part revenge for the wrongs perpetrated by the coal industry while, coincidently, providing him with enormous satisfaction at being able to take advantage of a side effect of the loathsome gas drilling. It was all exquisitely rewarding.

From time to time, Carl came across scattered remainders of former mining activity: broken picks and shovels, miner's knee pads and helmets, empty dynamite and powder boxes. Things that looked interesting and possibly saleable he put aside to retrieve on his way out. No sense leavin' these here antiques layin' around, he told himself, when people will pay money for 'em.

Every eight feet his light picked up the cross beams bracing the roof of the tunnel. He was relieved to see that none looked like it had deteriorated. Locust wood, he thought with respect, acknowledging the tree's strength and durability.

It was when he had been walking steadily downhill for almost an hour that he sensed he was beginning to go uphill again. After a while the tunnel seemed wider and higher, with what looked like a rudimentary ceiling above to keep the area dry. There was a coal car sitting on the tracks, shortly beyond which the tracks had been taken up. He saw debris here and there—splintered chairs, smashed crockery, a refrigerator lying on its side, whiskey bottles of all kinds. There were even some pinball machines. Carl rubbed his chin. What the hell we got here? Where was he? He shone his light around and it picked out a stairway with a broken railing going up to a closed door. "Yeh," he said softly. "I know where I'm at now."

The school district office was not a busy place for the next few weeks, with staff members taking vacations and only one board meeting planned. Pat met with the lawyer representing the Elk Creek mobile home park residents, and he agreed that the school district had an interest in slowing down the displacement of so many children. "The sale did seem very sudden. My requests for information to the sellers have been ignored," he told her.

She asked if he could find out more about the buyers, so the district could communicate with them to ask for a delay of eviction, at least for one more school year.

"I've been trying to find that out. It isn't easy. They seem to be a subsidiary of another corporation. You get into an endless loop, going from one site to another, and emails are not answered. You'd think it was set up that way on purpose." Then he added, "We're just country lawyers here. This is a city slicker kind of arrangement."

Pat reiterated their strategy. "If we can hold them off for two months, school will start again and the court may be willing to see this as constituting an unacceptable hardship on elementary aged children."

She also specifically invited Clem Duncan and his group to the upcoming board meeting, emphasizing that parents were encouraged to speak about their concerns. Then she called the media.

On Tuesday evening when the school board met, the room was packed. Parent after parent rose to speak, stressing the difficulties children had already experienced and dreading what another dislocation would cause. Children were frightened. They were crying themselves to sleep. There were eating disorders. More than one child had threatened to run away. Speakers took encouragement and inspiration from each other, creating ever more dire scenarios. It was a touching and moving display, captured in its entirety by the TV cameras. Pat did not cut anyone off and testimony went on for over an hour. The residents of Elk Creek Mobile Home Park did themselves proud.

At last there were no more speakers and Pat thanked them for informing the board of this urgent situation. She explained what she had learned from the lawyer, making sure that the ladies and gentlemen of the media understood that there was a residents' association prepared to buy the property. "They were not given right of first refusal, even though they had been negotiating to buy it for over two years."

Pencils scribbled, keyboards clicked, cameras recorded.

"I'd like our Superintendent to address this issue now. Dr. Strauss?" She turned to Jerry and he stood up.

"Thank you, all of you, for being here tonight. We are grateful that so many parents of children in our district came to give us the benefit of their experiences. You were unhesitating and sincere and painted a clear and explicit picture, a picture that is very disturbing." He paused for a moment, then went on, "Children are not second class citizens to us. They are the most important people in the world. They cannot be treated as if their welfare doesn't matter. They cannot be disregarded, caught in the middle of someone's scheme to make money, of someone's" ...there was loud cheering which went on for some time, and Jerry waited... "greed."

He was interrupted again by cheering, then continued, "We are committed in this school district to children, to their education and well-being. There are over forty children affected by this hurry-up decision on the part of unknown buyers and uncommunicative sellers, and families who would be hard-pressed to find affordable housing in the district. We cannot let this happen, either to the children or their families, and we will explore every possible avenue to keep Elk Creek Park intact."

People rose to their feet, clapping. The opening salvo, Jerry thought. I just hope we can find a way to make good on our promises. He's absolutely gorgeous, thought Pat. They love him.

The media eagerly took up the plight of the trailer park and for several days there were articles and pictures in the *Clarion* and stories, interviews and footage on TV. Jerry took calls from concerned citizens, including some in the gas industry, who wanted to assure him that they were not planning to buy the property and evict children. He received emails and several letters, one written in pencil that said only, "Bless you." That's a first, thought Jerry.

He wondered how Elliot would have reacted to the meeting and the subsequent media frenzy. Were his spies gathering data while he was at his undisclosed vacation whereabouts? Were they also keeping tabs on where Pat parked her car? Jerry hadn't told Pat about a possible connection between the Star Partnership listed on the eviction notice and the names he'd overheard about the charter school subcontractor. He had held back because, in the first place, he didn't really have anything but a hunch and, secondly, he didn't want his antagonism to Elliot muddying up what should be an impartial seeking of facts. But how to get the facts?

He had brought the charter school report in to his office and had studied it. There was nothing to indicate the name of the subcontractor that handled their business services. Before he contacted the charter school himself, he'd have a go at Elliot's files. Francine might be able to locate this information and, while he was at it, she should be able to find out who had made offers to purchase the Elk Creek School property right after the fire. He strolled down the hallway to Elliot's office, in front of which was the budget clerk's desk. Francine, it transpired, had been given a short vacation during this downtime. "I need to check on some figures," Jerry said with a disarming smile at Elliot's secretary.

"I'm afraid the door to Dr. Lucas's office is locked, Dr. Strauss," she answered apologetically. "Dr. Lucas is very particular about his files. I don't have a key, but I can ask Francine when she gets back next week."

Jerry resisted the urge to frown. This was not the way school district business offices were run in his experience. "Yes, please," he answered. "Mrs. Foster needs some data." That might unlock the door, he thought. If not, we try one of the custodians and if that fails to get the door open, I will break the damn thing down myself.

Chapter 24

They decided to have a day in the country. Pat had said, "You can't come to Cross County and spend all your time in the refined environment of urban Colton. What's that Land Rover for anyway? There are back roads, state and county parks and some breathtaking overlooks." Her voice became more serious as she went on, "And there are small towns consisting of company-built housing, all of it substandard, but still being lived in, and places where children have real trouble getting to school in winter."

There were only three school districts in Cross County. Besides Colton Area, there was Boundary Area covering the southern third, and Hemlock district to the east. Even though the county was relatively small, it was not feasible to consolidate the districts into one, given the barriers caused by the mountainous terrain.

Pat said, "We discussed consolidation a few years back. But there were objections all over the place. One of the school board association people asked this question when the subject of consolidation arose: What is the hardest animal to kill in Pennsylvania?"

"Yes?"

"The high school mascot."

"Hah! I can imagine the fight they'd put up if the 'Colton Critter' had to be scrapped for another school's identity."

"Even though no one is sure just what the 'Critter' is," Pat granted.

"Well, looks to me like a cross between a weasel and a porcupine," Jerry commented irreverently, "only less attractive."

"It's supposed to look mean!" Pat protested. "A force to be reckoned with."

"Or eaten?"

"I'm beginning to think I should never have revealed that painful fact," she said, making a face.

"Good thing you did, so I can be on my guard."

"Well," Pat continued, getting back on track, "in spite of all, I want you to see what the county is like, where children are living. Some of it has a very isolated feel."

Jerry became pensive at this. "It's hard to believe in this day and age, but could there be kids out there who are not in school?" he asked. "And certainly they would have no internet."

Pat nodded sadly. "Quite possibly there are hidden children and quite possibly they are disabled, mentally or physically. It's something I wrestled with when I was working for the county. We thought we'd found them all, but that was over 6 years ago."

There were also, she went on, towns and settlements that had vanished, but left their traces in vine-covered stone foundations, in abandoned fields and orchards. "And up on a hillside far from anywhere," Pat reflected, "you might see a cemetery with a hundred gravestones, and they are still being tended. You wonder what it was like when people lived around there: so much has disappeared. But who is keeping vigil? Who comes to make sure this measure of respect is given?"

"That someone is doing so speaks well of Cross County, that there are people who value the past."

They went on a weekday when nothing was scheduled. He and Pat both fixed picnic food, as she had assured him they would definitely want to bring their own. "No charming inns dot the countryside, no gastro-pubs in the little towns. Although," she added, "one can't entirely rule out running into antiques where we're going. Perpetual yard sales are the way a lot of people make ends meet, and things emerge every year."

Jerry had picked Pat up at her house and they were driving south on the old highway. Pat's last statement caught his interest. "Things?" he repeated.

"Mostly rusty tools and implements coming to light after the snow melts or when an old shed finally tumbles down. But last year a derelict garage yielded a Model A."

"What happened to it? The car, I mean."

"After the lucky finder reported it to the newspaper, he had dealers swarming all over. Sold it to the highest bidder, who turned out to be an antique car collector. Wanted it for parts."

"Ouch. That's as bad as buying an 1895 set of King Francis sterling just to melt down."

"The relatives are still not speaking to each other, so I understand."

They had come to the rocky face of the old road cut. "Stop a moment, Jerry," Pat requested, knitting her brow.

He pulled the car over and parked in the verge. Pat opened the door. "Go with me a little way," she said.

It was still early, the day's heat yet to come. Dew was on the grass as they walked to where the ravine plunged down. Pat paused. "I wanted to show you—this is where the train trestle was."

Jerry put his arm around her shoulders. They were both quiet for a few moments. He said, "It's gone, yet leaves a mental imprint for those who remember. You know, sometimes we leave tangible imprints, good or bad. But often an imprint fades, except for what is intangible."

"And then, one day, there's no one left to remember," Pat said sadly.

"That's one of the reasons I value antiques," Jerry said as they walked back to the car.

"Tangibles?" she suggested.

"Yes. You can hang onto something that otherwise would be gone and take the past it came from with it."

"You're an insightful man, Jerome Strauss," Pat said. "Cousin," she amended.

After they'd driven for a while, they left the paved highway for a gravel road that headed up and over a series of precipitous, heavily wooded hills. When the road leveled out, Pat said, "Boundary School District."

Here there were a few widely spaced houses, often with vehicles in various stages of deterioration parked about. Front porches held sofas, refrigerators, washing machines. Porch roofs sagged, support posts leaning this way or that, the whole seemingly held up by Virginia creeper. But, since it was summer, things conveyed a sort of decrepit and nostalgic charm, almost as if, Jerry thought, behind the patched screen doors, people's lives held an enviable self-containment, even a languid passion. "Faulkneresque," he murmured.

Some children playing in front of their homes stopped to watch the car go by. Pat waved to them and they waved back.

"I'd love to know how they like their schools, what they are learning," Jerry commented.

Pat smiled at him. He was so interested in children's education. It was sad that he'd had no children of his own. At least she assumed not. Perhaps it was because his marriages had been so unhappy.

They took a road that switch-backed up a hill and had reached the top, where there was a turnout. Jerry, at Pat's direction, came to a stop in the modest graveled area and they got out. It was only a few yards to the edge of a steep drop-off. "It's a little scary," Pat warned, "without any guard rail. But what a view!"

Beyond them lay a green, corrugated panorama of hills and valleys gentled-out in the mid-day light of high summer. There were glints from lakes and rivers and there were dark patches of conifer forest, the whole a verdant sweep of hill after hill, valley after valley, trailing off into distant haziness.

"There," said Pat, pointing southwest, "is West Virginia. And to the southeast, you can see the Cumberland Gap area of Maryland. On a day like this, we are looking all the way down into Virginia. But it's mostly Cross County before us."

It was hot and still. A red-tailed hawk was making a rapid and purposeful descent below them. Insects were subdued in the heat, and the faint ticking of the car, as the engine cooled from its climb, was the only sound.

"It's magnificent, Pat," Jerry said to her. "I can imagine what it must be like with fall colors. And in winter, when the trees are bare? You could see even more. The car altimeter read over 1700 feet when we stopped."

"Although with snow," Pat said, "this road would be closed."

"So, how do they get to school?"

"They quite often don't. Education takes a back seat to winter."

Jerry rested his eyes on the distances again. "Four states," he said with awe, "and no sign posted anywhere proclaiming such an extraordinary vista. Is this an indication of Cross County's innate modesty?"

"I'm thinking that it's best not to advertise it, at least until they put up something to keep people from plunging off the cliff."

They stood gazing out, quiet in the quiet noon. Jerry said, "I remember flying into D.C. from the West Coast once. As the plane settled lower on our approach to Dulles, we went over Harper's Ferry. The sun was setting behind us and lit up everything in front. It was a privileged gift to see that unmistakable geography laid out below, the way the Shenandoah meets the Potomac, and the long span of the railroad bridge. Being up here reminds me of that, the same perspective as flight. Gathering it all in from above. It's a free feeling."

Pat remarked, "That's the way I feel just being with you, Jerry. I have a sense of freedom."

He smiled and said, "Freedom from what?"

"Not 'from.' 'To.' Freedom to love you. You've let me love you." Realizing that she was getting too serious, she went on, "You gave me no objections. No demurrals. You didn't even put up a decent fight."

"I know when I'm outclassed," he responded, then added, "and anyway, wasn't it in my job description?"

"In the fine print," she said and was rewarded by his warm laugh.

They came back down to a main road that followed a river. After a stretch of cut-over uninhabited land, Pat pointed out a settlement on the opposite bank. Huddled under a steep hillside, were the remains of a town built by a coal company in the early 1900s for its workers: a single line of 3-story houses on the narrow space between river and hill—six identical wooden multi-family homes, spare, unadorned and cheerless. They had probably been white to begin with, but were now a dull, darkened gray. Bereft of any landscaping and in full view from the highway across the river, the houses sat sullen and exposed, facing the world with an injured air.

"People are still living there?" Jerry observed with surprise. A few cars were in evidence and even though it was July, smoke came from several of the chimneys.

"Yes, it's inhabited. And the smoke is from cook stoves. I made a few visits here when I was doing social work. I remember a lot of coughing," she said with resignation in her voice. "There had been a store and a school. The store was demolished by the company after the mines closed. Someone burnt down the school in protest. Arson. And not for the first time in Cross County."

"Nor the last."

Pat was silent and Jerry didn't press the subject. Some other time, he thought.

The county park Pat had chosen for lunch was in land that had once been a farmstead. As they walked from the parking area, they could see grassy depressions, testimony to where buildings had been. There was a little stream running through and picnic tables sitting at random. An old apple orchard stood slightly higher up the hill, and there was a tumbled-down stone wall covered in blackberry brambles. There were also primitive, but adequate, facilities.

"It's basic, but we can move a table under the trees and it looks like we have the place mostly to ourselves," Pat said, hoping he would like it as much as she did.

"It's absolutely charming," Jerry assured her, "all one could want for a perfect country picnic."

After their meal of salads and thin-sliced steak sandwiches, along with a generous handful of the seedy but sweet, carefully plucked blackberries, they strolled by the stream and then on a trail that wound into a grove of oak, ash and hemlock. Woodpeckers were busy tapping high up on tree trunks and chickadees were flitting in lower branches. They walked hand in hand, pausing to listen to the birds and the sound of the stream in the distance.

This day, Jerry said to himself, even while it is still unfolding, is a golden moment. It is the kind of day you thought existed long ago, sometime in your faraway past. But it is happening right now. How can I hold onto it? How can we hold onto each other? I will have this moment in my dreams, he thought. This place, this time with Pat, will come back to me again and again, ceasing to be real, yet bringing the vague feeling of having once happened.

Oh, come on, let's cut out all this unwonted sentimentality, he told himself.

Or am I already starting to say goodbye to her?

Chapter 25

In the afternoon they drove north, frequently passing evidence of bygone coal mining operations: blackened earth, stunted trees and boarded up mine entrances, hallmarks of former activities. There were not many settlements in this hilly area and the few they saw looked precariously sited, as if they were bracing themselves against impending disaster, the consequence of trying to defy gravity. On one side of the road, small wooden houses crouched in the shadow of a hillside rising above that appeared fully capable, should it take the notion, of coming down upon them. On the other side, the back of each house was shored up, usually with a motley assortment of miscellaneous materials, lest the slope, stealthily in the night, give way.

A former elementary school, now repurposed into a community center with notices of classes and activities in its windows, caught Jerry's attention. "A school from the 'Dick and Jane' era, but still used, so all is not lost."

Pat asked, "Are we better off with fewer, larger schools now when the bus ride is so long? It's really a moot question, I guess, because districts can no longer support all those small schools anyway."

They passed a hillside cemetery, immaculate and aloof, and they passed other hillsides almost completely covered with wrecked cars in a messy jumble of weeds and rusting metal. Pat shrugged when Jerry commented, "Are these actually operating businesses? I don't see any roads. Strange.

Junk yards out here. I suppose the fees to compact them aren't worth the scrap metal."

"Doesn't shed the best light on Cross County," Pat admitted apologetically.

Jerry said, "Still, blight here is less odious than blighted inner-city neighborhoods, to my way of thinking."

They headed to another park Pat particularly wanted Jerry to see. "This one is a favorite," she promised. "It's part of the state forest lands and has a swimming pond and stonework fireplaces. It was built in the 1930s and used to be a hunting camp. There's a trail to a vista point, dramatic as the first although, since it looks north, you only get Pennsylvania."

But as they got closer to the turnoff, truck traffic picked up, and it was plain things had changed. A new and raw road had been sliced through the woods at an angle to the park entrance with a sign that said *No Access. Gas Drilling. Rig Traffic.*

Although the picnic area of the park was intact and several children were splashing in the pond, the trail to the overlook was blocked, with a warning posted. And, in case that wasn't enough, standing guard was a formidable-looking person wearing a hardhat embellished with an energy company logo. Over the sound of children's voices could be heard the steady, low throbbing of drilling equipment and the growl of truck engines.

"When will the trail be open again?" Pat asked with a smile.

"Can't say, Ma'am," the guard answered, unsmiling. Clearly he was not interested in questions posed by park goers.

Pat took this as a challenge. "Have you gone up to the vista yourself? It's quite breathtaking. On a good day you can see five Appalachian Ridges from there."

The guard did not deign to answer.

"You know," Pat said to him, as they turned to leave, "a friendlier attitude would make our sacrifice to your enterprise a little less unpleasant."

This time the guard merely spat. Jerry felt his anger rise and realized they'd better go back to the picnic area, before he made the mistake of engaging in a very futile no-win exercise.

When he had calmed down, he ventured, "I thought they weren't supposed to be leasing drilling rights in public parks."

"Some parks, but not all parks."

They had poured two cups of iced coffee from the thermos they'd packed and were sitting at one of the tables. Pat took a drink and went on, "Oil and gas drilling have helped us in many ways but, because it isn't regulated effectively, there are great disparities with regard to protection and benefits."

"Direct benefits to education: zilch," Jerry stated.

"And all the infrastructure issues, environmental degradation, health concerns and social problems that occur."

"And then, when gas extraction is no longer profitable," Jerry added, "what will the county be left with?"

"Well, there's work to be done, my friend," Pat said resolutely.

Jerry looked at her. There was determination in the way she voiced that last statement, and he would not be surprised if she intended to take on causes beyond the school district. "In spite of all," he said, "I'm glad we saw this. I'd heard it was going on, that there were disruptive closures of trails and game lands. But what I see among the families here is a carry-on-as-usual attitude. Is this the adaptive nature of Cross Countians making the best of it, or are they oblivious?"

"Even if they are oblivious, I'm not. Given the amount of gas to be extracted and the tremendous profits to be made by the industry, the energy companies should be willing to make more accommodations. That is, the legislature should see that they do." She smiled at Jerry, thinking that he deserved more from his companion than a diatribe. "It hasn't really spoiled my day, Jerry," she amended.

"Nor mine, Pat. Are you ready to go back now and didn't we promise ourselves Deems this evening?"

Pat came out of her reverie. "Antiques! You just reminded me: yard sales! I *thought* we'd forgotten a seriously important activity. I know several places where you can count on something going on. We'll backtrack and see if there's any gold among the dross."

While most of the countryside they had driven through was sparsely settled, there was the occasional town or, more accurately, the remnants of a town. Late in the afternoon, they came upon one consisting of early 20th century brick row houses on both sides of the road, each with a narrow front porch running the width of the house. Here and there several people were in the process of winding up porch sales, putting things away or covering larger items with plastic tarps. Jerry parked and they got out, wandering among a few unpromising tables set out with canning jars and other household leftovers. They decided that it was not the best time.

Jerry declared, "The game is not worth the candle, as one of my old professors used to say. But wait..." Jerry had spotted a box of books.

Pat rummaged around in the box and found some 1940s advertising pamphlets for Jell-O and mayonnaise, with recipes from the era. "And see the plates the food is on! Fiesta in yellow and turquoise. And here are desserts tastefully displayed on green Depression glass. I think it's the 'Princess' pattern."

Jerry looked at her in amazement. "I didn't realize you knew Thirties dinnerware. Will you never stop impressing me?"

Pat explained, "There was a set of mismatched Depression glass, inherited from my grandmother, stacked on the bottom shelf of my mother's china cabinet. It's one of the few things from the house that my aunt kept for me. She said my father's mother referred to them as 'hardship plates,' bought at a time when people turned to cheap but cheery things. Bright clear colors, pretty patterns. I think they're still beautiful, but I'm afraid to use them."

"Don't be! You should enjoy them!"

Pat smiled at him "I like your attitude about antiques," she said, thinking again how comfortable she felt with him.

Her thoughts were interrupted by Jerry's sudden low, "Wow!" He had been going through the books and had pulled out a large leather-bound volume.

"Sell you the whole box, mister," they heard and, turning, saw a spare woman with the pinched face of poor nutrition and poverty. "You kin have 'em all fer two dollar."

"How much do you want for just this one?" Jerry asked.

"Dollar," she answered.

"No, it's worth more than that to me." He took out a twenty-dollar bill and handed it to her.

"Don't think I kin make change offa this here twenty."

"You keep the whole thing. I'm happy." He cradled the book carefully.

"Take them there with the recipes too," she said to Pat, who graciously accepted.

Not until they were back in the car and Jerry had dusted off the first of the grime did he show it to Pat. Her eyes grew wide as she read the title out loud: "*The History of Cross and*

Marten Counties, Pennsylvania. By Col. Marcus Parmalee Tyler. What a find!"

The smell of mildew was sharp as Jerry opened the book, handling the pages as lightly as possible. When they came to the title page, they both let out a little gasp. In faded spidery 19th century handwriting was the inscription: *To Maude. From your loving brother Marcus.*

"How do you suppose she came by it?" Jerry asked Pat later. "I didn't want to query her." They had gotten their barbecue to-go, and were sitting on Jerry's deck in the evening twilight. "Perhaps someone with a family connection brought it with him during his annual autumn pilgrimage at the hunting camp, to be read aloud in the evenings by the fire for the edification of his companions."

"And then it got left behind," Pat added. "I don't know where else it could have come from. The educated Cross County families lived in Colton."

"You know," Jerry mused, "all along, I was sure Cross County had hidden treasures, and I held out the hope that we might uncover one."

"The secret wealth of Cross County. And not natural gas."

"Oh," Jerry demurred, looking thoughtful, "there's that too, even though we saw much less in the way of the industry's impact today. But closer to Colton, with the large influx of workers and all the new development, it's different, and it has me wondering: as it spreads, will the extraction process and its ramifications cause, on balance, more harm than good for the county?"

"That's the main question," Pat said. "Over and above the obvious problematic areas, what could be permanently damaged or lost? But tell me, what's your impression of the county after our day?"

Jerry plunged in, "Well, I have to admit it's more beautiful than I imagined." He saw her quick smile. "Even more," he went on, "I'm impressed by your people. Tenaciously, even fiercely, they hang in there and survive, making what adjustments they can to climate, terrain and circumstances." Pat nodded and Jerry continued, "What they exhibit is, I think, the effect of remoteness, the self-reliance engendered by remoteness. 'We can take care of ourselves, thank you.' The land even looks that way. It gives the impression of a self-possessed, self-assured and slightly cocky piece of geography, as if it's saying, 'I'm directing this show.'"

She laughed, then said more soberly, "The two go hand in hand, land and folk, as they have down through history. And might a wholesale invasion by the energy companies erode the resiliency borne of remoteness? Could it destroy the defining character of both land and people, particularly after the industry packs up and goes?"

Jerry shook his head sadly, "And creates a scenario of closed businesses and abandoned housing. Over forty trailer park families dispersed for a handful of pretentious builders' houses. Well, darling, it hasn't happened yet."

But when it does, if it does, he won't be here, she thought bleakly. She smiled wanly at him and he took her hand in his.

"I do know what you're thinking, Pat," he said.

"About the future?"

"About our future, isn't it?"

"Yes," she couldn't deny it.

"Lately, it's always in the back of my mind," he confessed.

Although, he thought, surely it's more in our control than we think. Can't we shape the future as we choose? Why should it be a threat, dark and brooding, looming over us while we, powerless, wait for it to defeat us? But only if we know what we want, he reminded himself.

Chapter 26

It has been said that the Welshman, separated from his native land of unpronounceable place names, is a bashful creature. Among his countrymen he is sociable and notably choral, but take him away and he becomes haunted, as if seeking to return to the earth. The Romans, who overran Wales in 48 AD, regarded the small, dark Silures as inferior beings, an attitude adopted throughout the British Isles, and never quite rooted out. Consequently, when the Welsh immigrated to America, they came to work in the mines, with which they felt familiar, and to live in the wild and hilly places, like Cross County, and to expect being treated as lesser entities. Perhaps bashful isn't the correct word; perhaps it's more a case of keeping one's head down.

Carl's ancestors had come to Pennsylvania in the mid-1800s, first to work the anthracite in the northeastern part of the state and then, when the hard coal began to play out, to mine the soft coal of the bituminous region in the southwestern area. Whatever Welsh traditions there had been were long forgotten. Yet something clung to Carl still, an ineffable sense of the solitariness of the Welshman removed from Wales. Carl exhibited traits that had been present for more than a millennium. He hadn't a hint of why; he just had begun more and more to like being in the mine tunnel.

His earlier negative feelings associated with coal mining had diminished with the pure fun he was having. He had wandered as far as he could, checking to see whether he could find a place for the things entrusted to him by his grandfather and he'd decided, reluctantly, that it was too damp. Anyways, he said to himself, nothing's happened at the Park yet. He'd also checked for daylight sifting in above, an indication of another quake-activated opening, and had found none. Yep, safe, he thought smugly.

He had gone back a few times to the portion of the tunnel beneath The Pit. It was the only area that made him uneasy. It had the appearance, as far as Carl could tell in his flashlight's beam, of possibly being used. Someone could come down them steps an' then where'd I be? All them whiskey bottles an' I bet they're still throwin' trash down here. This was also the end of the line, as the tunnel was blocked a short distance beyond. He decided to steer clear of the former speakeasy site.

It was on one of the last days of his vacation, before he had to report back to work at the school district, that he made the find. Set back on a ledge cut into the rock was what looked like an old safety lamp, the kind with a carbide cap that detected increased levels of methane gas and deficient levels of oxygen. It was made of brass, Carl was sure, although covered with years of coal dust. Boy, I could use one of them, or mebbe I could clean her up and sell it out to Deems, he thought excitedly, and he reached to bring it down from its resting place. A rusty, bent nail affixed the lamp to the rock face and made it difficult to extricate. He had to tug and twist and, as he did, he dislodged the stone behind it, which went crashing to the floor of the tunnel. Carl shone his flashlight around the hole he'd been responsible for creating. It gaped emptily back at him except in one place, where a tin box was wedged into the corner. Aw, guy must have went and left his lunch pail, he thought and, not having much desire for so humble an item, was about to leave with his brass prize. A few steps later he hesitated. Don't really seem near so much like a lunch pail, a voice in his mind said. Let's have us another look. He went back to examine it, worked it loose and pulled it out. Heavy sucker, Carl grunted. Partially crushed by the rock, it would have to be pried open. Do that later, he thought. He headed home, pleased with himself in the special, secret way that comes from a successful clandestine endeavor.

It wasn't until the next week that he got around to opening the tin box. Inside he found, wrapped in strips of oilcloth and sturdy plaid flannel, over a hundred double-eagle gold pieces minted between 1910 and 1930.

They'd had three unspoiled weeks in July. Jerry had even become reconciled to Pat's house. They'd fixed meals in her kitchen, watched old movies and spent evenings listening to her collection of jazz. When Elliot comes back, he asked himself, must we be more circumspect? Or, unhappy thought, will we feel too inhibited to see each other? Will Elliot be keeping track of our movements? He fought off the idea. Maybe Elliot would fall overboard during his cruise or, more wonderfully, be pushed into the swiftly-flowing, inky-black river late at night by an irate ship's steward or fellow passenger he'd annoyed once too often. You uncharitable so-and-so, Jerry chided himself.

He was also able to get a lot done towards finalizing the new programs and initiatives being introduced for the upcoming school year. Pat often worked with him, going over his plans and making recommendations. Her input and suggestions also added the touch of reality; she knew how to put his ideas into a context which would be approved, and enthusiastically so, by the school board.

The month was almost over and Pat was leaving at the end of the week, Jerry soon after. Elliot was not due back until the first week in August. Francine had returned from her vacation. It was the moment of opportunity,

Jerry decided, to see if they could find out any more about the charter school's business service, and whether it was somehow related to the buyers of Elk Creek Mobile Home Park. It was time to breach his locked office door.

"The darned thing is," Jerry had said to Pat, "we don't know what we're looking for. Will there be written records? We're not at the stage where we can commandeer his computer files."

"You know," she said, "until you questioned it, I didn't think it strange for Elliot to keep his door locked all the time. I guess I supposed it was just his fastidious nature, that he was concerned someone would sully his pristine space."

"And maybe that is the reason."

"And maybe he has something he wants to keep hidden."

The plan of attack was for Pat to see Francine first and ask to look up some records dealing with the displacement caused by the school fire, then for Jerry to come wandering in, ostensibly to assist her. Pat began by greeting Francine cordially, told her what was needed for the next school board meeting, then going on to say how much she'd been missed and asked if there were anything she could do to help. "You've got extra work, I know. We really appreciate your taking over while Dr. Lucas is away. I'm sure he does too. He would be lost without you," Pat said with a smile.

At this last statement Francine, thin, plain, bespectacled, turned a deep crimson, cast her eyes down and in a whisper said, "Oh, I don't think so."

Ah, thought Pat, the wind blows from that quarter, does it? Elliot has her wrapped around his finger. I might have guessed.

As Francine unlocked the door, not yet able to look at Pat, Jerry materialized and followed them both into the office. Francine was still flustered and Pat took advantage, swiftly appropriating her in the search for data on transportation for the displaced students. This left Jerry alone to "help," noisily opening file drawers to aid Pat. He kept up a barrage of chatter, reading aloud the names of files, in case Pat might find them relevant to her search. Francine was soon overwhelmed and meekly stood by, her professional demeanor shattered by this assault on her hero's personal property.

"I really don't know if I should be letting you go through Dr. Lucas's files," Francine said miserably. "He would be so upset with me."

Pat answered brightly, "Of course he would, so we won't tell him. These are all public records anyway, and we promise to leave everything as it was. Now, where did you say you found the file on transportation expenditures, Jerry?"

Wishing to prolong their stay, Jerry turned to the discomfited Francine and said in his most soothing voice, "You are helping us immensely. You are also helping to keep children from being displaced by letting us seek out data to substantiate their case."

Francine managed a weak smile, since she had great respect for Dr. Strauss and accepted what he said without question, but there was a look of anguish on her face.

Pat realized that removing whole files would be suspicious, so when she found a few promising references, she announced, "Francine, I need to borrow this page to make copies for the Board. Oh, and these pages too."

"I'll do it for you, Mrs. Foster," Francine said eagerly, and left the room as if exiting a building about to collapse.

Free from scrutiny, Jerry had time to take a few photos with his phone. It would be better, he thought, if it were only Pat who wanted pages copied or otherwise removed, and not him as well. The phone put away, Jerry nodded to Pat and they left the office together just as Francine returned with the copies, Pat thanking her cheerily on the way out.

Back in Jerry's office they discussed their escapade in quiet tones.

Pat said, "I'm sorry we ran over Francine like that. She's such a nice, capable person and we had her practically in tears. And it doesn't help that she is, I'm sure, quite hopelessly in love with Elliot."

Jerry raised his eyebrows. "She is?"

"Yes. She turned beet red when I said how he relies on her, how he'd be lost without her, and she could hardly look at me after that."

"Well, well. Another useful conquest for Elliot. Oh, Pat, I'm sorry..." he began.

She shook her head. "Don't be sorry. I knew all along that he regarded our affair as beneficial to his position, if nothing else. Did I let him get away with anything? I don't think so. I never had to sway the Board to approve his expenditures." She paused a moment, then said, "Although the financial requests could have been concocted and how would I know?"

"You wouldn't know, nor would I. But that's one of the things we might get a clue about."

"From the few bits of information he's given me, it's clear he's very bitter about his ex-wife. I think the experience left him fundamentally suspicious. Of everyone."

"I guess that could be why he's so closed, so protective." Jerry sighed, then went on, "Well, let's see what we have from his files. There are a few photos we'll go over after I enlarge them to be readable, copies of various school expenses. I want to have a closer look at them."

But what, he wondered not for the first time, am I going to do if I find something?

Chapter 27

Jerry decided to postpone going over the copies and photos. Getting immersed in Elliot, he reasoned, would cast a pall over the last few days they had together. After Pat left for California, he finished preparations for the new school year, including leaving notes for Elliot on budget items. He enlarged and made copies of the photos he'd taken, although he didn't scrutinize them. Something told him to hold off; he knew it might spoil his vacation too.

But he did make it a point to see Francine and thank her again for helping them locate data, adding, "You're very important to the running of this place, and particularly now."

Her typical office composure having been restored after the setback caused by their raid, she replied, "Thank you, Dr. Strauss. I'm glad to help. I guess I hadn't thought about the trailer park children and that we're responsible for them."

Jerry nodded, glad to see her interacting normally with him. "While I'm gone," he told her, "if you need me for anything, just call. The district's functioning is my priority and I want to stay on top of things. Call for any reason, Francine. A school district must have its lines of communication open at all times. You never know what might come up." He had delivered this little speech in a serious tone, but ended with a warm collegial smile. It said, "You can count on me, and I know I can count on you."

Had she understood this intentional hidden meaning? Had the word "communication," which was apparently a debatable concept where Elliot was concerned, struck home? Jerry thought so. Her eyes opened a little wider behind her glasses and it seemed as if a light had been turned on, reminding her of what her role in the district was.

Jerry left soon after to visit his family in Connecticut, packing Col. Tyler's 1888 *History* to share with some of his likeminded friends and relatives. He also packed Eric Arden's book of case studies on ethical dilemmas in school districts, which Pat had given him. At the last minute, he added the copies purloined from Elliot's office. Perhaps, he thought, when I'm away from it all, I'll be less paranoid about him and able to look at things more objectively.

As he drove northeast from Colton and began to put some distance behind him, he got to wondering how much he should tell his mother about Pat. Just conjuring up her possible reactions to this news amused him no end and took his mind off the Elliot problem. And I'll call Owen next week, he told himself, and stop in Martensdale on the way back.

At Cider Run Antiques, the month of August was marked by a wealth of bounty from dealers' gardens. Bouquets of flowers in vintage pottery and glass vases graced oak wash stands and marble top dressers. Baskets of assorted vegetables, with "Help Yourself" signs, showed up on the front counter and the church pew. Cucumbers, tomatoes, squash, and peppers, along with the flowers, all looked effortlessly at home with the antique furnishings.

"Why grow 'em if you can't show 'em?" Elaine said provocatively, coming in the shop with an armload of gladiolas.

Keith, who was bravely fighting the summer doldrums with a game of solitaire on the computer, looked up as Elaine breezed by. It was a slow day and Owen had gone in the kitchen to have lunch, while Keith manned the front. It was a hot day too, but he noted that Elaine was her usual picture of cool sophistication in linen and pearls.

Elaine, intent on getting her flowers in water, swept on. She sniffed disparagingly as she passed an untidy assortment of zinnias crammed in a Jadeite jug on Sally Ann's Formica-top chrome-leg 1950s kitchen table.

Sally Ann, coming up the aisle, caught sight of Elaine. "Oh, what beautiful glads!" she exclaimed, thereby neutralizing Elaine's feelings of disapproval at the zinnias.

It was impossible not to be charmed by Sally Ann's simple sweetness. And it wasn't an act, Elaine knew. Sally Ann was a genuine item, even when dressed as she was this afternoon, Elaine realized as the full effect hit her, in some kind of, ye gods! Chiquita Banana outfit: a long sweeping skirt fitted tight across the hips and falling into tiers of deep, ruffled flounces, a puffed-sleeve peasant blouse with floral embroidery, Cuban heels and huge golden hoop earrings, topped with a colorful scarf wrapped turban-style around her head, the whole complemented by the mingled scents of anthurium and frangipani. The production was totally arresting and it stopped Elaine in her tracks. For a minute she was, uncharacteristically, without words.

Sally Ann, unconscious of Elaine's loss of speech, continued with what had been on her mind. "I wish I could grow flowers. I don't know why they always wilt on me. But Ruth told me to pick all the flowers I wanted from her garden while she's away, so I brought these in," Sally Ann beamed at her bouquet.

Elaine had to give her credit for the effort. "They look very nice, Sally Ann," she said. And, because the remarkable attire demanded recognition, ventured, "Arrayed for the tropical weather, I see."

"Do you like it, Elaine?" Sally Ann asked, looking pleased. "Paul is picking me up for dinner and we're going dancing. They're having a Latin band, he says, so I thought I'd wear something to fit right in."

"You're going to knock 'em dead," Elaine predicted.

"Oh! Do you think so?" asked Sally Ann, wide-eyed.

"They'll be falling all over the place. They'll be dropping like flies. They'll be at your mercy." Elaine started to move on.

"Do you think Paul will like it?" Sally Ann called after her.

"If he revives," Elaine called back.

In the kitchen, where Elaine went to fill a large green Bauer vase, Owen was just finishing his sandwich. "Hey, Elaine," he greeted her, tossing aside the *Antiques Week* he'd been reading. "Did you see Sally Ann?"

"Over the top," Elaine commented, "but somehow, and I don't know how, she carries it off."

"Well, all I can say is Paul is in for an interesting evening."

"Hah!" scoffed Elaine. "He should be used to her eccentricities in the wardrobe department by now."

Owen said, mostly to himself, "I hope he remembers to come in a little earlier this afternoon."

Elaine was running water and didn't hear, or she would have certainly raised an exquisitely penciled eyebrow. Conversations with a police detective usually indicated a legal or maybe even criminal topic, even though Paul Willard was a good friend of Cider Run and antiques buff as well. But she had work to do in her area and hurried off. Owen tidied his lunch things and went out to relieve Keith.

At 4:30, Jerry pulled into the Cider Run parking lot. He'd had a good vacation, ten days with family and old friends, plus a little antiquing in shops he was familiar with. Pat had been on his mind constantly, a benign and exciting presence, and they called and texted each other freely so that, as much as he missed her, they kept close.

The 1888 *History* was a sensation, not only because of its venerability, but also because of the inscription by the author. Various family members took turns assessing its value, but in the end it was decided that an appraiser in Pennsylvania could come closer to the mark.

And Mama knew without being told that something was afoot. The private phone conversations and the contented look on Jerry's face afterwards were inexorably giving it away. Finally, no longer able to contain herself, she broached the subject at breakfast one morning by saying, out of the blue, "So, is she Jewish?"

Jerry, momentarily taken aback by her unerring perception, particularly since he thought he'd been very discreet, found he was glad to have it out in the open. He winked conspiratorially at her and began the conversation happily, "Yes, actually. Her mother was Jewish, although she was raised Protestant." And went on to tell her all about Pat; could not, in fact, stop talking about her. It was obvious how much she had come to mean to him.

By the end of his stay, when everything was packed and the goodbyes all made, his mother leaned into the open window of the car, kissed him once more and said, "And when, Jerome, will I meet her?" This was delivered not as a request but as an expectation.

Bless this straight-forward mother of mine, he thought. "I hope," he answered with conviction, "soon."

He had strenuously avoided looking at what he referred to now as the Pilfered Pages. But he had finished the book on ethical dilemmas and opportunities for fraud, and it had refueled his concerns. There was so much money coming into and going out of school districts and it was, for all intents and purposes, in the hands of the business manager. An order for new desks or books or computers might carry with it an understanding that a particular vendor would get the nod in exchange for a small, or not so small, consideration. Who would find out? An influential community member might make the suggestion that a certain company supply the team's uniforms, even though they cost more than the low bid. Should one bow to pressure, particularly if life could be made difficult? While these sorts of things weren't news to Jerry, with each case he read, his thoughts went back to Elliot and his guarded behavior. All right, all right, I will have a shot at the PPs. He took the file out to do just that, but somehow got sidetracked, and the file was still unread when he parked by the orchard at Cider Run Antiques.

Chapter 28

The first impression Jerry had of Cider Run was that its age and charm had a powerful pull. He'd heard plenty about it, of course, from Owen and Eric Arden, but actually seeing the 18th century former cabin, its weathered gray limestone substantial and welcoming amid the summer leaves of old apple trees, touched the chord in Jerry that resonated to anything both beautiful and historic. He got out of the car and walked over to the edge of the parking lot, as he'd been told he must do in order to complete the experience, and gazed across the valley at the stunning breadth of mountainside and ridgeline. They were right, he thought, this place is unique. It stands on the brink of the Appalachians and is part of it, is made of the mountains itself. It's connected in time and place. No wonder Owen was eager for me to come.

And what awaits me inside? he wondered, going back to the entrance. He didn't ask Owen when they'd spoken earlier if Ruth were there today. Suppose Owen had said yes. Would he not have come? It didn't seem fair to Owen or Ruth, or himself, if he couldn't face her after all these years. So, shaking off his unease, he opened the door and breathed in the familiar slightly musty, slightly acrid, exhilarating redolence of antiques shops.

Two steps beyond the door, Owen came at him like a whirlwind, pumping his hand and grinning that grin of his and talking a mile a minute. "You made it! You've gotta see Sally Ann; you won't believe her getup. And Paul Willard is going to be in later, so you'll get to meet him today. You can stay for dinner? Lynn has got everything planned. Oh, and Keith is over there, on the computer. He's the expert on sports and military stuff I was telling you about. Did I mention Elaine?"

Jerry, laughing, interrupted the dialogue, "Owen! Let me catch my breath!"

"Oh, sorry, Supe," Owen apologized. "You want to have a look around, don't you? I can tell you who the dealer is if there is something that looks interesting."

"Owen, *everything* in here looks interesting. This is one spectacular place. Tell me more about its history..." and the two went off.

Elaine, at the front, watched this encounter with interest. In his excitement about Jerry showing up at the shop today, Owen had praised Jerry's character and accomplishments to Keith, Elaine and Sally Ann, leaving out no detail about his boss, including where he'd come from and his association with Owen's academic advisor.

Sally Ann said she'd be thrilled to meet him. Keith said he was looking forward to telling him all Owen's embarrassing traits. Elaine just looked thoughtful. Something sounded familiar in the description of this school superintendent's background, although she wasn't sure why it should. Then he walked in and it all made sense. He was tall and strikingly good-looking and conveyed elegance and urbanity, even though wearing a polo shirt with khakis, and she instantly knew what it was. There could be no doubt. "Thank heavens," she murmured, "Ruth is not here."

"Huh, Elaine?" Keith said absently, and at that moment a customer came up asking a question, and Keith happily responded.

Well, well, Elaine said to herself. That Ruth had moved down from New England when she retired from the school where she was principal was understandable: her brother and his family lived here. That she had been involved with a school superintendent and had to end the affair was only speculation on Elaine's part. But from hints gleaned during conversations spanning the last three years, Elaine had been pretty sure that was what had happened. And here he was: Owen's Supe, the Former Man in Ruth's life. And she could see why. He must have really been something, Ruth, my dear, Elaine thought, not unkindly. She went off to be helpful to any customers who were around and to have another look at Jerry.

Jerry and Owen toured the shop in a constant flow of high-spirited discussion about history, antiques and dealers. In the intervals between appreciation of individual pieces of furniture and other antiques that particularly appealed to Jerry, there were introductions and conversations.

Sally Ann seemed to have forgotten what she was wearing and shook Jerry's hand completely unselfconsciously, as if there were nothing in the slightest bit unusual about her appearance. "I'm so glad to meet you, Dr. Strauss," she said in conventional tones, unaware of how bizarre this sounded coming from someone resembling a fruit icon. "Owen has told us what a great job you are doing in Cross County. I know Colton pretty well; that is, I did. But Owen says it's improved a lot."

Jerry thanked her and asked politely about her experiences in Cross County.

"Oh, it was over 20 years ago, when I had just gotten married and Rosie was born and my husband took off, so I lived with my mother-in-law and it was pretty hard, but she was the kindest thing in the world, and not just to make up for her son's leaving us..." Sally Ann was nothing if not forthcoming.

This was more than Jerry wanted to know, but he listened attentively and when she went on to say "...and so I had a social worker and between her and Rosie's grandma, I got back on my feet again..." his curiosity got the better of him.

"Was her name Pat Foster by any chance?" he asked.

"No, her name was Hodges. The social worker was Pat Foster, though. She couldn't have been nicer. And she was pregnant herself. I often wonder what happened to her. Mrs. Foster, I mean. Mrs. Hodges died." Here Sally Ann looked as if she might cry, so Jerry paused.

Owen, used to Sally Ann, jumped in. "Mrs. Foster is now president of the Colton Area School Board. And she's terrific!"

That she is, Jerry thought to himself, and it was especially gratifying to learn about Pat's effectiveness from someone she'd helped.

"I'm so glad!" Sally Ann exclaimed. "If you see her, please tell her hello from me. But wait, my name isn't Hodges anymore. It's O'Neill, but it won't be for much longer," and, smiling happily, she held up her left hand to show off a sapphire engagement ring, which matched the sapphire blue of her eyes. "I'd love to see Mrs. Foster again," she added. "Maybe we could come down sometime."

"I think she'd be very pleased if you visited," Jerry encouraged. And since, like Elaine, he couldn't let the outfit go without comment, said, "And you must wear just that, because it is such a knockout."

"Oh, I couldn't," Sally Ann protested, her distinctly individual take on what constituted appropriate dress for an occasion activated. "It's not right for Cross County. But I'll come up with something." At that she fluttered away, giving Jerry and Owen a little wave of her hand over the turban and her swinging earrings, a cloud of scent following in her wake.

Keith was introduced and, as Jerry expressed interest in his collection of Civil War memorabilia, they went into

Keith's area to continue their discussion. Jerry was intrigued even more by the sports equipment and in particular by the wooden shafted golf clubs. *Niblick,* he read on one tag, *Mashie,* on another. And *Spooner.* "Keith," he said, "you've just sold some sticks."

Owen and Jerry came to a dealer's area that had the feel of a dining room in an early New England home. There were blue transferware ironstone serving pieces set out on a polished pine table, pewter candlesticks, a sterling porringer and spoons of coin silver. Ranged around the area were several spindle backed chairs and two oak plant stands. Pattern glass reminiscent of Sandwich sparkled in the light of an electrified kerosene lamp with a blue floral decorated globe. The whole went together beautifully.

Owen noticed Jerry's absorption and said, "I can't remember if you told me you knew Dr. Arden's sister Ruth. She had an antiques shop in Maine before she moved to Martensdale. She has such great stuff. There was a sideboard here, pine, which you don't see that often. Also a china cabinet. But they were sold at the beginning of the summer. She's gone on a buying trip this week. Too bad, or you could talk with her."

Jerry had not been able to get a word in edgewise, so left it without having to answer, except to say, "Takes your breath away," which was quite true, but whether for the goods or for the proximity to Ruth, Owen was not to know.

"Take your time, Supe," Owen instructed, leaving to carry the golf clubs up to the front counter.

Jerry let it all wash over him for a few minutes, analyzing how he felt. Relieved, he had to admit, and glad to have in this way eased into a reunion of sorts with Ruth. He knew there would be a meeting of the two of them sometime in the future and he felt more prepared having seen her area, if only to provide common conversational ground.

And this was where he was, standing there musing, when Elaine found him. She sailed right into her agenda by saying, "Lovely and classy, don't you think? Just like Ruth herself," and then she waited to see Jerry's reaction.

"Ah, you must be Elaine," he said. "Owen told me *you* were the classy one around here and I can see why."

Thus disarmed, Elaine had to smile at his tactics. Oh, he really is a charmer, she thought.

Jerry went on, "I was noticing the Limoges china in your area. How is it selling?" he asked, hoping to draw her away from the topic of Ruth.

But Elaine was not to be dissuaded so easily. "Here in central Pennsylvania it's somewhat of an exotic item. At Christmas it sells, but during the rest of the year, only the collectors buy Limoges, searching for that one pattern of little pink flowers from among the hundreds that Haviland produced. New England, now, where Ruth came from, is a different story. Much more urbane. Of course you know Ruth? Owen mentioned you were a friend and colleague of her brother," Elaine probed.

No way around it, Jerry thought. "Yes," he answered, "we knew each other in Boston, but I haven't seen her in ages," delivered as casually as he could.

"I'll tell her you were in and admired her area," Elaine offered affably. "I'm sure she'll be pleased."

Or not, thought Jerry. But he replied, "Yes, do. That would be kind of you," and was spared further comment when Owen came with the news that Paul Willard was in the shop, so they walked up to the front counter.

Sally Ann had just departed, after making a brief appearance in her astonishing concoction of ruffles and fragrance as Paul, glassy-eyed from the experience, was introduced to Jerry. "I've been hoping to meet you," Paul said, starting to make a recovery, "but perhaps we should go back into the kitchen, where there are fewer, er, distractions," he added, the stunned look returning, as he contemplated the retreating figure of Sally Ann swaying gracefully towards an unsuspecting customer.

Jerry laughed appreciatively. He could see why Owen felt at ease with Paul. This soft-spoken man with his shy, sad-eyed smile was certainly not what Jerry had pictured for a police detective. They adjourned to the kitchen and, seated with soft drinks, they discussed the fire at Elk Creek Elementary School.

"The reason I feel justified in telling you what I know," Paul began, "is because no one ever asked for confidentiality; the county said they wanted a full public disclosure."

Jerry and Owen exchanged glances, and Paul went on, "We were asked in when it was clear that the locals were dragging their heels. As a matter of fact, it was the *Colton Clarion* that made the request to Martensdale, wondering if our police department could help. After that, the county sheriff must have felt pressure to do something, so we were given the green light to go ahead with our investigation. And we sent in our report, which definitely raised some disturbing questions. After a week we got a call claiming they hadn't received it, but had decided they didn't need us."

"As if they could figure it out themselves, what with all the arson in Cross County's infamous past?" Owen suggested.

Paul nodded. "You might think. But when I looked back into those cases, only two or three out of dozens were ever prosecuted. No," he continued, "they needed help and this one was tricky. Even identifying the body was a stumbling block. And I'm convinced the remains were not identified beyond the shadow of a doubt."

Jerry looked up sharply. Owen looked sick.

"When this was mentioned in the report, along with the coincidence of an unlikely Florida vacation by the nearest residents and their subsequent disappearance, the arrival of a blizzard with its already-announced snow day, an offer to buy the adjacent mobile home park, plus an unsolicited bid by one of the energy companies on the burned-out school soon after the event, someone must have decided we were coming too close for comfort."

"Who," Jerry asked, "actually made the call firing you?"

"Oh," said Paul, "it was the Colton Chief of Police himself."

Chapter 29

"The Borough?" Jerry asked, surprised. "Not the County?"

"He said he was speaking for the sheriff. Apparently there was some arrangement that if the sheriff was out of town, the report would go to the borough authorities. Needless to say, when we were informed that it had not been received, we said we'd send another one right away. The reaction was that he had been instructed to tell us 'Don't bother,' and they'd do their own investigation. My chief told me it would be best to put a lid on it and leave things alone, given Cross County's reputation for insularity and truculence."

Paul spread out his hands in a gesture of defeat, but his words were still in a fighting mode. "I haven't forgotten nor do I want to let it go. The more time that elapses, the colder the trail, but that doesn't mean it still can't be solved. Somehow. And you, Dr. Strauss?" he encouraged.

Jerry said, "From the beginning I've had the impression that the fire was a subject not to be discussed, and I was the only one who was interested in answers. I guess I feel a responsibility to learn what I can. As you might imagine, I've been warned off asking questions. Owen has helped by researching the newspaper archives, so he may be regarded with suspicion himself. I do have a few ideas though, some of which resulted when I was trying to find out more about the charter school, built by the power companies for 'their' kids." While he didn't mention Elliot, he did allude to the fact that there might be a link between the group contracted to handle the business side of the charter school and the buyers of the mobile home park. "It may be only a fluke, but 'star' appears in both names. I hadn't mentioned that to you, Owen, or anyone else yet," he added.

Paul looked thoughtful. "There are many energy companies from Texas working the Shale," he said. "I'm sure you've seen a star logo on trucks. In fact, I believe the bid to buy the school came from a star-branded corporation. As you say, it may be coincidence."

Owen suggested, "Or a bunch of crooks hit on a name so common that no one would think twice about it."

Jerry said, "Could be a strategy all right. If we were able to track down the couple who went to Florida, we might learn something."

"We tried," Paul responded, "but ran into a dead end. Didn't help that their last name was Smith. No, for all we know, they never came back from Florida. 'Moved away,' was all we got. Officially, the case is on hold, but I would very much like to clear it up."

Jerry said, "Our priorities, of course, are the children displaced by the school fire and the ones about to be affected by the sale of the mobile home park. There are over 40 families living there who would not be able to find housing in the area if they are forced out. The buyers apparently plan a complete razing of the park and a smattering of luxury homes built on the site."

Paul gave Jerry his shy smile, saying, "You even made the *Martensdale Times* with that one, the school board meeting when all the residents got up to speak. And the 11:00 news. They aired your remarks in their entirety. So when Owen said you'd be in town, I was definitely hoping we'd have some time together."

Owen's brow had been furrowed for a while and now he said what was on his mind. "Why did you question the identification of the, uh, remains? I mean, how does one, uh, determine...?"

Paul answered his friend, "Good question and that was to be the next stage of inquiry. Without going into too many details, we learned that the superintendent had been over six feet tall. All we had to work with were charred...oh, sorry," he interrupted himself when Owen began to turn green. "To get to the point, when we were allowed in the mortuary, it did not seem that this individual could have been more than five foot ten. Of course, things had gotten scattered in the fire..." At this juncture, Owen made a speedy retreat out of the kitchen and a brief hush fell over the two at the table.

"And then the family had the remains cremated...But," he said, rising, "let's get together again. I'm afraid we're up against the gas industry and the powerful lobby that exists with the sole purpose of not upsetting them."

"*If* it's the gas industry. I'm not so sure that's where the responsibility lies," Jerry said. "There are copies of emails and vouchers I haven't had a chance to go through yet, but which might yield a few clues."

Paul looked interested. "Oh? Hmmm. Perhaps you have another perspective, being there among them. I don't think we overlooked anything, but we weren't given what you'd call free rein either. Tell you what, why don't I come down for a visit. We can invent a plausible reason, I'm sure."

Jerry laughed. "Already have a reason. That fascinating fiancée of yours wants to see an old friend who lives in Colton."

It was close to midnight when Jerry finally left Martensdale. Owen and Lynn had treated him royally with a cookout supper on their back porch. They grilled sausages and sweet peppers, served a salad of tomatoes and greens from their garden, steamed ears of corn-on-the-cob and Lynn had made a dessert of peaches, nectarines and blueberries. The two Griffith boys, aged seven and five, behaved themselves admirably and didn't even complain when it was time for bed, although they were seen sneaking down to listen in to the grownups' conversation and had to be dispatched back upstairs by Owen twice. Jerry brought the 1888 *History* from the car and, as he had guessed, Owen was blown away by it, incredulous about how Jerry came upon it. He gently turned the pages, amazed at the wealth of history on residents who fought in military campaigns, going back to skirmishes with the Native Americans. "Keith is gonna love this," he exclaimed. "Do you suppose I could keep it for a week or so? One of our founding partners at Cider Run is a retired history professor. He'd know what this baby is worth, and he could help find a conservator. Oh, look at this!" Owen had come to a section titled *Robberies*. "'A series of insidious affairs occurred at Deems Mill...'" Owen read aloud. "'These desperados,'" Owen went on, "'lurked in the darkest recesses of the mountains surrounding Elk Creek and made incursions for purposes of plunder.'" Despite the fact that it was written in the dry formality of Victorian prose, Col. Tyler managed to leave out no detail in recounting robberies, murders and barn burnings.

Jerry was glad to let Owen borrow the book, as he clearly understood how to handle an antique volume. He would also, Jerry knew, have a great time finding interesting facts with which to regale his fellow dealers at the shop and students and colleagues at the high school. "Go ahead and dazzle 'em," Jerry had said, to which Owen had replied, "I'm finally going to be able to one-up the kids."

They had another short conversation before Jerry left. "Looks like we're still far from putting things together," he said. "But we'll get Paul down to Colton and go at it again."

"You can count on me, Supe," Owen responded, then added with a lop-sided grin, "Don't worry about my stomach; it's always been like that."

As he drove back to Colton, Jerry's mind was full of the events of the day, running from thoughts about Cider Run's unique ambiance, his growing appreciation of Owen, Col. Tyler's exposure of the lurid side of Cross County's past, and the enlightening conversation with Paul.

Detective Willard was as Owen had predicted—articulate, intelligent and thorough. It wasn't surprising that he thought the gas industry, or at least someone connected with an energy company, was responsible for the fire. But Jerry's experiences with the power company executives had not led him to believe they had any interest in being devious in pursuit of uncertain gains. On the contrary, they had been helpful and seemed to make extra efforts to establish good relationships with the school district. Barn burnings, he reflected soberly, and the tradition continues. Or was it an outsider who took advantage of a long-standing Cross County phenomenon, giving it an opportunistic twist?

As he neared Colton and thoughts of Pat began to take over, he recalled with a pang that she would not be back for another two weeks. Two weeks! Too long! But Elliot was back now. Jerry knew he was going to have several weeks of concentrated work with Elliot, seeing to the myriad items associated with a new school year. And along with that thought, he remembered he still hadn't delved into the PPs. Had he already made up his mind that Elliot, whom he didn't like for several reasons, was a criminal? He decided it would be abysmally unprofessional to start looking for evidence of wrongdoing with a prejudiced attitude. Just because the guy was cold and humorless and secretive and had mistreated Pat...almost mistreated Pat, he amended...didn't mean he was a barn burner. I think, he told himself, I'll put the PPs away for now and give Elliot the benefit of the doubt, at least while we've got work to do together.

Then his thoughts turned to Cider Run Antiques. A really superior shop in every way, and the dealers he'd met were even more interesting than he'd imagined. Sally Ann, you absolutely couldn't make her up. And Elaine, another original. Keith struck Jerry as a true expert in his field of antiques—definitely a visit to Deems BBQ should be planned. He didn't want to think about Ruth and had resisted the urge to go over in his mind what emotions he'd felt being in her bailiwick, as it were. But in the solitude of the late night drive, memories of her came back to him. They were not of the lover, when they met each other so eagerly in Boston, nor of the disillusioned and resentful words she'd said when they parted. What flashed into his mind was a picture of Ruth, pale and still in her hospital bed, and he again felt the anguish of that time.

Chapter 30

With only a week left before she flew back to Pittsburgh, Pat started thinking, as she put it to herself, about what she wanted to do with her life. She was reclining in a chaise lounge on the redwood deck overlooking the beach at her brother's house. The sun was warm and the breeze off the Pacific cool. A glass of white wine from lunch was by her side. This is living, she thought contentedly, and I am privileged to enjoy it once in a while. But it wasn't her life and she knew it.

Like Jerry, she'd had a good time visiting with her family. Johnny had gotten leave and spent several days with them. And yet, it was the phone calls and texts with Jerry that she looked forward to. "Ah, me," she said aloud to no one, as no one was around at that moment. "What am I going to do about him? It's at the point where I simply must be with him."

He did say his mother wanted to meet her, and that was sweet, but in the meantime, in the larger context of her concerns, what about Cross County? She knew it so well. She knew how much it needed to be looked after. Families in Elk Creek Mobile Home Park: good people and what could she do? The conviction that she had responsibilities was getting stronger, and sitting in the California sun in the lap of luxury, she told herself, was very removed from the realities of Cross County.

On the other hand, from this distance she had perspective to reflect and to prioritize. She began to formulate some plans.

Several things needed to be put into motion. The sickening feeling that Elliot might still pose a threat had to be dealt with. She was sure he understood that their sexual relationship was over, but it was an ambiguous situation. She needed him for the smooth operation of the school district, but under no circumstances would there be a resumption of the affair. The solution was clear. She and Jerry would get married, the sooner, the better. In fact, it solved her other big concern: not wanting to live without him. That taken care of, she went on to the next area.

The eviction. Something had to be done. All right, the school district would take them to court. It might be only a costly delaying tactic, but she knew she could count on community support and a liberal interpretation of the child welfare laws. She'd call the district's lawyer first thing in the morning and have him file a brief. The school board's approval could come later.

Another problem remained, and it was becoming more critical. What good did the gas industry's boost to the economy do when it threatened to destroy the beauty, enjoyment and perhaps the very fabric of the county? Where could she be most effective in helping to stem the tide of careless destruction, to harness the extraction process for its benefits without spoiling everything? To work toward a future after gas production ceased in Cross County? She pondered this a long time, and in the end came up with the only feasible course of action for her.

But first she needed to tell Jerry of her decision for them to get married. On the phone? In a text? Wouldn't do. She was the one proposing, after all. No, better wait till she got back.

Pat drained her glass and went down for a walk on the beach.

Jerry came back to the mid-August relative calm. With the exception of the football team's daily practice, things were quiet. Most of the teachers and administrators wouldn't return for a week, and it left him free to tackle work which needed to be done before school began. There were fewer disruptions, less chit-chat about vacations and more time one-on-one with Elliot. Which, he reflected with surprise, was going a lot better than he'd anticipated. Elliot seemed to have thawed over the summer, and his interactions with him were, while not exactly warm, quite pleasantly courteous. Jerry had to admit, again, that Elliot knew his business well and had an excellent grasp of the financial intricacies of the school district.

Francine, on her part, had not spilled the beans, and when the three of them were working together on teacher salary schedules and she had been asked by Elliot to find something in his office, she gave Jerry a conspiratorial little smile over Elliot's head. Jerry kept his resolve not to go through the PPs, in order to keep an open mind about Elliot. The more their relationship went well, the more he was beginning to feel the whole idea of Elliot being guilty of anything was absurd. But where Pat was involved, it was a different story.

She'd be home soon and he wanted to be with her most desperately. But being around Elliot had a dampening effect on him. Was it because Elliot and Pat had once been intimate? He got sick thinking about it, but it had to be accepted as having happened. Maybe that was at the root of all his suspicions and misgivings. Time I got over it, he said to himself, although the idea of Elliot observing her car parked at his house, or his at her house, made him very uncomfortable. What were they to do then? Not see each other? Escape to a motel in Martensdale? This brought him face to face with his past, when he and Ruth used to meet in Boston for the weekend. Was his relationship with Pat going to end that way too?

These depressing thoughts were interrupted by a call from Pat, all excited, saying she had important things to tell him, too important to go into on the phone, and that she couldn't wait to see him.

"Darling, darling, Pat, you don't know how I've missed you," he said. "Can't I meet you in Pittsburgh and we'll hide out for a few days?"

Pat sensed, beyond Jerry's words, the constraint in his voice. "Elliot's presence getting to you? Don't worry, Jerry, we won't let him stop us. Now, did our solicitor get in touch with you about the lawsuit? I understand nothing has happened yet at the Park, but he says we should go ahead anyway."

It was during this time that one of Eric Arden's graduate students arrived to do research for her dissertation, a possibility that Jerry and Eric first talked about soon after Jerry had taken the position. When Eric called to set up the student's visit, he told Jerry, "She's looking at the economic and social impacts of natural gas drilling on half a dozen school districts in the state. It should be a good study."

"Glad to help," Jerry replied, "and our business manager will be a valuable resource for her. I'm sure he'd be more than happy to fill her in on the fiscal and logistical consequences we're facing with this influx." And impress her with his suave superiority. Stop that, Jerome, he told himself.

They talked a bit about Jerry's experiences with the energy companies and also of their willingness to partner in vo-tech education. "Just to give another side. It's not all heavy trucks making the roads impassable for school buses, although we've had a few instances." Then Jerry mentioned that he'd been to Cider Run at last. "The place is impressive, the setting truly beyond compare, the dealers a real kick, and the goods superlative!"

Eric chuckled, "Liked it, did you?"

"I'm looking forward to going back. Do you know Sally Ann? Are there more like her?"

"They do have some characters all right. But you may run into Ruth, you know. I think it's time we talked about things."

Jerry agreed. "I'm hoping perhaps this fall after school gets underway."

After Jerry had rung off, Eric sat for a while in thought. Jerry seems different, he decided. Less superior-sounding, less edgy. Could Cross County have mellowed him?

Celeste, the graduate student, proved to be appreciative and unobtrusive, carefully taking notes in her interviews with Jerry. Since he had a balanced approach to running a school district amid the boom of drilling, knowing both the positive and negative effects on Colton Area, he was able to give her many insights. At golf on Saturday he arranged for Celeste to meet with several gas company executives and engineers. Then he turned her over to Elliot and, besides seeing her in the district office, did not give her much thought.

The teachers and administrators were due back on Monday and, in addition to the new course offerings, Jerry had made some changes in assignments and put in place the anti-bullying policies. Not for the first time, he felt the lack of an assistant superintendent, a director of curriculum and a counseling staff. But you work with what you have, he reminded himself. He was thankful he had Francine, since Celeste seemed to be taking up a great deal of Elliot's time learning about revenues and expenditures...or whatever. Francine was able to step into the breach and supply him with information, and did so willingly and cheerfully. It was a pleasure to work with her and he let her know.

To implement his new policies, Jerry had set up sessions of in-service training on anti-bullying and child abuse awareness and arranged for two consultants, both well-known experts, to lead groups of teachers, administrators and support staff. He'd already gotten approval earlier for the expenditures, but wanting to follow precedent, he thought he'd ask Elliot about consultants' fees in the past. Elliot's office door was closed and when he knocked there was no answer. He glanced at his watch and realized it was after 12:00. He turned to Francine, who was still at her desk.

"Dr. Lucas has gone to lunch, Dr. Strauss," Francine said, and added, "with Celeste," and couldn't help elaborating, "He takes her to lunch most days."

Jerry looked for signs of distress on Francine's face, but she appeared composed although, perhaps, a little resigned. Just as well, Francine, he addressed her in his mind. You don't want to get bogged down in sentiment for Elliot. "Could you, please, get some data for me then? These are top-of-the-line people who are doing our workshops, and I'd like to know what the district has been paying for consultants over the last couple of years."

"Right away, Dr. Strauss," Francine said with a smile, and disappeared into the inner sanctum. A short time later she laid a file folder on Jerry's desk. "This should be everything pertaining to payments for consultants. It's probably more than you need, but I thought you might want to see the range."

"Francine, this is super," Jerry praised her, impressed again by her efficiency.

As he went through the papers in the folder, he learned that the district had the occasional consultant in to give a workshop or assist with operational aspects during the years preceding Elliot's arrival. Last fall and winter, however, there was a surge in the use of consultants, and many payments were made to experts who had been brought in to assist with technology upgrades, transportation planning, structural matters, heating, ventilating and air conditioning, cafeteria guidelines, and on and on. Good Lord, Jerry thought, there were over a dozen of them. *I must discuss this with Pat.* He noticed that Hank had signed or initialed the payment requests, ranging from $500 to $2495. District policy permitted payments for services less than $2500 to be approved by the superintendent without further approval from the school board. But still, what in the world, Jerry wondered, had these people been doing here? Before he returned the file to Francine, he made copies and put them in his briefcase to take home. *Later,* he told himself, *when I don't have to see Elliot. Later, when I've talked with Pat.*

After dinner, when he hadn't any luck reaching her and in the lull of waiting to call her again, he brought out the PPs, the charter school summaries, and the copies of files Francine had given him, and stacked them on the table. He had decided that he no longer wanted to put things off. He wanted answers and if these documents could help in any way, he must sift carefully through them and try, if possible, to find inconsistencies.

The ironstone pitcher was still in the middle of the table and, as he took it up, its contents, a few roses, some mums and a spray of asters, looked querulously at him, as if to say, "So where is she? Where's the one we've sacrificed ourselves for?"

"You'll have to be content with me for now," Jerry said to them, moving the arrangement to the kitchen countertop, where it regarded him with a reproachful air.

Then he dug in and it was 2:00 AM when at last he quit. He realized he had not called Pat nor had she called him back and, partly because of this and partly because of what he'd been reading, a sense of estrangement from her had wormed its way into his mind.

Chapter 31

In his rented room above the Sure-Shot Taxidermy, Carl sat looking at the contents of the tin box. "Holy Cow," he said over and over. "Holy Cow." The beautiful gold coins, freed from their imprisonment and spilled out on the bed, winked back at him, as if they were overjoyed to see the light of day after their long confinement. "There must be a hunert of these suckers."

He chucked some take-out containers off a small table and brought over handfuls of gold to mound in gleaming piles. Then he pulled up a chair and sat staring at the bounty, transfixed, running his hands through the coins, as if he couldn't get enough of the sheer weight of them, their satin-like feel. "Holy Cow," he said again.

He was in possession of something which, he was pretty sure, was worth thousands of dollars. Or maybe tens of thousands, he thought. Slowly the possibilities dawned on him. I could buy me a new truck. Hell, I bet I could buy me my own place. Then Carl remembered that the fate of the trailer park was in doubt and he began to entertain more altruistic thoughts. I could help get the folks a house. Pappy won't have to go to a Home after all. And Seth. I could pay for college for Seth.

He picked up a few coins and let them run through his fingers. He studied their markings. There were gold pieces from before the Second World War, Pappy's war. There were ones from before the First World War even. Here was one bearing the date of 1927 with a little P. P must stand for the

Philadelphia mint, Carl thought shrewdly. Another 1927 coin had a *D*. That there other mint, he reckoned, Denver, most like.

A new thought struck him. How was he to find out what they were worth? And how could he be sure they were telling the truth, even if he was looking over their shoulder at a computer screen, which he didn't trust in the first place? Carl rubbed his chin. And how, he asked himself, would anyone ever believe he hadn't stolen them? This thought troubled Carl because, in a way, he had stolen them. Well, removed them from where they'd been. Wasn't that stealing?

That got him thinking about who might have stowed them behind the ledge down in the mine. It had to be either a miner or one of the foremen, anyways a mining guy. All them $20 gold pieces. He musta bought one every time he got paid. Suppose he was saving up for his family or somethin', Carl thought. So he hid his loot away and then what happened to him? Was he killed in a mining accident? Carl searched through the coins. The latest date he found was 1929. Maybe there'd been a mining accident that year. Or suppose someone stole them from the first guy and hid them in the mine. Carl's head began to spin with all this conjecturing

What he'd do, he decided, was put them back in the box and put the box under his bed for now. He'd figure something out. He was rich and he'd figure something out.

His morning golf game had been rained out and he had still not made contact with Pat. Jerry sat back and looked at the papers he'd gone through last night. After all his work, he had come to the conclusion that he was simply not able to tell whether the figures for various expenditures were genuine or not. The only thing that stood out were the payments made to consultants, but what exactly had they been paid to do and did they do it? He could find nothing in what he had. Was this information in another file somewhere? To learn whether these expenses were bona fide, he'd need to search through Elliot's files again, which didn't seem likely, or actually talk with Elliot about it, which would reveal his distrust of the guy and blow everything. He could enlist Francine, but didn't want to run the risk of getting her in trouble. Who else might know? Pat, of course, but that would have to wait until she was back.

I should put Paul Willard on the case, he thought. There was no way on earth to prove anything without a full scale audit, without bringing in someone who could access files and analyze them. The bits he had now were only that. Bits of information that could lead in a wrong direction, the accusation of an innocent person. No, his hands were tied. He had to sit on things for the present.

Jerry, like Carl, wrapped his questionably-obtained material back up and put it away. He'd get more data eventually and he'd figure something out.

On Monday the teachers and administrators were back and there were meetings most of the day which required Jerry's presence. On Tuesday orientation workshops for staff were held, more loose ends were seen to, and Jerry met with Elliot to finalize transportation details. On Wednesday the consultants arrived to lead the in-service training sessions. "A Fresh Start" was the theme teachers and staff had come up with for the new school year, and a banner proclaiming this unlikely goal hung over the door of the district office. Jerry looked at it ruefully as he left to go home Thursday evening. A fresh start: wishful thinking. Too many questions were still unanswered. Tomorrow, he reflected, he had scheduled visits to each school in the district to help out, give encouragement, and do whatever needed to be done.

Saturday he could relax and play golf. Monday was Labor Day and on Tuesday school started.

And, in between, Pat would be back on Sunday.

They had talked several times. She had wanted to know everything that was happening this last week before school started. She told him about her trip with friends to Ashland and the Oregon Shakespeare Festival. They had loving words to say to each other. But beneath the surface, and Jerry knew it was all on his part, something bothered him.

What was this perplexing feeling that had come over him regarding Pat? He didn't like it. He didn't like wondering if she knew about the abundance of consultants. It wasn't fair to her, his thinking this way, but it had crept into Jerry's mind and wouldn't leave. What else had she known about and gone along with? He couldn't imagine her not being scrupulous in her examination of Elliot's expenditure requests, but had their affair, and again he felt sick at the word, blinded her to what might have been going on? Was he blinded now too by his desire for her?

It occurred to him that he had not discussed a couple of very important things with her. He had not told her how "star" kept cropping up. For all he knew, she may have been aware of one or more groups doing district business with "star" in their name.

But, more oddly, they had never really discussed the fire. Yes, they'd gone to the school site together, she'd wept a little over Hank, but they didn't talk about it. Maybe because he knew it would make her sad. And he hadn't asked her who she thought might be responsible. They had, like nearly everyone else in Cross County, avoided the subject. Now he had met Paul and, equally important, Sally Ann. He'd arranged for them to come down. It was time to lay out to Pat what he and Owen had learned. It was time to talk with her about the fire.

Chapter 32

After golf on Saturday, Jerry had lunch with his foursome. He had decided that if Clarence were there, he'd go to his table, make friendly conversation, and see what he could learn about the charter school. With the meal nearly over and people beginning to leave, Jerry realized that Clarence was not going to show up. He had to take the bull by the horns.

"Darn," he said to an engineer in the group, "I was hoping to get a chance to talk with Clarence about Power Learners, how he thought the new school year was going to shape up and all." Well done, Jerry, he congratulated himself. That sounded plausible and you managed not to choke on the name.

"'Fraid not," the engineer responded. "I don't think we'll be seeing him here anymore."

"Oh?" Jerry asked. "Did he break one of the club rules? Take too many mulligans?"

The party at the table laughed and Jerry went on, "Gosh, I'm wondering how I can talk with him, since we're in the same business, in a manner of speaking."

"That's going to be difficult," was the answer he got.

Another power company official leaned over from the next table and elaborated, "It's no secret. We had to send him back to Texas."

"Lord! Texas!" exclaimed Jerry. "Extreme disciplinary measures for a course infraction!"

"You betcha," someone drawled. "We take our golf mighty serious compared to y'all up here."

Another said, "We don't tolerate no course 'fractions."

"That's right," added someone else, squinting menacingly to emphasize the gravity of the crime. "Mulligans are shooting offenses where we come from."

The engineer stepped in, "Aw, come on, boys, quit tryin' to lead the Super astray." He said to Jerry, "We didn't have a choice. He'd been hitting the bottle just a leetle too much for his own good. Anyhow, he's gone. Although, I thought he wasn't leaving till next week, didn't you?" he asked the father of the budding Annie Oakley.

"What I heard was he didn't stay around long enough to catch up with his tail."

Must be a Texas expression, Jerry thought, and went along with the general laughter.

So that was that on Clarence. He'd have to initiate another approach to learning about the charter school's behind-the-scenes management corporation.

In the afternoon, Jerry went back to the Elk Creek School site. It had been something he'd had on his mind to do again. It might be, he thought, a way to get in touch with what happened there. A device, he realized, but sometimes we see things we hadn't noticed before.

Jerry parked by the chain-link fence at the end of the lane. In the two months since he and Pat were there, weeds had burgeoned wildly, growing thickly everywhere. Vines covered the fence and grasses had shot up, tasseled heads about to burst with seeds. There were even a few saplings amid the ruins. The blackened remains of the school were hardly to be seen. In the cavity of the school's foundation, all was a tangled mass of verdant growth. It struck Jerry that here was dramatic testimony to the power of Nature, who would not let herself be kept down but, set free by the fire, welcomed all comers, allowing them to sprout, take hold and strut their stuff in defiance of, or because of, what humans had perpetrated. Both flora and fauna. Doubtless millions of insects now thrived in this environment and dozens of small creatures had found homes in the protected, sheltering cover. Maybe not as grand as the Phoenix rising from flames, but still impressive: an abundance of robust new life emerging from the ashes. If there's a lesson here, Jerry thought, it's that neglect is powerful to behold. But the school itself was, in effect, obliterated. So much for enlightenment, Jerry sighed.

His reverie was interrupted as he became aware of the sound of a mower, which had been distant and was now getting closer. In one respect the school district had not shown neglect, but had seen to it that the grass in the playing fields was kept mowed. Should another facility be built on the site, periodic cutting in the meantime would help discourage the proliferation of weeds. While they couldn't sanction the use of the fields for organized sports, the school board agreed to turn a blind eye if those living nearby wanted to have an occasional game. The district would be liable in case of accidents, of course, but no more so than when other unsupervised fields were used. Jerry decided to have a word with whomever was doing the mowing, and strolled over to where the driver, wearing a Sure-Shot Taxidermy cap, was just turning his vehicle to cut another swath.

Carl recognized the Super at once, shut off the motor and sat waiting. He thought, now what? Is he gonna get on me for workin' Saturday? I wasn't gonna put in for overtime. Well, maybe I was, but I ain't now.

"Mr. Morgan," Jerry greeted his middle school custodian with a pleasant smile.

"Afternoon, Superintendent," Carl returned warily.

"Mr. Griffith has told me what a standout Seth was on the team last year. We're all very proud of him."

"Yep." Is the Super tryin' to butter me up? Guy's smart; don't do to have any funny business with him.

"I hear he'll be on the team next spring. We should have a good season."

"Yep. Reckon should." Don't he want me to get this mowin' done? I'm happy settin' here, I guess, jawin' with the Super. It's up to him.

"You heard, didn't you, that Mr. Griffith is looking into athletic scholarships for seniors? I'm sure Seth would qualify."

Well, this was news! This, with the gold, and they might be able to swing it. Carl rubbed his chin. "Aw, he ain't that good, I don't think," his Welsh reticence coming out.

"He's very talented, Mr. Morgan, and it is certainly worth a try. Does he want to go on to college?"

"Yep, says he does. I guess his grades have bin ok too."

"You have one great kid and we'll do all we can to see that he has a chance." Jerry, who was facing the path to the trailer park, now said with a nod in that direction, "Your parents live in the mobile home park, don't they? I met your grandfather there. He's a wonderful old gentleman."

Carl, getting more favorably disposed by the minute toward Jerry, became almost voluble. "Pappy's gonna be 92 nex' month. I don't know what we're gonna do if they throw everyone out."

Jerry looked serious. "We're going to try not to let that happen. There will be a lawsuit for starts. And with the new school year, we're pretty positive the court will rule in our favor to keep children from having to move."

Carl nodded, then seized by another thought, gazed off into the distance. "He were a War Hero, you know. Pappy. He saved some officer's life and got a medal. He got lots of medals. An' a bench dedicated to him."

Dreamland! The missing plaque! Jerry said, "And he watched out for Mrs. Foster when she was a little girl. He was caretaker for the old Mitchell place. But you probably knew that. Quite a guy, your granddad."

"My dad, he got black lung from workin' in the mines. Pappy had to take care of him for a long time." Carl wasn't sure why he was telling Jerry all this. Somethin' 'bout the Super, he thought. You can trust him. Not like the Doc. I was crazy to work for him. I bet I could tell the Super a whole bunch of things he'd like to know.

Jerry could imagine how hard life had been for them. Sturdy folks. He had nothing but admiration for their courage and perseverance. "Well," he said, "you probably want to finish before it gets any later. Thanks for talking to me about your family. We'll fight the good fight to keep the Park." Jerry held out his hand, and the two shook hands.

Carl sat for a moment before he started the mower again. It was a new experience. Carl turned it over in his mind. To be treated that way by the Super hisself, respected like, and without nothin' in return. 'Cept to keep the kid on the right track. Yep, he'd do that. And he would, from that point, do just about anything for Dr. Strauss.

Jerry walked back toward his car, the sound of the mower receding again. He was thinking about the Morgans and how hardship had been a continual feature of their life. And suddenly, like a revelation, it came to him in a moment of intense awareness that he held the very same attitudes as Pat about these people. Oh, yes, he told himself, he'd acknowledged it intellectually before. But that was with the detachment of an outsider and lacked an emotional component. This was different. He felt it keenly and it had the effect of startling him and at the same time cementing his affinity with her. How could he have doubted her? When would he see her? Tomorrow? Or would she be too tired from the transcontinental flight to see him? Then they'd get together the next day, Labor Day. Oh, damn! There was another Rotary picnic!

Shadows had begun to lengthen and he could hear crickets chirping in the high grass. It was the time when, sun making its retreat and summer almost over, regret about what one hasn't accomplished can easily dominate and Jerry was feeling defeated. Mostly, he thought, it's because I've been away from Pat for so long. But it was also because of the fire. In spite of Paul's vow of determination, he was beginning to consider it a lost cause, that they'd never find out who was behind the arson. Being at the site provided no useful information. The place bore little resemblance to what it had once been. It was well on its way in the process of sinking back into the earth and it would take its secrets with it.

Absorbed in these reflections, Jerry hadn't noticed that he'd come to the derelict house until he was right in front of it. He paused, saying to himself, can't hurt to check it out. He walked up three sagging steps to the porch. The floor boards creaked loudly but didn't raise anyone. There was no doorbell, so he knocked. He tried to look in the front window but it was implacably covered by a shade. He knocked again and after knocking a third time reached for the door handle, then thought better. Not a good idea, he reluctantly concluded, reading in his mind the screaming headline in the *Colton Clarion*: SUPERINTENDENT OF CASD CHARGED WITH UNLAWFUL ENTRY. Just contemplating what delicious repercussions this could cause put him in a jauntier frame of mind, and he set out on a tour around the house.

The windows on the side yielded nothing, as those that weren't too grimy to see through had their shades down. He noticed that the garage, leaning dangerously, had tire marks leading to it although the door was closed. As Jerry rounded the corner of the house and came into the back yard, he was halted by a loud exclamation of "Oh! Sorry!"

On the back porch stood an elderly man, replacing a hearing aid and talking all the while in a steadily modulating voice, until he had adjusted the volume to his satisfaction. "Damn things. Can't stand 'em. Sorry I didn't hear your knock. Wouldn't have heard it anyway out here." This last was said in an almost normal tone. He went on, "I'd shake howdy but I've got furniture wax all over my hands." He looked around for a rag, found one and commenced a rapid cleaning.

Not only did he seem pleased to have a visitor but, to Jerry's amazement and delight, the old fellow had been applying wax to a beautiful oak and chestnut icebox, the door of which was open, revealing a zinc-lined interior. Jerry realized he must have been ogling and had forgotten his manners. He said, "Yes, I did knock and that is one gorgeous piece you have there."

The old man grinned. "Like antiques, do you?"

"You might say so!" Jerry replied with enthusiasm. "But let me introduce myself."

"No need. You're the Superintendent of Schools. Dr. Strauss. I'm Ed Deems," who had by now wiped one hand clean, and Jerry, mounting the steps onto the porch found himself, for the second time in less than ten minutes, shaking hands with someone unexpected.

"Would that be Deems as in Deems Barbecue?"

"One of 'em. There's a large amount of us. I'm the guy that buys the antiques, also cleans 'em up."

Jerry said, "I've seen your handiwork and admired it. Do you ever sell too?" he asked hopefully.

Mr. Deems laughed. "My arm's been twisted in the past. Could be again."

Jerry almost forgot what he was going to try to learn from the present owner, distracted as he was by the icebox and the possibility of antiques. But he needed to take advantage of the opportunity, so started in with, "I was hoping to talk to the people who used to live here when the school burned down, but I guess that isn't you."

"No, they'd gone off to Florida before that happened and liked the life there so much, they moved down."

"You bought the house from them?"

"If you can call it a house," he said with a snort. "Just a place to store things and do repairs and what not."

"I don't suppose you have their address or know how to get in touch with them."

"That's what others asked, back in the spring, and I had to say I didn't."

Jerry's heart raced a little as he said, "And now?"

"Still don't, and it was stupid of me to let the chance go by. We did talk on the phone the one time recent, oh, maybe in June. That is, I talked to the Missus. She said she hoped I didn't mind they left some old things here and I told her if she meant the cast iron stove, I could certainly understand. She said the stove and the other heavy stuff, and I was welcome to all of it. She told me to enjoy the stove, as it reminded her of their lucky break. Too bad I never got her phone number or anything," he finished with a look of self-disgust.

"Lucky break?" Jerry asked. "How so?"

"She said it was like the check, the one that was sent by whoever treated them to a month at the condo. Had a star design on it."

Chapter 33

At the Saturday night poker game, starting again after a break for vacations, the private back room at The Pit was heavy with cigar smoke. It was a boisterous group, eager to resume its ritual of gambling, drinking, smoking, profanity and exaggerating, mostly about sexual exploits. For Mel and the other female Pit staff who were unlucky enough to get stuck working on one of these Saturday nights, it was a trial, although the tips, more accurately bribes for silence, were very good.

Mel had been in and out, taking orders and bringing drinks. Each time she came back the room was smokier, the noise level higher and the men bolder with their fanny pats and suggestive comments. Some of the guys, the older ones in particular, she tolerated, feeling sorry for them. She knew about their situations, their loneliness and, in some cases, their overbearing wives. But with Elliot it was another matter. He acted as if she should fall all over herself being attracted by him and nothing could be farther from the truth. He'd even given his fellows the impression that she was interested in him.

"Mel, tell me how much you've missed seeing me," someone said to her.

"She ain't missed you, son. She's missed the Doc over there."

"Hah! You can tell by the way she's pretending to ignore him that she can't wait to get him in bed."

Laughter, coarse and crude, followed these remarks. Mel said nothing. Elliot, on the other side of the table, smirked and had another sip of his drink. It seemed to Mel that he was not drinking as much tonight, which was fine with her, as it meant less interaction with him.

He'd only spoken to her once tonight, other than ordering drinks. It was unpleasant enough and also said in a voice that others couldn't miss, "When you get off tonight, Mel, I'll make up for being away. It's been hard on both of us," the last part accompanied by an offensively familiar look.

Hoots and cheers went up from those who were close enough to hear and Mel did what she'd always done, turned on her heel and walked away.

It was ugly and she hated it, but she needed the money. She and Jamie needed the money. Even though he was making a decent salary driving for the energy company, his child support payments ate up much of it. So a few minutes of crap, she said to herself, she could stand. And they had the band too, which was getting some gigs. OK, Mel Morgan, you can put up with the creeps, although she'd never let on to Jamie the extent of what she had to deal with.

It was later in the evening when Mel heard someone say, "Too bad about Clarence," and she realized Elliot's sidekick was not there. That seemed strange, as they always sat together. Was this why Elliot was drinking less? His friend had been a heavy drinker, she knew. Mel paid attention, if only out of curiosity, to the talk that followed about Clarence.

"I thought he'd be here tonight. One last game, he told me."

"Hey, when Uncle Tex says he wants you back, you don't have no say in the matter."

"Well, he didn't ought to have gone without saying goodbye at least."

"Did he say anything to you, El? You and him were good buddies."

Elliot said darkly, "Clarence let me down."

"You mean with all the drinking? He let everyone down and himself most of all."

"Yeh," said Elliot, and talk resumed about other matters.

Jerry did not leave the Elk Creek School site until it was nearly dark. While the "star" connection that Ed Deems said so casually had hit home, Jerry knew he should hold off thinking about it until later. To help get his adrenalin under control, he brought his attention back to Mr. Deems, who was still expressing dismay at his sin of omission.

"And when everyone wanted to find them, too."

"Everyone?" Jerry asked, still a little dry in the mouth.

"Well, for a while anyways, especially the *Clarion* folk. No, and I had to tell them the house was a cash deal, so the bank didn't even have a clue." Deems went on, "But I dunno why we're standing out here when you want to have a look inside," and he motioned Jerry to come in, holding open a tattered screen door.

Jerry was glad to have this distraction, a few minutes to think of other things. He entered the room off the porch and found himself among a beguiling assortment of antiques. And even though some were in various stages of disrepair, he gave a long, low whistle by way of appreciation.

Mr. Deems chuckled, glad to have like-minded company. Then, in the manner of many people with a hearing loss, he did all the talking, launching happily into a running commentary on every piece: what it was, how old it was, where it came from, what he aimed to do to fix it up. Jerry admired an apothecary cabinet, hardware store bins, an oak and glass display case, several wooden wall-hung telephones, a walnut Victrola...

"...but I had to toss out the 78s. Benny Goodman, Glenn Miller, Tommy Dorsey..."

"Yike!" exclaimed Jerry, interrupting him for the first time. "You didn't!"

"Did. Deep scratches in all of 'em."

"Oh, then, that's different," said Jerry's practical side.

"It wasn't easy, mind."

"I imagine not."

"Had to be done."

"It would have killed me."

Mr. Deems nodded. "Not too many people understand the agony of having to throw away original vintage items just because they're completely useless."

Jerry wasn't sure he followed this reasoning precisely, but decided it probably made sense in context. Indicating the assembled pieces, he asked, "Will all these go out to the restaurant? And where will you put them?"

"That's a continuing point of contention in the family," Mr. Deems allowed. "Several near relatives have offered to 'store' them for me, which means the next thing you know the grandkids will have gone off to Martensdale and furnished their apartments with them."

"Unto the next generation." Jerry prophesized.

"Well, long as they have the proper respect for 'em. I'm doing some teaching of respect myself. There are several teenagers live in the trailer park yonder I employ regular to do my lifting and hauling. They're good kids and keep watch on the place for me. Wouldn't want to lose them, but I read in the paper that you are going to court to see that don't happen."

"We're pulling out all the stops."

"Well, I'll be pleased to testify for the school district." Then, spotting another item, Mr. Deems said, "Look at this here document box," pointing to a substantial quarter-sawn oak piece. It was about 2 feet long, a foot deep and 6" high and had dovetailed corners and brass hinges, with a beveled panel on the lid. "Came out of a bank that went belly up."

"It certainly is a beautiful piece. What are you planning to do with it and is there any chance I could take it off your hands?"

Mr. Deems cast an eye, first at Jerry, then at the document box. "Got to clean it up some, but then, hell, I'll put your name on it."

"I'd be much obliged. Name your price."

One unforeseen thing after another today, thought Jerry, as they shook hands goodbye in the gathering darkness. "This has been a real treat for me. I'm very glad you were here when I came by," Jerry said sincerely.

"Couldn't have asked for a better visitor," Mr. Deems stated. "Last guy that showed up I wouldn't let in. Said he knew the people that was here and they wanted him to have a look around, but I sent him on his way. Something about him I didn't trust."

Another surprise, thought Jerry, or have I intuited it already? "Did you happen to find out who he was?" he asked.

"Oh, I knew who he was all right. It was that business fellow from the school district."

As Jerry began the drive back into town, images from the afternoon flickered in his mind: Carl Morgan sitting motionless on the riding mower in the middle of the field, late sun slanting on the tall grasses around the ruined school, century old wooden furniture haphazardly arrayed in the dim rooms of the house. But then, almost against his will, he could not keep from mulling over the information from Ed Deems. That damned "star" has turned up again, he thought, and it seems as if Elliot had some interest in the old couple's house. What in the world does this mean? A connection between Elliot and the fire? A whole new and chilling area of speculation began to rear itself, and Jerry was frankly horrified at where it might take him. Or is there a completely reasonable explanation? Enough of this, he told himself, and pulled into the parking lot of a supermarket. A break for buying groceries, then a stop at the liquor store to get a couple bottles of wine, and he was functioning more rationally. He started thinking ahead. Tomorrow evening she'll be back and, surveillance by Elliot or not, I intend to have her in my arms and shortly thereafter in my bed. Or hers. Much rather think about that.

It had slipped his mind that his landlord was having a family reunion over Labor Day weekend, so he forgot about the guest parking it involved. He was particularly dismayed to find one of the rental cars blocking his garage. He parked where he could and went inside by his downstairs front entrance, leaving the wine and groceries on top of the dryer, then headed for the door again to politely request access to his garage. And I may as well chat a bit about the charter school while I'm there, he thought, because they'll no doubt offer me a drink and... At that moment, he distinctly heard the sound of footsteps above him and with a sinking feeling knew someone was in his apartment. An automatic, unquestioned assumption that one of Elliot's informants was bugging the place kicked into his brain and, oblivious to what a confrontation could entail, Jerry went charging up the stairs two steps at a time. As he did so the door opened at the top.

Pat was standing in the doorway, radiant, a glass of wine in one hand. "My love," she said, as Jerry reached her, "can we get married?"

Once again, she hadn't planned it this way; it just came out. Like so many things I do, she thought, and then had a terrible moment: what if he says no? To postpone this calamitous prospect, she changed the subject and kept talking.

"...and I got the Redeye so we'd have today together, and then this! The car had been towed from the parking lot, so I got a rental and went to the body shop to survey the damage. Luckily, they can have it fixed in about a week and I can go over to Pittsburgh to pick it up. Can you credit it? An airport shuttle bus driver, careening around the lot, five sheets to the wind..."

Jerry took her in his arms and she stopped talking. "Just let me hold you, Pat," he whispered. "Just let me know you're here." He closed his eyes to seal in the picture of her standing there, standing there asking if they could get married. Oh, it was priceless! She had come to a decision about their lives and she was not going to beat around the bush. Pat, my lovely, Pat, I would get married to you in a split second. But he couldn't say it. Nor could he say what would dash her hopes, that he had ruined every relationship he'd ever had in the past and it was inevitable that he'd ultimately ruin this one.

However, he would make an honest response to her enchanting offer. He held her at arm's length, placing his finger on her lips, as she seemed about to speak again. "Yes, my darling, we *can* get married. No impediments and no one to speak now or forever hold his peace." He smiled as he said this, letting her take it as she would, until the time came to tell her of his very real fears. "But at the moment a more immediate plan is on my mind."

Later, when they were lying close together, Jerry stirred and sighed a long, drawn-out sigh.

"A contented sigh?" Pat asked, so tuned to him, so sensitive to his nuances, that she knew at once there was something bothering him.

"Yes, love, I am contented. Very contented with you."

"And the sigh?" she persisted.

Where to start? Not the time for self-confessions. But there were things that needed to be discussed. "I've uncovered more than I bargained for these last few weeks. The book you lent me set me off, and then I talked to...but let's not get into it now. Are you hungry? Why don't I fix something and we can try to catch up. I think we may be facing what Eric Arden would agree is a hell of an ethical dilemma."

Chapter 34

"So this reference to 'star' crops up again and again," Pat said.

They were still sitting at the dining table, the large deli salad he'd bought for the picnic having been hungrily consumed. He had recounted everything he'd found about the use of "star" and about Paul's investigation, everything, that is, except what Paul had said about the identification of the body.

She went on, "It does seem such a commonplace symbol. But Owen may be right and its very lack of originality would make it forgettable. Let me see if I've got all the allusions you've noticed. Clarence, who has now left in disgrace, didn't dispute that 'star' appeared in the Power Learners' management service. Then, Clem Duncan's letter to the trailer park's residents listed the buyers as Star Partnership LLC. And, coincidentally, he thought that it was Elliot who'd cooled them off attending that school board meeting," she added, looking at Jerry. "OK. Now, Paul Willard. He told you there was a bid on the school property soon after the fire and he remembered it as a company with a star logo or the word star in the name. I think I remember that too. There is bound to be a file somewhere, probably in Elliot's office, which would corroborate that. But the last thing you told me, Ed Deems and the cast iron stove—that gave me goose bumps."

"There was one more occurrence. According to Mr. Deems, Elliot showed up at the house and wanted to, as he put it, 'have a look around.' Mr. Deems, however, took a dislike to him and wouldn't let him in."

"What could he have been looking for?" Pat wondered.

Jerry shook his head. "Some evidence that might compromise him?"

"Oh, lord, Jerry, does this mean what I think it means?"

"Even if it does, there is no way anything can be followed up on, let alone proved, without arousing Elliot's suspicion. We're between a rock and a hard place on this one."

They were both silent for a while, thinking about unpleasant possibilities.

Jerry said, "Also, I unearthed a whole slew of payments to consultants when I was looking for precedents on fees. Francine who, by the way, has left the Dark Side and come over to us, pulled out Elliot's files on consultants for me. There were many more consultants brought in than I would have thought—over a dozen last fall and winter, right up until the fire. I assume you were aware of what they got paid for."

"I can think of one or two, although requests only go to the school board if the amount is over $2500," Pat explained. "But a dozen! I should look at those files, Jerry, because if something isn't right, I want to know about it."

"So you see why I sigh."

Pat reached for his hand. "And none of this you told me when we talked on the phone. You only had nice things to say. There I was, all carefree in California while you, my poor darling, were digging and sifting your way through this mess." She gave his hand a squeeze before releasing it.

"And it could get messier," he said.

"Good thing we have Francine. How did you win her over?"

"Francine realized where her loyalties lay, particularly after Eric Arden sent one of his graduate students here to gather data for a dissertation. Elliot spent an inordinate amount of time with Celeste. Fortunately for Celeste, she was only here a short time."

"And was able to extricate herself from his clutches before any damage was done. It isn't amusing, I know. And I am not looking forward to seeing Elliot again. How long may I stay here?"

Jerry said, "As long as you can stand me. I'm sorry, Pat. This isn't much of a homecoming for you, I'm afraid. Pretty heavy stuff."

She nodded. "It's OK, Jerry. You've been shouldering it alone and I want us to share it. It's my school district too, and I have a responsibility to find out what has been going on."

"Not entirely alone. We have Owen, and Paul Willard has turned out to be a perceptive ally. He had gotten well into his investigation, putting together the circumstantial evidence: the elderly couple going away so conveniently, the bid on the school property, the mobile home park sale, even the timing of the fire to coincide with a blizzard. Who had detailed weather information ahead of time? One person: Elliot."

Pat looked away into a middle distance. "No," she said. "Two people."

"Two?" Jerry asked.

"Hank had the same information source," Pat said in a quiet voice.

"Ah, yes, of course," Jerry admitted. He could see that something was beginning to trouble her. The fire, he decided. But what if the body were misidentified? Apparently she had not read Paul's report. "Let's go back a bit in the sequence of events," he said to her. "Who was instrumental in the decision to close the school? There were some comments that it was grudge arson against the superintendent."

"What is so ironic," Pat said, bringing her attention back to Jerry, "is that Hank was not in favor of closing the school.

It was only after he'd had a meeting with Elliot, discussing ways to cut costs, that he seemed reconciled to it and Elk Creek was the smallest school. I made the point that new housing was going up, and families were starting to move into the area. There would be more children, I argued, not less, and more income from property taxes. Then, shortly before the fire, Hank had come around and was actively opposing the closure. As was the school board; they would have supported Hank and not approved the decision to close Elk Creek."

"So Paul's theory, that the haste to buy the school property and the mobile home park is linked to the fire, begins to look exceedingly plausible. With the 'star' tie-in it looks even more plausible. But the questions remain: who is using the term? Is it only one person or several different groups, and is Elliot involved? And short of an all-out audit with devastating media coverage, which would only damage the school district, we can't get any answers."

"Looks that way," she said sadly. "What's our next move? Or do we even have one?"

"Only one, as far as I can see now," Jerry answered, "and that's to have Paul Willard down to go over his report, while we fill in our bits." He was thoughtful for a second and then said, "It's still an enigma, about the stifling of the report. Paul said when he got the call about the county not having received it, he told them he'd send a copy out right away. Instead of agreeing, they said to forget it and they'd do their own investigating. It sounds like someone paid them off or, as Paul assumes, someone in the energy industry put the pressure on. But I've come to know the gas executives around here and it just doesn't sound like them. They've been more than helpful and..." Jerry noticed that Pat's eyes were filling with tears.

"Oh, Jerry," she said in a hushed voice, "that was my doing. I'm the one who wanted the report suppressed."

It was the last thing Jerry expected, this unanticipated confession, and he was without words for a few moments. No wonder she didn't want to talk about the fire, he thought, and then realized how troubled she'd been. He broke the silence. "Why, Pat?" he asked gently.

She wiped her eyes, "I would have told you sooner, but I thought it wasn't something to concern you about. Now I see it is, the fire itself and all the ramifications and complicating factors."

"Were you trying to protect Hank?" Jerry made his voice as calm as he could, but he was still shaken by her admission.

"I'd been worried about Hank for a long time. I knew he was getting more and more in debt because of a gambling problem. It was too close to home, too close to my own family's history."

"And you thought...?"

She looked at Jerry, met his gaze squarely and said, "Yes. That perhaps he'd chosen this way to end his life." She let this sink in, then went on, "I don't know if he was trying to put out the fire or not, but I was scared silly that the investigation had delved into Hank's affairs, and this was what they'd concluded in the report. A fine man forever tarnished. Do you see?"

"Yes, I see. Tell me, did you read the report?"

She shook her head. "No. All I knew was what Elliot told me."

"Elliot?" Jerry asked with a frown.

"He said he'd learned that it would make Hank look bad. I asked him what we should do, and he told me he thought he could keep it from coming out."

Jerry nodded. "And he hadn't read it himself?"

"I don't know, but I've heard that one of his card playing buddies is the Chief of Police, who would have read it before it was, as I understood and hoped, destroyed."

Things were starting to become clearer. Jerry said, somewhat apprehensively, "I think it's time you knew what was in the report."

"From what you've said about it already, I don't see how it puts Hank in a bad light. What more did you learn from Detective Willard?"

Jerry took a deep breath "This will not make matters any easier. But one of the main concerns the investigation team had, and which was clearly stated in the report, was lack of certainty that the body had been correctly identified."

"That the...the what? *Not* Hank?" Pat said incredulously. "But, who?"

"Someone not as tall, for one thing. Remember, identification was done on the basis of Hank's car and keys. Did anyone around here disappear about that time? This was to be the next stage of the investigation before it was prematurely ended."

Pat thought for a moment. "Well, yes," she said with a wrinkled brow. "Our middle school custodian, but he was always taking off, sometimes for months at a time, so no one gave it a second thought."

"About how tall was he?" was Jerry's next question.

"Burt Hodges. Let me see. Maybe about five nine or ten. But Jerry, if not Hank, then where is he?" Her eyes appealed to Jerry for some kind of answer.

"Precisely. Where, then, is Hank?"

Jerry got up and put his arm around her. She rested her head on his arm and they were quiet together for a while. They hadn't an answer to the question they'd posed, but both knew there were several possibilities: none palatable, all unconscionable and one grisly.

Jerry brought himself back to practicalities. "It's late," he said, "and you're probably exhausted from traveling all night."

She looked up at him. "But I feel lightened from this burden of guilt I was carrying. I mean, I know what I did was wrong. But now I realize I was led into it for some reason."

"I have another bit of information, but this is good news, a surprisingly cheerful note to end the day. Let me move that rental car, so I can get my behemoth into the garage, and I'll bring your luggage up. And if you're not asleep yet, I'll tell you about Sally Ann."

"Sally Ann Hodges!? She was such a sweetie! Do hurry back and, Jerry?"

"Yes, love?"

"I'm so happy we're getting married."

Chapter 35

By the next morning they had a tacit understanding to leave off talking about the fire or speculate about Hank. It wasn't as if they hadn't been stewing on it most of the night. Swirling around obsessively in both their heads were possible, yet thoroughly untenable, scenarios. Had Hank engineered what looked like his own demise in order to escape his debts? Was he now residing in some South American country? Was it part of the plan to have an unrecognizable body found in the school? Had Elliot helped and covered up for him? Was there some scheme to finance this venture involving buying and developing the school property?

And yet it was all preposterous. Pat had known Hank well, knew he could never endanger the life of an innocent person. Jerry remembered that a fellow Rotarian called Hank a "gentle soul." But gradually the ugly speculations were put in the back of their minds, put away where thoughts, in a semi-conscious state, often get infused with insight. It was judicious, as well as saving unnecessary distress, not to take them out and air them until some time had passed and they could meet with Paul Willard.

Pat was very glad to hear about Sally Ann. "She was only nineteen that year and had a brand new baby. Her husband had deserted them, the same as his father did when he was born. I got her on welfare, helped with social services. We had her working on finishing her high school diploma, and she did that in no time, and we got her divorce from Lester

Hodges finalized. You'd think she'd be beaten down, but what spirit," Pat recalled fondly.

"You should see her now. Naiveté and flair, rolled into one."

"I can't wait to see her. When are they planning to come down?"

"In two weeks. I thought things would have eased off a bit by then."

The beginning of school was always hectic and would take most of their time and energy. In the meantime, this last weekend was to be a lull and they treated it as such.

"About the Rotary picnic tomorrow," Jerry said. He had asked Pat if she would accompany him and, since she knew everyone, she was pleased to be his date for a social event. They were finishing breakfast, once again on the back deck, although this time the clothes she was wearing were her own. He went on, "Last night we ate all of the Greek salad that I was planning to take tomorrow. Any suggestions?"

"Maybe it will rain," Pat replied, burying her nose in the paper. "Oh, dear, the weather forecast is not cooperating." She looked up in time to see Jerry moving her coffee cup out of reach with elaborate surreptitiousness. "Stop that!" she ordered.

"Disloyalty to the Rotary Club calls for severe punishment," he intoned imperiously.

"Withholding your coffee is punishment indeed," she admitted.

Jerry knew this light and pleasant exchange had a lot more going than was observable. In spite of still being enormously concerned, the humor and mutual consideration which defined their relationship provided a well of comfort. It enabled them to postpone finding strategies for disagreeable lines of inquiry, for what might prove to be very destructive lines of inquiry, to step back and follow a conscious inaction. He was rather in awe of what the two of them had achieved over a few short months. Could he, perhaps, at last consider himself marriageable? But he wasn't ready to explore this with Pat yet.

Pat did not bring the subject of marriage up either. She was content that he had accepted her so readily, and was confident that when they could, they'd quietly elope.

With a leisurely Sunday and an enjoyable Labor Day gathering, then two weeks of new school-year challenges, they were able to get a needed respite from their concerns. Unexpectedly, because it was in such variance with their recent mindsets, their working relationships with Elliot were pleasant and productive over those two weeks. Privately, both of them wondered if they had been mistaken in their deductions about Elliot's behavior, and maybe had been miraculously saved from making a major error in judgment. No further attempts to evict the trailer park residents had taken place, and Pat was hopeful that the threat of a lawsuit had made the buyers back off.

She went back to her house after a few days, her car was repaired and delivered by a driller who needed transportation from Pittsburgh, and in her mailbox at the district office the next week there was an envelope containing the key to her kitchen door. Jerry breathed easier, tackled scheduling glitches and program confusion, met with parents, board members and individual teachers, had many lively conversations with students, and spoke with eloquence to the *Clarion* reporter about new school initiatives. Friday evening was a home football game and, although the Colton Critters went down in defeat, fewer incidents of underage drinking than usual were noted. The school year, as always, was off to a great start.

The last Saturday afternoon of summer was warm and still. On the wooden deck Carl had built years ago behind his parents' trailer, old Mr. Morgan, bright-eyed, ensconced in his wheelchair, chatted with the people who had come to wish him a happy birthday. It seemed to Carl that the entire Park had turned out and many others from around the county. Pappy's really enjoying this, he thought to himself. He don't look near so old as 92. I bet he's sharper than half these folks. I gotta get him to tell me about what he done in the war one more time. Maybe Seth can write it down while he's saying it, so's we can have a record like, 'cause you never know. With this last sobering thought, Carl remembered what the Super had said. They were going to do everything in their power to keep the Park from being sold. Well, I got me a pretty good idea of who it is wants to buy it, but no way to prove it. Can't prove lots of things.

The party had wound down and Carl saw that his grandfather was leaning toward him and looking keenly at him. Carl asked, "You want another piece of birthday cake, Pappy?"

"Naw, not now, but thank you, boy. What I want is a talk with you 'bout next year. I think it's time we sold the Parker."

"Sell the Parker? Why ever for? That was gave to you in appreciation for what you done."

"I want Seth to go to college is why. He'd be the first one in the family to go. That there fancy shotgun could pay for it."

"Aw, Pap, goin' to college costs a lot more'n what you could sell the Parker for. Anyways, I heard Coach was gonna help get Seth a scholarship." The gold coins, well, what to do there still needed working out.

His grandfather considered for a second, then said, "Sell it anyway, Carl. Seth is gonna need a car. That should get him something real nice."

Carl knew better than to argue with his granddad. Obviously, he had his heart set on helping Seth and this was the way he figured he could. Carl conceded, "I'll see what I can do, Pap." To himself he thought, maybe if I set a high enough price...

"And don't you get notions 'bout asking some astromical amount so's no one will buy it. There's lots of folks who collect guns and they'll know what it's worth."

"Yes, Pap," Carl said, chastened.

"You go talk with Ed Deems, but don't sell it to him, hear? He'll think he kin get a low price on account of having knowed me for so long. Let him give you his information, but then take it up to that place in Martensdale where all the collectors go."

"Yes, Pap," said Carl.

"You'll know if the guy's honest. I always said you was one could smell a rat." His grandfather nodded affirmatively after this last statement.

"Yes, Pap," said Carl. Huh, he thought, Pappy's right. I knew somethin' was fishy with the Doc and t'other guy, that Texas lush. From the start I could tell they was up to shady stuff. Spyin' on everyone like that. Shouldn't of kept takin' their money, but leastways I never did anything I oughtn't of done.

"See you pay attention to that new Super of yours, Carl. He's all right. I wouldn't put it past him to marry up with Pat Mitchell. You kin see they're courtin'."

"Yes, Pap," Carl said, and thought, more'n jes' courtin', and why shouldn't they? Much better'n her with the Doc. Good thing the Super come along when he did. No telling what might of happened to Mrs. Foster if he hadn't.

Mr. Morgan settled back in his wheelchair. "And, Carl?"

"Yes, Pappy?"

"I believe I'd like some more cake now, if you'd be so kind to bring me a piece."

Jerry had thought Deems Barbecue would be a good place to meet with Paul and Sally Ann. Pat concurred, although there was a possibility that Paul might be recognized. "He was down here for a week," she said. "I remember him as very well-spoken, polite and patient. And to think I was the one who called him off! At least I can apologize and explain."

"I'm quite sure he would have been pulled off anyway and the report suppressed, given the situation and the players."

They hadn't resumed their speculations out loud to each other. But, Jerry thought, with Paul as a sounding board, it should be more productive than circular thinking that went nowhere. And he didn't want to spoil the reunion of Pat with Sally Ann, an event which could include high drama, emotion and amusement, in equal parts. "The big question in my mind..." he started to say as they drove out to Deems Township.

"Yes?" Pat asked, anxious lest they not be of one mind in explicating their concerns to Paul.

Jerry went on, "...is what will Sally Ann wear? She told me she'd find something appropriate. What's appropriate for Cross County? What you're wearing?"

This last-of-summer evening, Pat had on a swingy denim skirt with sandals and an apple green linen shirt. Jerry received a grateful look for having alleviated her anxiety and she said, "Let's see, how might Sally Ann approach this sartorial challenge? Coal miner's daughter? Appalachian hillbilly sweetheart? Or, in a more up-to-date mode, Shale worker's girlfriend? I wish I'd seen her as the fandango queen. I bet you were wondering where you'd landed."

"And she brought it off without any self-consciousness. Owen says she usually wears something vintage to complement her antiques. That must give her plenty of scope for her creativity," Jerry said, as they turned into the lane leading to the restaurant.

The rocking chairs on the porch were almost all filled. There were people waiting for tables and those who had finished and were lingering to chat in the warm evening. It was particularly busy, being a Saturday, but also because there was live music tonight. Jerry had made a reservation with Ed Deems himself for an outside table, not wanting to leave anything to chance. He had explained who would be joining them and Mr. Deems had said, "You'll want a table a bit apart. We can do that. And, by the way, I'm almost done with that document box you fancied. I think you'll be pleased how it turned out."

As they mounted the steps, Jerry spotted Paul sitting in one of the rocking chairs, talking with a man on his left. On his right, chatting with the person on her other side, was Sally Ann. Jerry did a double take: she had short honey blond hair, the same shade as Pat's. Since he'd only seen her done up in the turban affair, he didn't know what to expect, but he was definitely not prepared for the next surprise.

Paul got up to greet them and so did Sally Ann. Totally confounding any of their predictions, she had on a swingy denim skirt with sandals and a linen shirt in golden yellow, hers tied in a knot at the waist. She rushed over to greet Pat with a squeal of "Oh! Mrs. Foster!" and Jerry watched with pleasure as the two hugged each other, tears and laughter intermingling.

Looking at their nearly identical outfits, Paul observed, "I don't know how Sally Ann does it, but she does." And then, shaking hands with Jerry, said with his sad-eyed smile, "Copy of the report is in the car. I can see we won't get to it for a while."

"I remember this place, although it was much smaller then," Sally Ann was saying, after they'd ordered and been seated with their drinks. "I only got to go here the once but, oh, my, was the food ever good!"

"Especially after Cross County cuisine?" Jerry suggested.

Sally Ann, who did not think this an unusual question, nodded, answering, "Not only that, but there were antiques everywhere back then, too. I thought they were just beautiful and now that I'm here again, I think it's what started me off collecting."

Paul, who had been looking around appreciatively when they were inside, added, "It certainly would nudge one in that direction. And the thing about the antiques here is that the display, as huge and varied as it is, all *belongs*. Nothing seems out of place to this particular locale, to its history and way of life."

Pat agreed with a nod. "It really has evolved into more of a museum," she said. "They don't sell the things and if you want an interpretive tour, one of the owners has, I swear, total recall about each item."

Food was served and lived up to all expectations. Conversation continued about Cross County, the antiques to be found therein, Jerry's acquisition of Col. Tyler's book, from which Owen had read to Sally Ann and Paul selected bits of alarming county history, and the superb dinner.

"But one thing I must know," Jerry said to Sally Ann, "before I burst with curiosity, is how you came up with the same thing to wear as Pat. You told me when I was at the shop that you'd find something appropriate, but this is extraordinary."

"Oh, not at all," Sally Ann answered with perfect equanimity. "I remembered Mrs. Foster was blond, so I asked Paul what kind of blond, and I started there."

Jerry still looked mystified, not understanding that hair style and color were an integral part of any outfit, while Sally Ann breezed on, "And when he said we'd be going to Deems Barbecue, well, that meant only a denim skirt would be right, and since it's September and we're out in the country, the top had to be yellow, and in linen because it's still so warm. And sandals for the same reason. It just seemed appropriate."

"It's uncanny," was Jerry's comment.

"Oh, do you think so?" Sally Ann said. "I thought I was being practical."

Paul, chuckling at Jerry's response, said, "With Sally Ann there's no predicting."

Slices of apple pie, made with local apples, came next, and then a graniteware pot filled with fresh hot coffee was set down on their table, the hurricane lamp was lighted, and their server withdrew.

Jerry noticed that Sally Ann and Pat had begun an earnest conversation, punctuated by trading phones to show photos of Pat's Johnny and Sally Ann's Rosie, now an administrative assistant in one of the state offices in Harrisburg. They were both animated, and not wanting to disrupt a joyous occasion for them, he and Paul decided to go ahead and quietly begin their discussion of the fire.

Chapter 36

It had been growing darker for some time and the lamp cast a welcome flickering glow. Crickets chirped steadily under the trees and cicadas shrilled now and then in the distance. The musicians could be heard inside the restaurant testing sound levels. Nighttime, closing in, lent a feeling of welcome isolation.

Paul looked out into the deepening shadows. If anyone were within earshot, the background noises would cover up their conversation, he reasoned, and he turned to Jerry. "I'll leave a copy of the report with you, plus our notes on follow-up, so you'll have a complete picture. It's essentially as I explained when we met. The frustrating thing is that we were pulled off before we could get any farther."

Jerry said, "Yes, and I know more about that now."

Paul looked curiously at Jerry, and he started, giving Paul all the information he had gleaned, describing Pat's role with regard to the report and her concern about Hank, going on to the various incidents of suspicious behavior on Elliot's part and his card games with the Chief of Police. "By the way, Pat is planning to apologize to you tonight."

"Even though she was deliberately misled." Paul shook his head. "Yes, I remember meeting with Dr. Lucas," he said, and looked thoughtful.

Jerry went on, telling Paul about the additional contexts in which "star" had appeared since they'd talked last, his and Pat's theories about Hank and the improbability of those theories. He even gave a possible name to the remains found in the fire. Nothing got left out and, because Jerry had an orderly mind, there was orderliness and logic to this sequence. Paul asked a few clarifying questions but, to Jerry's relief, seemed to understand completely.

"We thought, both of us," Jerry continued, "that after a couple of weeks had passed, we'd have insights, that stepping away for a spell would give us new perspectives. It hasn't happened. Everything is still unexplained and unexplainable. There is one thing though."

Paul raised his eyebrows.

"Elliot. We may have been wrong to suspect him of being complicit. He has been a good working companion, particularly lately, and it would be unfair in the extreme, as well as potentially crippling to the reputation of the school district, to come out and accuse him." What else could he say? That suspicions on his part could have been exacerbated by jealousy? No, at least not for now.

When Jerry had finished, Paul sat back and let his mind play over what he'd been hearing. He recalled how raw and grim the school looked in the cold bleakness of last February. Then he came back to the present and this lovely evening, the richness of this verdant setting. The contrast made the subject of their conversation seem faraway and fantastic, as if it were a dark and grotesque shape seen vaguely through the whirling flakes of a snow globe.

Jerry waited, letting Paul digest what he'd been told. He was certain about this detective and, far from dumping everything in his lap and withdrawing, was ready to work with him to find out what had happened.

"As I told you, the case is on hold. But my chief told me to go ahead after I related our conversation to him. I don't think there will be any procedural problems with continuing the investigation," Paul said with a smile.

Pat, sitting close by Sally Ann, caught Jerry's eye. They had come to a pause and she had sensed that Jerry and Paul had too.

"More coffee, darling?" Jerry asked, then was aghast at how, without thinking, he'd addressed her when others were present. I've got to watch that, he told himself.

Paul appeared to have taken it in stride and Sally Ann showed no signs of noticing the endearment at all. In fact, it had seemed so normal to Pat that she simply answered, "Yes, please," passing both of their cups to him. As he poured, she said brightly, "I guess you've been serious while we've been larking. How far have you gotten?"

"To where we left it two weeks ago. Except that I told Paul we were giving Elliot the benefit of the doubt, for now anyway."

Pat nodded at this, then turned her attention to Paul. "I owe you a sincere apology, Detective," she said with a chagrined expression. "Has Jerry mentioned that I asked Elliot to use his influence with the Colton police chief to have your report suppressed?"

"Yes, he's told me, but also the rest of it. There was nothing in the report detrimental to your superintendent, Mrs. Foster. You were purposely used to keep other information from surfacing."

"Still," Pat said, "it was wrong and I am sorry for what I did, especially," and she gave him a smile, "since you were so nice when you interviewed me in February."

"He *is* nice, isn't he?" purred Sally Ann. "That's exactly what I thought when he first interviewed me." She looked at her sapphire ring and then winked at Pat.

Jerry glanced at Paul and, had it not been so dark, could have sworn he'd blushed.

There were a few warm-up chords from the band, and Sally Ann looked with interest toward the lights of the restaurant. Paul suggested, "If you two want to go in first and find some seats, we'll be along. We're really just wrapping it up."

Sally Ann was ready in an instant, pausing only to bestow a kiss on the top of Paul's head. Pat said vaguely, "If you don't mind..." and quickly followed.

Paul cleared his throat. "Let me detail the steps we need to take now. Most of it I can initiate from Martensdale, but I'll need some help on your end."

Inside the packed restaurant, Pat managed to get a table. Someone had said to her, "Take ours, Mrs. Foster, we're just leaving" and Pat and Sally Ann gratefully accepted.

"You always knew so many people!" Sally Ann enthused.

Pat smiled, "It comes in handy sometimes, doesn't it?"

Sally Ann was watching the four-member band set up, a slight frown on her face. "Wait!" she exclaimed, "I know one of those guys!" and she was on her feet, swiftly threading her way around tables to the stage. Pat saw her say something to the person holding a banjo, and the next moment he had jumped down and was embracing her enthusiastically.

Pat thought, Jerry was right on the mark about Sally Ann. Naiveté, yes. Flair, yes. And a delightful social sense. She noticed that Sally Ann was being introduced to a young woman and was shaking hands with her. With a feeling of quiet happiness, Pat thought to herself: I do believe at this moment that my whole career as a social worker has been justified.

Jerry and Paul arrived at the table, as Sally Ann came back flushed and excited. "Do you know who that was?" she asked Pat.

"Jamie Hodges, I think. It's hard to tell through the crowd."

"He's Rosie's cousin! The last time I saw him he was still a teenager, but I could never forget him, he was so kind to us. And I met Mel, his girlfriend, too!"

No more could be said after this, as the lights dimmed, a spotlight picked out the stage, and the crowd hushed. The banjo started first with a paced, melancholy solo riff in a minor key. When the final chord died away, there was a pause, as if the players needed to draw breath before going on and then, with a sudden burst of wild exuberant energy, the rest of the band kicked in and took off. Bluegrass, sweet and crazy, homegrown and down-country. Just right, thought Pat. Just right, echoed Jerry's mind. Paul gave Jerry and Pat the thumbs up sign. Sally Ann looked ecstatic. "Rosie's cousin!" she mouthed to Pat.

Jerry was glad to stop thinking about the fire for a while. Paul, who was used to switching easily off unpleasant subjects, had been worried about him and was thankful the music provided so much diversion. He had laid out the next part of the investigation for Jerry, and it couldn't have been easy for him, Paul thought. He respected the way Jerry seemed to accept what needed to be done.

They were served a pitcher of cider and, in between sets, talked about the musicians' considerable talent and bluegrass in general. Two of the numbers were vocals with Mel singing solo in one and a duet with Jamie in another.

"That's Mel Morgan," Pat explained to Jerry. "She's a great-granddaughter of old Mr. Morgan you met at the trailer park."

"So a cousin or second cousin to Carl," Jerry surmised.

"Everyone is related down here," Sally Ann said happily, reveling in the newly-found distinction of being part of a Cross County family.

As the first half of the show came to its closing number, Paul announced, with reluctance, that he and Sally Ann would have to leave when the band took their break. "Sally Ann's on at the shop tomorrow and I have a report due. Otherwise, you couldn't get me to leave this place.

"Or me!" Sally Ann exclaimed. "Look. Even Mel is wearing a denim skirt."

Mel had strummed a chord on her guitar, preparing to back up a vocal by Jamie. He stepped into the spotlight and took the mike, then he addressed the crowd. "Before we take a little breather, I'd like to do a special song I wrote for all of us workin' the Shale."

Cheers and whistles went up from the dozens of single men who packed the place. Many of them knew Jamie, since he drove for one of the companies. They could be sure that, even though a native of these parts, he would speak to their concerns.

"And for all their sweethearts," he said, at which he turned and smiled at Mel. This brought out more whistles and when the noise died down, he took up his banjo. He set the tune with a few bars of haunting, sad melody. The other players waited while he began a slow lament.

They sent me up to Pennsylvania, said I'd make a lot of money.
Had to leave my home behind me, had to leave my Texas honey.

The rest of the band then came in, with Mel singing harmony in the choruses, providing a subtle grounding to the high lonesome of Jamie's voice.

Drove two thousand miles to a hostile, northern ground
Where the forest's rough and rugged and the winter hangs around.
And I'm workin', workin', workin' the Marcellus Shale
And it's cold, cold, I tell you, when the snow's thick on the trail.

Oh, we're bunkin' all right, I guess, and eatin' plenty fine,
But the women, lord, the women, they won't give us any time.
And I'm workin', workin', workin' the Marcellus Shale
And it's lonely, man, it's lonely, when the night winds start to wail.

Don't hold me back, you slow-poke, got to haul my frackin' load!
Get that yellow-bellied school bus off this here drillers' road!
Hey, I'm workin', workin', workin' the Marcellus Shale
And I'm prayin', yes, I'm prayin' that these blessed brakes don't fail.

But each evening when the daylight fades, I'm tired to the bone,
And that Appalachian moon above makes me long for home.
Oh, I'm workin', workin', workin' the Marcellus Shale
But I'm weary, oh, so weary, when the moon begins to pale.

Well, there may have been some huntin' in these Pennsylvania woods,
And there may have been nice scenery 'fore we came and got our goods.
Still I'm workin', workin', workin' the Marcellus Shale

Here Jamie paused, and then continued very slowly in a much quieter voice, the instruments all holding fire,

And I never thought I'd say this, but I hope the land will heal.

The last flourishes from the banjo and guitars were drowned out as the room erupted into applause, people standing up clapping and stomping in robust appreciation. Jamie grinned at the band members and they took several bows. He grinned at Sally Ann, or so it seemed to her, and then they retreated off the stage into a break room. Sally Ann stayed on her feet, clapping her heart out, her pretty face bright and eager, her mind made up to come back just as soon as she could and reconnect with her rediscovered very own wonderful extended family.

Carl, there to watch his friend perform and help haul equipment to and from the van, was thinking, can't say I agree with all Jamie said in that there song, but he knows his business. Hmm. An' there's the Doc. Probably keepin' an eye on Mel. Carl couldn't help noticing the Super's party. Huh, he thought, it's that detective guy. Now what do you s'pose he's doin' here?

Chapter 37

During the following week Jerry assembled the materials Paul had asked of him. He sent copies of all the documents he'd run across in which "star" had appeared, including the trailer park notice to residents and, with a little help from Francine, the bid on the school property. He wrote up the description of the cast iron stove conversation he'd had with Ed Deems. He also made a copy of Burton Hodges' personnel file and included the invoices for consulting work for the district and payment information pulled from the PPs.

He had told Paul on Saturday night about the company used by the charter school to manage the business side of their operations. "Someone named Clarence, now recalled to Texas for partaking too liberally of the good life here, was on their board. He was teased about the name and its 'star' reference. But I can ask the school outright what the group is called," he said to Paul.

"Maybe not a good idea yet," Paul answered. "This has to be done in the least conspicuous way we can manage. This Clarence person: if you can get me a last name we'll try to locate him. We'll tell him there's going to be an audit and we'll need his help."

Jerry smiled at this tactic and, to identify Clarence, came up with one of his own. Since he couldn't find the board members listed on the Power Learners' website and didn't want to wait until Saturday and golf, he had Francine call the school.

"...to check on a board member whose last name seems to be missing from our list," she said, per Jerry's instructions. "We want to recognize local 'Friends of Education,' those who have contributed their time to improve the quality of education in our area over the last year. Let's see, Clarence is his first name. Oh! *Was* on the board? Yes, it's an award for his participation, a nice certificate," she lied adroitly. "You don't have an address by any chance? No? I can try through his company? And his last name is?" She ended the call and turned to Jerry and whispered, "Halvorsen," intrigue dripping off each syllable.

"Francine, that was brilliant," Jerry rewarded her.

Pat, meanwhile, had looked into the records on consultants hired by the school district over the past year. "It's true," she told Jerry, "that if the service or purchase is over $2500, there needs to be Board approval. But almost all of these were under that amount, $2200, $1900, and so on. I certainly didn't hear about most of these. I'd ask Elliot, but how to do it so he doesn't think we suspect him of something?"

"You probably can't," Jerry answered her. "We'll have to table it for now."

It was the next day that one of the secretaries came hurriedly into Jerry's office, out-of-breath, looking furtively behind her as she blurted out, "Dr. Strauss, Ed Deems is here and would like to see you. I wasn't sure if you knew him and..."

At which point, Ed Deems poked his head in the door, a wide smile on his face, one hand resting on the handle of a furniture dolly. "Got it all done, Super, and I must say it looks swell."

Jerry rose to his feet, murmured, "It's all right," to the secretary and strode out to meet Mr. Deems and his burden with eagerness. "The document box is absolutely beautiful!" he exclaimed. "What a superb job of refinishing you did."

They carried it into his office and placed it carefully on a table, Jerry stepping back to admire the effect, which greatly pleased Mr. Deems.

"Turned out real nice," said Mr. Deems, opening the lid. "And look here, even the innards. 'Course I didn't have to do much but give her a bit of a wax-up inside."

"It's a credit to your handiwork as well as your antiques spotting ability," Jerry lauded him. "Tell me your price," he said, reaching for his wallet.

"On the house, Super," Mr. Deems grinned. "I'm honored it will be residing with a man who's got some savvy."

"But you put a lot of labor into it, not to mention the price you paid," Jerry protested.

"Practically stole it. Guy threw it in with a bunch of other pieces. Tell you what: you bring your friends out to the restaurant from time to time and I'll be pleased."

Jerry laughed. "I'd do that anyway. It's the best place around." He accompanied Mr. Deems and his furniture dolly back to the front entrance. "After I show it off for a bit here, I'll be taking it home so I can have it all to myself."

"You could," Ed Deems affirmed nodding, "even though it's too pretty a piece to shut up anywhere for long. That's why we started putting things out in the restaurant, so folks could appreciate them. Don't know what we'll do with all the furniture though. Got stuff everywhere around the place, in the kitchen and filling up the restrooms. Maybe it's time we sold some. So's I can keep buying," he said with a chortle as they shook hands goodbye.

By the end of the week Jerry and Pat had done what they could to further the investigation, except for one thing which remained: Hank. Jerry had read the report and given it to Pat to read. They were discussing it late on Saturday at Jerry's house. It was the doubt about the remains that was most problematical.

"Is there anything," he asked Pat, "you can think of that might aid Paul with the identification of the body? I suppose there might be dental records."

"I wouldn't think so. Burt had the usual gap-toothed look of a lot of country folk around here," she said despondently. "At least I can say that Hank had no missing teeth. It's awful, but I still want to believe it was Hank who perished in the fire. Otherwise..."

"Very, very worrisome. And we'd all rather avoid gruesome publicity, no way around it."

They were quiet for a while, each thinking how repugnant it was to talk about this subject. Pat broke the silence first. "The urn with the cremated ashes was interred next to his wife, who passed away from cancer ten years ago, and their two children, who died in infancy." She paused for a second. "In many ways he's had a heartbreaking life."

"I can understand why you wanted to protect his reputation," Jerry said sadly. "Well, I'll call Paul on Monday and see where he is on this and what else we can do."

Damn, he thought to himself, surely somewhere there's more information. Someone must know something. Elliot's alleged spies? I wonder how I could find out who they are? *If* they are.

To Pat he said, "Eric Arden's book did arouse my suspicions but, you know, everything about Elliot's role in this is conjecture on our part. Has he been moonlighting doing the charter school business operations? Conflict of interest, I suppose, and he may be up to something in the way of profit-making, but to infer that he's involved in arson and homicide, if it is that, is pretty far-fetched. I've been thinking that we might actually make use of him. He has his fingers in many pies and he has been quite helpful lately."

"He has been very cooperative, I agree. Maybe if you made it a point to talk with him about, oh, some of our concerns regarding the trailer park and what to do about the school site, he might have information he's willing to share."

"It's worth a try certainly. I may ask him to speculate about the fire. I'll set up a meeting with him next week. Take him out to lunch, see how it goes."

"But, Jerry, you'll approach it sensitively?"

"Oh, yes." And I hope, he thought, I can pull it off without my other feelings betraying me.

On Monday morning, Owen pulled into the parking lot of the high school and parked in the space marked *Reserved for Assistant Principal*. He was eager and excited, ready to uncover secrets of the Parker. "A Man with a Mission," he said to himself, narrowing his eyes to a steely glint and checking the effect in the rearview mirror.

Over the weekend, October had firmly established itself with several early frosts. All along the way from Martensdale the leaves were turning, quietly transforming the landscape. Sumacs were starting to flame and maples were going from yellow to gold. Shades of russet were showing in the underbrush. Soon the trees would form a tapestry, a sweep of jewel-like hues, interspersed among the dark green of the conifers. It was the time of year when the Appalachians have the power to break hearts by sheer beauty.

As he drove, Owen pondered again what Keith had said about Cross County's wildness and loneliness. It was impossible to imagine any lurking menaces this splendid day, he thought with cheerful confidence. As the morning sun warmed the air, the mists rose to reveal far ridgelines, and he saw a V-formation of geese heading south. Autumn was fleeting though, Owen reminded himself. Blink and you might miss it, things changed so swiftly. But that sense of brevity brought a needed stimulation, telling one to hurry up with what must be done before the color fades and winter sets in.

He looked around with renewed appreciation. The season's charm lent appeal to each humble settlement he passed, made every back road going off into a hollow beckon seductively, and rendered a glimpsed rustic cabin with smoke rising from its chimney irresistibly idyllic. And who knows, he thought with a kick, maybe one of them holds a clue to the guy with the Parker.

So by the time he got to Colton, Keith's and Lynn's fears notwithstanding, Owen was raring to go.

Chapter 38

Jerry ended a phone call with Paul and sat for a while in deep thought. They'd had a long conversation, but were far from definitive answers.

Paul had put things in motion and had come up empty handed. "You won't believe how many corporations, groups and other entities have 'star' in their names. I think Owen was correct in his assessment of its being a useful cover."

"Nothing doing then?" Jerry asked.

"Not yet, but I have some ideas before we give up along that line."

As for Hank, there was no information on his leaving the country or entering another country, and the same for Burt Hodges, although Burt did not hold a U.S. passport.

"Frankly," said Jerry, "I'm glad you didn't learn that Hank had his passport stamped at a border crossing somewhere and is on the lam."

"But here's another mystery," Paul told Jerry. Clarence, it transpired, was due to arrive at the company's headquarters in Houston a month ago but never showed up.

"Disappeared?" Jerry asked.

"Vanished. His wife has filed a missing person report. He was supposed to have left Pennsylvania in August, and hasn't been seen either here or there."

Jerry said, "I asked the golfing group about him and their assessment was that he'd high-tailed it out of here earlier than expected."

"And went...where? No passport info on him either. Well, it's a big country. At this point I'm guessing he's hiding out, nursing his addiction. If that's the case, sooner or later he'll show up in a drunk tank."

Jerry pictured Clarence as he'd last seen him, belting down whiskeys on the deck at the country club. "It's a possibility," he allowed.

"Burt Hodges. Any ideas?" Paul asked next.

"Pat said he had more than a few teeth missing. And that Hank hadn't. Sorry, that's all we could come up with," Jerry apologized.

"That's helpful. I remember thinking at the time that the superintendent of a school district would have paid more attention to dental health. One more thing you should know. We've decided to make discreet inquiries into the Colton Police Department. The fact that the Chief of Police was instrumental in quashing the report has my chief riled."

Jerry gave a whistle at this news.

"We'd also like to find out who the card players are and see if there's anything to be learned there, but it's going to have to be done obliquely. Perhaps a member of the wait staff at The Pit has kept his ears open," Paul suggested.

"Owen is friendly with all the high school kids, and high school kids know everything that's going on. He may be our best bet."

Paul chuckled at this. "If you can get him to take time out from his quest."

"Quest?" Jerry asked, mystified.

"I hear through the Cider Run grapevine that someone from Cross County has shown up at the shop offering a valuable shotgun for sale, and Owen has been given the job of finding out all the particulars. If, of course, he can locate the seller, who didn't give his name. Need I say that Owen is beside himself with eagerness for this enterprise?"

Jerry laughed heartily. "Sounds like Owen."

"Which reminds me," Paul went on, "one of the dealers at Cider Run has skills in forensic accounting. If it's all right with you, I'd like to make copies of the materials you sent and have Keith take a look at them. He'd be able to spot discrepancies and inconsistencies better than we, and he might find similarities which could shed light on the 'star' angle."

"I've met Keith," Jerry said. "In fact, I bought some antique clubs from him. Sure. Go ahead. If he has questions or needs more data, please tell him to give me a call. Not that I can raid Elliot's office again."

"However," Paul put in, "Keith's findings could take us in an uncomfortable direction, and I know that both you and Pat are concerned about a trail leading to your business manager."

"We'll have to deal with that when it happens. If it happens."

Paul promised to check back with Jerry at the end of the week and sent his regards to Pat before he rang off.

Jerry thought about what his next steps would be. He was dismayed, as was Paul, by their lack of progress. At least, where Elliot was concerned, nothing had pointed in his direction. No news was better than bad news, particularly as he'd arranged to have lunch with Elliot later in the week, and he wanted to keep prejudice to a minimum going into that meeting.

Then Paul's mention of Owen and his quest came into Jerry's mind, and his mood changed dramatically. He could imagine Owen madly pedaling his bicycle around the county, knocking on doors, hot on the trail of the elusive firearm, and the image was so plausibly Owen and yet so comical, that it neatly balanced out the feeling of being stymied.

Meanwhile Owen, armed with the license plate number and a description of the pickup, had settled on a plan to drive around Colton each evening after work in ever-widening circles. Daylight was not lingering as long, so he figured he'd better get started right away. On Monday afternoon he made the first circuit. Although he saw several trucks similar in age and condition to the one Keith described, none had the identifying plate. He did, however, pass the Sure-Shot Taxidermy on the old highway, but since it was after 5:00, the place was closed for the day. On Tuesday he had to stay for the school board meeting, with a staff dinner beforehand, so was unable to go back to the taxidermy or continue his search.

By Wednesday he was getting antsy. He had made afterschool appointments to meet with several students and their parents in order to discuss scholarship options. He hoped they could get through early...so I can hit the taxidermy place, he said to himself, and maybe take a few roads out a bit before I lose the light. Dang! This could take all month. As he was idly looking out his office window into the parking lot, he saw his first appointment, Seth Morgan, stroll out of the building. Nice kid, Owen was thinking. Then he noticed a battered black pickup truck pull in and park, and he saw Seth go up to it as Carl Morgan emerged.

Since it was a warm and fair October day, Jerry took Elliot to the country club for lunch. He was surprised when he learned that Elliot had never been there. "It's well-appointed, and the food and service are good, what you'd expect from the energy industry. May as well take advantage of the place before golf season ends."

"I don't have time for golf," Elliot said, when they were seated and had ordered, although he softened it by acknowledging that he knew people who played there.

Jerry took his cue. "Did you know Clarence Halvorsen by any chance?" he asked. "I heard he was on the board of the charter school. I wanted to have a chat with him and see if he could shed some light on what they're planning."

"Can't say I know him," was Elliot's reply.

"Oh, well, that's water under the bridge anyway, because he appears to have left town," Jerry said.

He noticed that Elliot was on guard at mention of the charter school, or was it Clarence? So he began talking about the good start to the school year. Time for flattery, he decided. "I can't imagine what we would have done without you these past few weeks, helping smooth out transportation snags and coordinating the new breakfast program, as well as the projections you're doing on district revenues and upcoming expenditures."

Elliot shrugged off the praise, commenting instead on the last topic. "We don't know what the legislature is going to do, or how much support we can expect when revenue policies change. That's a wait and see."

"And so is the local economy, with some gas companies pulling out in other parts of the state. If, or more likely when, the boom goes bust, what will be the impact, either directly or indirectly, on schools?"

Elliot shook his head. "We need to continue to keep expenses down in any event. Not build a new school, certainly."

Another lead-in, thought Jerry. "Speaking of Elk Creek School, it's been bothering me that there's been no investigation to speak of. I have questions and, I'll admit, fears, as I'm sure you do too. What's your take on the fire?"

"Oh, grudge arson, without a doubt. We heard all the stories about Cross County's history in that department. There was no point in probing; everyone shut up like a clam."

"Wasn't there supposed to be a report by an investigative team? What did they come up with?" Jerry said this as casually as he could.

"I only heard second-hand," Elliot replied. "It sounded as if Hank may have been more involved than we thought, but the Chief of Police, who was acting for the county, felt it was better to protect Hank's reputation, so the media were told it was never received. The report would have raised more questions than it answered."

So, thought Jerry, some half-truths, just in case Pat had said anything to me about the report. No use pressing any farther along this line. "A bad business," Jerry said by way of tacit agreement.

Jerry thought Elliot had made up his mind to be a little friendlier, because he told Jerry he was looking forward to this school year with the new programs starting up. "Tell me again about how you convinced the energy people to fund vo-tec offerings. You said it happened here?"

Touché, Elliot, Jerry said to himself. You clearly want to change topics.

While the lunch with Elliot was not a success from the point of view of learning much that was definitive, it had been a pleasant meeting, a normal kind of occurrence for school administrators. It had made, Jerry hoped, Elliot feel secure and, as he told Pat later, perhaps secure enough to get careless.

Chapter 39

"It was just too easy!" Owen wailed. "I never got a chance to do any exploring! The whole thing just fell into my lap. Plop!"

Lynn tried to look understanding. He really is disappointed, she couldn't help thinking, his big adventure fizzling out. "Oh, Owen," she said with sympathy in her voice, "but think how much grief I've been spared, worrying about you."

"Still, how can I face Keith when I didn't do anything?" he complained bitterly. "I was so sure I'd have stories about all the cool places I went and the antiques I found and the dangers I confronted to learn about his silly gun. Carl Morgan is going to fill me in before the game and that's that. I mean, I didn't get to go anywhere or see anything suspicious or even scary!"

"Poor baby," was Lynn's last remark on the subject.

On Thursday Jerry got a phone call from the garage in Martensdale that serviced his Land Rover. A part they had ordered, under warranty, Jerry remembered with satisfaction, had arrived and needed to be installed, and could he bring the car up? He decided to go late on Thursday, stay the night and get the car done in time to drive back before the Friday evening football game.

"Maybe," he said to Pat, "I can meet with Paul, find out what he's learned. Do you want to come along? See Sally Ann in her native environment?"

"As intriguing as the idea is, I have meetings I can't miss—the lawyer in the trailer park suit, some parents concerning I'm not sure what, Francine and Elliot about proposed changes in state aid for the district and, last but not least, a hair appointment. No, Jerry, you go ahead and I'll see you for dinner and the game."

"Dinner it is."

After school on Friday, Owen met Carl at the Elk Creek Mobile Home Park. It was a soft, autumn afternoon and the maples in the park shone out, resplendent in orange and red. Owen, who had been there briefly on his spring bike jaunt, looked around appreciatively. "I can see why no one wants to leave this place," he remarked to Carl. The two were walking up to the Morgans' home from the entrance area where Owen had parked.

"Couldn't pry 'em out," Carl seconded. "Them buyers would of had, maybe still will, a fight on their hands. But Mrs. Foster and that Super of yours, now, they say they ain't gonna let that happen."

"You can bet they know how to fight too," Owen added with a grin.

This Carl Morgan, Owen thought, I can see why Seth is such a great kid. His dad may not look like much, but he's a spunky, caring person. He wants me to meet his family, his grandfather who owns the gun. This is a damn honor, thought Owen humbly. Maybe I'll have something interesting to tell Keith after all.

This Mr. Griffith, Carl was thinking, he's like the Super. I think I'll hang out with him a whiles after we see Pappy, and let him in on a few things. Yep. Might just do that. 'Bout time someone knew what's been going on.

Pat went to her meeting with the school district lawyer and they discussed strategies for the up-coming hearing about the mobile home park. While the buyers seemed to have let things lie for the present, the district did not want to lose momentum. The meeting left her feeling positive, and also reinforced her sense of purpose. She went into the next meeting in a mood of optimism.

The parents she met with had come in from one of the farther areas of the school district. They told her she was their last hope. Pat listened with her social worker side coming to the fore.

"It's like this, Miz Foster, we heard you was helping kids like these a few years back and then you din't come out anymore. People don't know what to do so don't do nothin'. Maybe you can get someone to come out and talk to them?"

It transpired that, while not the parents themselves of a disabled child, they knew a family who had two sons, motor and speech disabled, and this couple was seeking help for them. From their appearance and demeanor, Pat could tell how concerned they were, and how little they had in the way of resources themselves.

Pat was immediately mobilized. "We'll have someone out there as soon as possible," she reassured them. "I am so glad you brought this to my attention. Yes, you did the right thing, coming to the school district office." She got directions to the home of the children, names of everyone involved, the phone number of a neighbor, and went off to meet with Elliot, a sense of urgency pervading her thoughts. Here was a real problem, here were people, children in fact, suffering from neglect and ignorance. Funding proposals be damned.

Pat sailed into Elliot's office and put her briefcase down on the conference table with a loud *thunk*. Elliot looked up questioningly at this atypical behavior on Pat's part. Francine was not there yet, still doing paperwork for the meeting.

"Elliot," Pat said, getting right to the point, "I've just learned there's a family in the district, up north, way back on Springs Road, almost to the Marten County line, who have two children with severe hearing and speech impairments, one of whom has limited mobility. They're school age and have never been in school."

"Oh, no, Pat!" Elliot exclaimed. "Why haven't we heard of this before? Did they recently move there?"

Pat was gratified that he sounded so concerned. "No, the couple who came in to tell me said they'd lived there for years. Elliot, we must get someone out, someone who can help, say the right things, put them at their ease while evaluating the situation."

"But not you, Pat, although you know best how to do that."

"President of the school board, not county caseworker? I suppose you're right. Darn, I wish Jerry were here. He would take this on, and have them eating out of his hand."

"Up in Martensdale again?"

Pat nodded, a bit disconcerted by Elliot's remark, but too immersed in the plight of children in distress to pay much attention. She looked at her watch. "He should be on his way back to Colton soon. The directions are straight forward enough, and he'll be passing that end of the county coming down. I'll see if I can catch him."

Deciding not to make the phone call in front of Elliot, Pat stepped out into the hall. Jerry's phone, however, was on voice mail mode. She left a brief message, giving him the gist of the problem, and headed back into Elliot's office.

"No luck?" Elliot asked, and Pat shook her head.

Francine came in shortly after with fact sheets she had prepared on school aid changes proposed by the state legislature, and how these could impact district revenues. Pat put her other concerns aside for the moment, knowing she had to be able to understand the latest baffling information from Harrisburg, and somehow communicate the salient points to her fellow board members. And the public, she reminded herself, as she refocused her attention on the meeting.

It took a concentrated effort to translate proposals laid out by legislative committee, and when, at last, they were finished, Pat realized she was overdue for her hair appointment. Francine left to run copies of their summaries, and Pat scrambled to put things back in her briefcase.

"Elliot, I must go," she said rising. "Colleen is staying late for me as a special favor." She hurriedly copied the note about the children and handed it to Elliot. "Here are the directions. You have Jerry's number; will you call him?"

"Yes, of course. Or, actually, I'll have Francine contact him, as I'm heading into another meeting myself."

"Thanks, Elliot."

"By the way, I've been wanting to talk to you about a few things. Maybe we can get together after 6:00?"

He sounded so sincere, and Pat was so distracted in her haste, that she answered, "By all means," as she rushed for the door.

Jerry stepped out into the late afternoon sunlight of Martensdale. He'd spent the last hour with Paul, hearing what he hadn't wanted to hear. Fraud led the discussion.

"I didn't do the heavy lifting on this one," Paul had explained. "It was Keith Mackinnon's scrupulous analyses. You were right in what you suspected about the books being cooked by your business manager, last fall and winter, right up to the time of the fire. He must have been making quite a sum on the side: overabundance of questionable consultants, abnormally high prices paid to certain vendors, suggesting the possibility of kick-backs. Obviously padding the budget here and there."

"The usual," Jerry said with a sad smile. "Well, I'm relieved it didn't go any farther. At least the integrity of the school district isn't totally compromised by his behavior.

The task now is getting him replaced as soon as possible with as little publicity as possible," he said in a confident voice.

Paul waited patiently until Jerry had finished and then, in his mild and diffident manner, went on, "But I'm afraid that isn't all."

Jerry felt a surge of adrenalin knowing he would not like what was coming next.

"I'm afraid it's only the tip of the iceberg," Paul said. "Star Partnership is decidedly involved, and that's where the serious stuff starts."

Jerry ticked off the connections. "Star Partnership, LLC, listed as buyers of the trailer park. Star in the name of the management company used by the charter school. Star on the check that paid for the Smith's timely Florida vacation. What else?"

"Star making a bid to buy the Elk Creek School property after the fire," Paul added.

"Yes, that's right. But the question is, can we tie Elliot to these entities?" Jerry asked.

"I think we can," Paul answered. "And this time we have Sally Ann to thank."

Jerry got into his car, still incredulous at the damning information which had been brought to the surface.

Sally Ann, in her enthusiasm to reconnect Rosie with her Cross County roots, had gotten in touch with Jamie Hodges and invited him and Mel to visit her at Cider Run. They'd toured the shop and had lunch and then, warmed by good food and Sally Ann's accepting and encouraging 'nature, talked about their lives and hopes for the future.

"The thing I picked up on when Sally Ann recounted this to me," Paul had told Jerry, "was that Mel works as a server at a place called The Pit."

"Site of the notorious Saturday night poker games."

"The same. And that your business manager was often in the company of a heavy drinker named Clarence."

Jerry shook his head. "And he told me he didn't know him. No wonder I sensed wariness on his part at that point."

"And Clarence has now disappeared. Why would Elliot lie to you? What was he hiding? This set us to digging a little more into the 'star' thing and finally we found what we were looking for. Clarence's wife in Texas, at her wit's end, has come up with names of all the people her husband had talked about in Colton. Elliot was one of them. She said he called him a 'business associate,' and that they had a corporation that went by the name of Star something."

"I guess I should have known," Jerry said with resignation in his voice.

Paul asked, "Do you know where he went? On his vacation, I mean."

"Not exactly. Something about a cruise and he wouldn't be reachable. Pat thought the Rhine."

"Hmm," was all Paul said.

Jerry shut the car door and sat for a moment. It wasn't that he was wondering what to do about Elliot; it was out of his hands for now. Paul had been in touch with the Cross County Sheriff and would be coming down to help lead a very quiet, but very thorough, investigation into the suppressing of the report. The Colton Chief of Police was being questioned this afternoon. "Of course, what we've learned so far doesn't establish a direct link to the fire itself," Paul had conceded. "Or the former superintendent."

"What I would like to know," Jerry put in, "is whether Elliot read your report."

"That is the first question they are planning to ask. If the Chief of Police admits that Dr. Lucas read the report, or that he was told about our uncertainty regarding the identification of the remains...well, we may have something."

And we've got a huge problem for the district in terms of damage control, Jerry thought morosely. As they shook hands goodbye, Jerry reminded Paul about the big homecoming game he had invited Paul to earlier. "Come down tonight if you can. Owen's wife and Keith and his wife are planning to be there."

Paul replied with a smile, "Only if there's enough time for Sally Ann to get dressed to her demanding specifications."

After Jerry left, Paul made some phone calls and then sat in thought for a while. He had an unpleasant feeling about what was going on in Cross County, and Jerry was heading straight into it. Flinging himself into it at full tilt, he thought with a sigh, and I had better get down there. Homecoming and all the accompanying hoopla as only a small town does it, complete, no doubt, with the fire company parading its rolling stock. Paul realized such a major distraction could easily be used by someone unscrupulous, someone who might be feeling nervous at this juncture. He called Sally Ann, who promptly started pulling together a suitable outfit.

Jerry's first concern now was not just how to think about this appalling thing that was emerging, but how to behave in a normal manner. He was, he admitted to himself, very much entangled in the Colton Area School District; he was damned fond of it, in fact. And he needed to talk with Pat.

He took out his phone, turned it on and switched it to speaker mode, then put it in the console holder. There was a voice mail from Pat and it brought him out of his gloomy thoughts. Disabled children: a problem they could work on and he was quite sure it would have a beneficial solution. He started the car and headed south on the road to Colton.

In the lowering October sun of this golden time of year, each bend in the highway offered another visual feast. Hillsides appeared enchanted, palettes of a hundred glowing colors. Jerry was getting the full measure of Cross County's ability to weave a spell. He relaxed, let himself appreciate the unparalleled panorama of autumn, and began to think of Pat. We will get married. It will work; I'll see to it.

The road to Colton, winding between the hills, intimate and beckoning, was drawing him along, irresistibly drawing him in. "Ah, the road to Colton," Jerry said as he looked around, "the road to Colton..." then found himself finishing the sentence "...is paved with good intentions." Surprised, he gave a short laugh at the uncanny relevance of the old proverb, as his phone registered a call from Francine.

Chapter 40

There is an unwritten, but time-honored, rule in most school districts that the superintendent and high school principals should attend every major home game. For small districts this practice is particularly important and, in the case of football, it amounts to a sacred obligation.

Of course, in a town the size of Colton, everyone goes to the game anyway, and for homecoming not only will the volunteer fire company often use this occasion to show off its equipment, the high school band marches down Main Street, behind which, in Pied Piper fashion, an ever-growing crowd follows and is led out to the football stadium. Restaurants close early to give their employees time off for this crucial sports event and don't reopen again until after the game, allowing patrons to heartily celebrate a win or with equal fervor recover from a loss.

This meant that when the high school principal had to be out of town, Owen was designated to go to the game in his stead, a duty he was more than pleased to undertake. It was also a perfect reason for Lynn to come down, along with Keith and June. Keith couldn't get away in time for the four of them to have dinner together first, but Owen promised they'd visit an authentic Colton hot spot after the game. "There's a place called The Pit. It'll be jumping Friday night," he told them. "Could be an interesting evening."

Jerry had a look at the time after he finished his conversation with Francine. Close to three hours before the game started, and at least two hours of daylight left. Good. He could have a short visit with the family to establish rapport, raise awareness about special education programs the school district offered, and arrange for follow-up. He checked the information and directions Francine had given him. Down south, close to the Boundary Area district. Springs Road, in the vicinity of Jacks Mountain. He'd take the bypass around Colton, feeling confident in where he was going because it was near the locale he and Pat had been to that day in the country. He gave Pat a call, but could only leave a voice mail. "Hi, darling. Francine called with your message and I'm following the scent. Probably won't make it back for dinner, but see you at the game." Then he added, "I love you."

"This here's Coach Griffith, Pappy. He's the one I bin tellin' you about, gonna help Seth with goin' to college."

In the presence of the small, bright-eyed nonagenarian, sitting alertly in his wheelchair, Owen had a gulp of excitement. Here was someone who, though wounded, had doggedly gone under enemy fire and saved the life of his commanding officer during World War II. He'd been awarded medals for valor, Carl had said, and received personal tributes from the officer's family. Owen extended his hand and it was taken in the firm, dry grip of, Owen also realized, the owner of the Parker himself. "I'm honored to meet you, sir," Owen said reverently.

"Son," countered Mr. Morgan, "it's you as whom we're tickled to meet. Seth can't talk about nothin' else. We're that thankful for what you done, him and the team."

"Seth's a super kid." Owen warmed to the subject. "He's not only an outstanding athlete, but he's doing very well academically." Owen wondered briefly whether he was being patronizing, but at Mr. Morgan's eager nod, went on, "We're pretty sure there won't be any problem in his getting a full scholarship to Martensdale, or quite possibly anywhere else he wants to go."

Carl pulled a long face at this last statement.

Mr. Morgan cast an eye on Carl. "Quit yer scowlin'," his grandfather scolded. "I kin see what yer thinkin'. Seth oughta go wherever he wants." To Owen he said, "An' he'll need a car, that's what I bin tellin' this grandson of mine. Why I'm sellin' the Parker."

"I tol' you, Pappy," Carl interjected. "You don't need to sell it."

Mr. Morgan ignored Carl and went on, "Time I sold it. I ain't huntin' no more nor Carl here ain't gonna use it neither. But, lookee, if it's goin' to a friend of yours, no matter he sells it on down the line, that's OK. I'd like that real well."

They talked for nearly a half hour more, Owen explaining about Keith and the shop and, atypically, finding himself talking about his family and growing up in a coal town. Mr. Morgan listened with interest and Carl looked thoughtful. Then Mr. Morgan talked about the war until he began to grow weary. When Owen said goodbye there was another firm handshake and a wink from Mr. Morgan. "You take that there gun up to your friend in Martensdale. He'll know what it's worth. And come back and see me. You can bring your friend along too. That right, Carl?"

"Yes, Pap. Mr. Mackinnon's real nice."

"And, Carl, you go dig out the Parker from wherever you bin keepin' it and see Coach here gets it."

"Yes, Pap," said Carl.

Mr. Morgan sat back in his wheelchair, a pleased look on his face. "I think everything's gonna work out jes' fine now."

"Yes, Pap," said Carl.

"Damn and double damn," Jerry swore to himself. Another unmarked road, climbing up a hillside, only to peter out in a barricade of fallen trees, or turn from passable to boulder-strewn, or narrow itself into a dirt track. All the while his phone stolidly registered *No Service*, and still no Springs Road. "Damn, damn," he swore again. This was farther than he'd thought. But he decided he'd better keep going as long as there was daylight.

I am getting a thorough dose of the contrariness of Cross County, Jerry thought as he drove. The sunlight, slanting in lower now, washed the hills in luminescent amber. All this incredible, alluring beauty, he mused, but when you try to get somewhere, you find it's impenetrable. You can't penetrate; you can't get far enough in, and your only option is to withdraw. Like a fascinating woman who won't have you. Just so far, leaving you frustrated. Is this another secret of Cross County, he wondered with amusement? A sensual, an almost sexual experience, but not all the way: never fulfilled. And yet you keep on trying. He laughed at the idea of such an analogy. Cheered, he drove on, while the sunlight began to fade and, in the gathering dusk, he saw a sign that read *Jacks Mtn. Road.* Close enough, he thought. Maybe Springs Road branches off of it. I may as well try.

Owen followed Carl out to Sure-Shot Taxidermy and, while waiting, peered in the windows of the shop, now closed for the day. Glassy eyes looked back at him, giving him an idea: could the taxidermy figure into the gun quest adventures he'd tell Keith about? No, probably not. After all, Keith was a hunter, Owen remembered. But there was plenty to recount: how the gun had been in the family of the officer whose life Mr. Morgan had saved, and how it had been used in Africa on safari, how the family had felt such gratitude for Mr. Morgan that they wanted him to have it. Lots of dramatic stuff for Keith.

Carl came out carrying the wrapped-up Parker and they carefully loaded it into the trunk of Owen's car. Once again,

Carl had that look from when Owen told about growing up in coal country. "You goin' to the game?" he asked.

Owen nodded and Carl went on, "You got a little time, we could go somewheres hereabout you might like to see."

"Sure," agreed Owen, thinking it had more to do with the Parker's history. "And then let me buy you supper, before I have to be at the stadium."

"It ain't far," said Carl. "We can take my truck."

Elliot called Pat at 5:45. He was, Pat thought, kindness itself. Could they meet for a drink before dinner? There were a number of school district items to discuss that, in the whirl of meetings and new school year activities, had gotten put off. "And I haven't had a chance to tell you about that Rhine cruise I took. I know you were interested."

This was too much for Pat to pass up. Imagine hearing about his vacation! Elliot had seemingly turned over a new leaf. Maybe no longer being lovers meant they could be friends. Maybe they could have a friendly and normal relationship. She told him she'd be glad to meet him. Jerry's message had said he'd have to postpone dinner. I guess I could actually have a meal with Elliot. That would be different.

She opted for 6:30. But what was open in town? Nothing during the lead-up to the game, with the parade and all. And she wasn't going to suggest her house.

"As unlikely as it sounds," Elliot told her, "The Pit is open, but only the part not visible to the street. If you don't object, we could meet there. It isn't as bad as some think, and they make a very good Martini."

Jerry headed up Jacks Mtn. Road. "Rock-strewn, rutted and wretched," he alliterated out loud, as the Land Rover bumped up the hill, giving the impression that at any moment it would bottom out. "Sorry, Beast," he said to it.

"But that's what you were brought on to do: suffer gallantly in the service of Colton Area School District." He winced as the car hit a partially buried rock. No wonder these kids have been hidden for so long, he thought.

He saw no houses, which struck him as odd, because Francine said there was a neighbor. Maybe on the other side of this damned mountain, he thought. But, wait, there was a house up ahead, set back, beyond which the road apparently came to an end. There was a gravel patch on the side and he pulled in. Someone must be there, he thought; he could see smoke curling up from behind.

Jerry parked and got out, taking stock of the dismal nature of the place. It was only a cabin; couldn't be more than one room wide. It was already getting dark, and the gloom was reinforced by the heavy forest growth around and beyond. I sincerely hope I've come to the wrong house, he thought. What a horrible place for children. He mounted the steps to a derelict porch, thinking that this was above and beyond awful, and also becoming aware of an unfamiliar scent in the smoke. Kind of like, what was it, ammonia? The porch held an array of junk and cast-off furniture which, from long habit, his eyes flickered over and they rested for a second on a small table holding a mass of magazines. He had just raised his hand to knock when the front door flew open, and Jerry found himself looking into the barrel of a no-nonsense 12-gauge shotgun.

Chapter 41

"**O**h, man! Oh, man!" exclaimed Owen, shining his flashlight in a wild arc. "Oh, man! Wait'll I tell Keith!" He adjusted his helmet light and grinned at Carl.

Carl would have grinned back, but being conscious of his lack of several teeth, he rarely smiled. "Yeh. Thought you'd like this place," he said casually, belying the fact that he was tremendously pleased at Owen's reaction to the mine tunnel.

They'd climbed down the ladder Carl had put in during the summer and were standing on the tracks. In addition to flashlights and helmets, Carl had brought jackets for the two of them. He'd been keeping extras in the truck so he could take Seth sometime, but when his grandfather got Owen talking about coal mines, he thought, what the hell, Coach here oughta get a bang out of this.

He also had an agenda item, namely to tell Mr. Griffith about the Doc, and this seemed like the place to do it. For too long he had been carrying around the burden of knowing about Elliot's activities, and it had gotten heavier than he could shoulder. Carl needed to unload.

He'd already talked with Jamie about the Doc's attentions to Mel. Jamie was, not surprisingly, livid. Carl tried to calm him down. "Now don't you go an' blame Mel. She din't do nothin' to bring it on. Fact is, she always looked disgusted and walked away fast as she could."

"I ain't blaming Mel," Jamie answered. "But if I ever get that son'fa bitch alone I'm gonna break every bone he's got."

"Ain't a good idea, Jamie. He's the type will get even. He's mean and low down. You don't wanna provoke a viper."

"I'll kill him."

"Listen, Jamie. I got a feeling he ain't gonna be around here that much longer. Jes' a feeling."

Now, in the mine, Carl planned on telling Owen all he knew. Coach is thick with the Super, he reasoned. Once the Super knows what's been goin' on, the Doc is gonna be history. Hey, in fact, they're friends with that detective guy from Martensdale. Yep, the Doc is gonna be history.

As they set out in the deserted mine tunnel, Owen forgot about everything else: the game, the time, even supper. He was so fascinated with the experience and the bits and detritus of mining operations scattered about that he couldn't stop talking. At one point he picked up a dented tin lunch bucket. "Can I keep this?" he breathlessly asked Carl.

"Ain't mine. Don't think anyone else would want it. No use carryin' it along," Carl said, as Owen cradled it under his arm. "We kin get it on the way out."

"Wow. Keith will never believe this!" He had a moment's reflection on what Lynn's reaction to his adventure would be, but was enjoying himself too much to let it dampen his enthusiasm.

Carl had a thought. "Din't you say you was into games and such?"

"Big time," Owen answered.

"Know where there's some old pinball machines up ahead, stuff got thrown out and jes' layin' around."

"Pinball machines? Are you kidding? Hey, lead the way."

Carl hadn't begun to talk about Elliot yet. Owen kept him busy, asking questions and making observations, and they made a few excursions into branching tunnels. Every knee pad, fuse box and pick was worthy of delighted scrutiny to Owen. I'll tell him on the way back, Carl decided.

By the time they got to the area beneath The Pit, close to an hour had passed.

Since black and gold were the colors of the Colton Area School District, Sally Ann used them as her wardrobe theme for the evening. Black and gold had been chosen for school colors in the late 1800s in honor of the black gold—coal—that was enriching the community. The Critter as mascot came during the Great Depression, after an earlier mascot, the Coyote, had been put on the list of Pennsylvania predators to be shot on sight.

Sally Ann had donned black tights, a black skirt and black turtle neck sweater, completing the ensemble with a 1960s vintage golden yellow plaid silk scarf. She was quite urbanely chic, turning heads as she and Paul, with Lynn and the Mackinnons, made their way into the stands at the stadium. Only a few years ago her outfit would have been deemed condescendingly ostentatious but now, with energy company executives and their families here, dressing with a touch of class was no longer automatically viewed with contempt.

Paul, meanwhile, was worried and kept consulting his watch, as they seated themselves in the area reserved for the Superintendent and High School Principal. Lynn was distraught. She'd called Owen at least four times and got no answer. Paul, on his part, had tried to get Jerry with no luck. The group discussed possible school district crises that could have caused their delay, and tried to convince themselves that things would work out soon.

Paul knew it could be far more serious, but kept his thoughts to himself. Sally Ann looked around for Mel and Jamie, as she was going to meet with them before Mel had to work a shift, but didn't see them anywhere.

And Pat, thought Paul. Where is she?

Jerry considered the present menace confronting him. Heavy-set, powerful-looking guy holding a gun, probably loaded with buckshot. Night coming on, isolated location. All right, Jerome, he said to himself, how are you going to handle this one?

The voice holding the gun rasped out, "What you want, mister? What're you doin' here?"

What possible reason could he have to be there? Buy meth? That would never be believed. His ignorance about the proper conventions regarding drug purchases would give him away in an instant. On the other hand, he had stopped at an ATM before he left Martensdale and had two hundred dollars in cash, so with practiced skill in negotiation he plunged in.

"Hey, don't get all heated," delivered in a pleasant, though slightly aggrieved, tone. "I came all the way up your damned road to make a deal."

The gun was not lowered one iota. "What're you talkin' about? I don't make no deals here."

"Friend of mine said you might." Jerry heard the gun click. "Said you had a piece of furniture, could be worth the drive." Jerry pointed to the table supporting the magazines and thought, this sure as hell better work.

The gun was lowered slightly. The gaze shifted to the table in question.

"Said it might be worth refinishing; that's what I do. Buy antiques to restore. I'm always looking. So is he."

The voice got harder. "Don't think I believe you, mister. You ain't the first one come up here in a fancy car. I think we're going to take a walk around back."

"Hey, my friend said..." God, thought Jerry. This is going to be difficult.

He was rudely interrupted. "Who's this friend and how the hell would he know about some table settin' on my porch? Huh? I don't know what your game is, mister, but I ain't takin' no chances. Let's walk," he grunted.

Jerry shrugged as if he were used to this kind of drill and said, in as confident a tone as possible, "Ed Deems." He was going to continue, starting with an explanation about the barbecue place, but it wasn't necessary. The gun was lowered.

"Damn, Ed!" the voice exploded. "He oughta' know better than send some rube up here. OK, mister. Cost you $100."

"Would you take $80?"

"You got cash?"

Jerry nodded, reached for his wallet and took out four $20s.

"I'll help carry it to your car."

The first sight that greeted Owen when they came to the area beneath The Pit was the coal car, resting on the last bit of track. The first thing Carl saw was Elliot, coming down the stairway, illuminated from above.

"Douse yer lights, Coach!" Carl ordered in a sudden fierce whisper.

"Huh?" said Owen, engrossed in appreciation of the coal car and playing his flashlight over it.

Light blazed up as Elliot flipped a switch. It was then Carl noticed that Elliot held a pistol, aimed at them.

"You got the wrong guys, Doc," Carl began. "We ain't been snoopin', jes' explorin'."

Elliot came closer, and Carl had enough presence of mind to put his hands up.

"Now, Doc," Carl began, as Owen stood looking in total disbelief first at the gun and then at Elliot.

Elliot said in a cold even voice, "No one can hear us down here. No one even knows about this place. I could shoot you without any trouble. Take those helmets off."

Owen said only, "Why?" and it came out high-pitched and squeaky.

"None of your business why, Griffith. People are trying to pin things on me and I'm not about to let that happen. Get over here and get down." He indicated the floor by a support pillar.

As Owen stood dazed, Carl obeyed and sat down on the floor. Elliot whipped around and slugged Owen in the stomach, and Owen crumpled, helmet and flashlight flying.

"Hey! Coach din't do nothin' to deserve that!" Carl protested.

Elliot ignored him and took a length of cording out of his pocket. When he had secured the two, he said, "I'll be back," and went up the stairway, turning off the light and slamming the door at the top.

Pat parked in the lot behind The Pit. Elliot had suggested the location, the street in front being clogged with cars parked for the parade and game. Although Pat had been to The Pit a few times, as she climbed the stairs to the back entrance, she realized it had even more of a seamy look to it. There were only a few lights on inside, no doubt so customers would be discouraged from thinking it was in full operation.

Elliot met her at the door and locked it behind her. "They asked me to keep it locked," he explained, when she looked questioningly at him, "as they aren't fully staffed until the game ends."

He went on, "I got a table for us in one of the private rooms in the back. They've already brought us a bottle of chardonnay—I know how much you like it. Was that right?" he asked.

My, thought Pat, he is doing his best. She knew this was a deliberate stance to seek her approval, but even so, she couldn't help having a sense of relief at the lessening of suspicion his behavior tonight brought forth. So, seated at a table in a very dimly lighted back room, she smiled at him as he poured, clicked glasses to wish the Critters luck, and complimented him on the choice of wine.

"I'm so glad you could meet me, Pat," he said. "I was afraid you were still mad at me."

"Why should I be mad at you, Elliot? You've been absolutely indispensable this fall, solving all sorts of problems at the district and keeping things on an even keel."

"I was thinking about the summer. You weren't well and I wasn't the best of company."

What an admission, she thought. "Forgotten, Elliot," she replied, smiling at him.

"And then," he went on, "after I got back, I got immersed in new school year issues, not to mention Celeste."

"Celeste?" Pat asked.

"The young woman doing research here. Down from Martensdale, one of Eric Arden's graduate students. Didn't Jerry tell you about her?"

"I think he mentioned her," said Pat. What is he doing? she thought. Trying to make me jealous?

"Oh," he said, "I guess I shouldn't be surprised Jerry was closed-mouthed. That really, Pat, was what I wanted to talk to you about."

Jerry and a grad student? Come on, Elliot, she thought; you can't be serious. Aloud she said, "About Celeste?"

"No. About Jerry."

There was a long pause while Pat took a drink of wine and put her glass down again very slowly.

Elliot continued, "About Jerry and someone named Ruth." He paused, then went on, "Ruth Arden."

Pat composed herself as best she could and said simply, "Let's have it, Elliot."

Jerry carefully navigated the dark road down the mountain and headed back to Colton. It was obvious his gun-toting host was a businessman, even if not a great one. I guess the least I can do is give him a few days to relocate his operation before I blow the whistle. He admitted to himself that he was still in a state of semi-shock at his escape, and he vowed to repay Ed Deems a hundred times over. Then he turned his attention to Pat and the time. Already late for the game. Phone still out. He kept driving north and when he had finally crossed the all-important, invisible line of cell phone service, the phone miraculously rang. It was Paul, at the game. Where, he asked, was Jerry?

"Sorry I'm late. I got sent on an errand and ended up in the wrong place. I'll explain when I get there. Tell Owen, please. And tell Pat I'll give her a call."

"Well, there's a problem, Jerry," Paul said in his quiet way. "Neither of them are here. Both Pat's home phone and her cell aren't being answered. Lynn has been trying to reach Owen with no luck. Do you have any idea where they might be?"

"Not at the game?" Now what, Jerry thought, and felt a sense of foreboding. "The last thing I knew Pat was going to a hair appointment. She had a meeting with Elliot and Francine first. But that was over before 4:30. Or so I thought. Owen...I don't know. I think he was going to see someone about the gun."

Cheering had erupted and Paul had to wait until it settled down. He went on, "I can't really talk here and there is some new information. Sally Ann is doing fine with her friends. Why don't I meet you somewhere? Your place?"

Jerry gave Paul directions, tried to reach Pat to no avail, and continued on, hoping desperately all the while that Pat would be at his house when he got there.

Pat had been listening to Elliot's recital, hardly touching her wine. Now, when he paused, she realized her mouth was very dry and she didn't feel she could trust her voice. She took a drink and put the glass down with care.

"I hesitated telling you, Pat," Elliot was saying. "But I felt you should know what he's been up to. Those trips to Martensdale. I imagine Ruth's being so close was too much for him not to want to rekindle an old romance."

Pat's phone rang. She took it out of her jacket pocket, saw it was Jerry calling, and quickly hit the *Decline* button. She put it on the table.

Elliot continued, "Celeste doesn't think the people at Cider Run are aware of the extent of their relationship, but she couldn't help guess, being several times with Professor Arden and his family. It all came together for her when she met Jerry."

Pat looked down. "I don't think I want to hear any more, Elliot," she said.

"No, I'm sure you don't. It gets more involved and messy, but I'll spare you." With this statement he gave her an offensively sympathetic smile.

"Look, Elliot," she said, "if you don't mind, let's change the subject. Tell me about your vacation. I'd like to hear about the Rhine." In case I want to run away, she thought, and right now that's exactly what I'd like to do.

The phone rang again and Elliot picked it up. "You'd rather not talk to Jerry right now, would you? Here. I'll cut him off," he said, ending a call which had registered *Paul Willard* and pocketing the phone.

"Thanks, Elliot," said Pat, still dazed from Elliot's disclosures, and not sure what to think. Could she believe Elliot? How far should she go to corroborate with Jerry what Elliot had disclosed? Did she want to accuse Jerry, interrogate him? Her head was spinning. Jerry seeing someone else. Jerry being dishonest. Jerry duplicitous. I will not cry in front of Elliot, she told herself.

Elliot said, "I also wanted to mention that some discrepancies on the books from last fall and winter might look suspicious when we have the next district audit."

Pat paid attention here. "What discrepancies?" she asked, still shaken but coping.

"I tried to cover them up as best as I could, to save Hank. But he was in debt and had me pad expenses for him. I should have spoken up sooner, but I know how much he was respected and, after the fire, I thought I could just take care of it without anything having to come out."

Pat found her wits. "Where *is* Hank?" she asked succinctly.

"Oh, Pat, you poor thing," said Elliot in a deprecating voice, as if she were daft. "You know where he is, there next to his wife."

"No, Elliot, I don't think so."

"What do you mean? What makes you say that?"

"If you read the report that came out after the fire, the one we decided to suppress, you would know what I'm talking about."

"No, I didn't. The Chief wouldn't let me," Elliot said decisively.

Pat was quiet. Maybe he didn't read it, maybe he's telling the truth. "Well, Elliot, I did and there was doubt that the remains had been correctly identified."

"Good Grief! What a shock!" he exclaimed. "Who in the world did they think it was? The arsonist, I guess."

"They don't know. Speculation is on Burt Hodges."

"Burt?" Elliot asked, looking perplexed. "Why Burt?"

"He's been missing since the fire."

"And many times before. Pat, I have no idea about Burt. Except that he should have been replaced years ago, given his record of absenteeism."

Pat shrugged. She knew she was probably on dangerous ground, and should quit this line of inquiry. She hoped one of the wait staff would come in; it seemed very quiet in the place.

Elliot changed the subject. "The Rhine is spectacular, Pat. Did I mention that?"

She answered absently, "I'm glad you enjoyed it," then gave him a frank look. "What happened to Hank, Elliot? Do you know?"

Elliot drew a long breath. "He was way over his head in debt. That's all the information I have," he said in an annoyed tone.

Frustrated by this game of cat and mouse, she decided to draw him out. "And was he part of the Star partners too?"

Elliot must have realized the implication of what she had said, because Pat saw his eyes go hard and cold. He got up from the table and came around to her side. He grasped her hand.

Pat could hear her phone ringing in his pocket. "Give me my phone, Elliot," she commanded.

He took it out and threw it across the room where it smashed against the wall and ceased ringing.

Chapter 42

In total darkness and lashed back-to-back against a pillar, Carl contemplated their options. Won't do no good to shout, he reasoned. He tested their restraints. Nor waste energy tryin' to wriggle out. Think up what to do when the bastard comes back.

Owen stirred and let out a little groan. "Coach! You all right?" Carl asked.

"Yeh," Owen said weakly. He was determined not to fall apart. I must be in denial, he thought. I can't believe this is happening.

"Glad to hear you're OK, Coach," Carl replied. "Gotta 'pologize to you," he said.

"You don't owe me an apology, Carl," Owen said. Gaining strength, he went on, "I wanted to see this place."

"Naw, not that. I was gonna warn you about the Doc. He's a bad sort. Pretty sure he was the one got Burt to set fire to the school an' who knows where Burt's at now? Always wantin' me to spy on people. Pretty sure he's behind the sale of the park too. He's a bad sort," Carl repeated.

Owen was stunned. Carl had known all along. He could see how Elliot had scared him into silence. That Carl would speak up now showed a great deal of bravery. The enormity of their present predicament hit home to Owen. "Carl, we're in trouble," Owen said resignedly, spirits sinking again.

Gotta keep him goin', thought Carl. "Hey," he said, "Couple good ol' Welsh boys like us oughta be able to think up somethin' ta outwit that snake."

Owen managed a little laugh.

Carl tried again. "Coach, you got kids, ain't you?"

Owen gulped, thinking of Robbie and Gil. With an effort he answered, "Robbie's seven and Gil's five. God..."

"They shootin' squirrels yet? I can skin out a squirrel quick as you please an' make it into a real nice hand puppet. Bet they'd love it. You bring 'em down sometime, Coach, and I'll demonstrate."

Owen knew he had an obligation to keep his end of the conversation up; Carl was doing all the work. "I'd like to have them down. Lynn is here now for the game," he got out, before he choked up.

"Yeh," said Carl in a quiet voice. "Me an' Seth was gonna go too."

Owen thought, change the subject before we both lose our minds. "Where are we anyhow? I couldn't see a damn thing before he clobbered me. You're right, Carl. He is a dirty son-of-a." Get mad, Owen, he told himself.

Carl was relieved that Owen had rallied enough to be angry. "Near as I can figure, we're down below The Pit."

"Where they sold the illegal booze and all?"

"Yep. Got a bunch of junk down here. Where I saw the pinball machines."

This took Owen's mind back to the carefree life at Cider Run and the uncertainty of his ever seeing it again. "Aw, hell," he swore, in much the same way as Carl.

The two were quiet for a few moments.

Carl broke the silence. "OK. I bin thinkin' we need to plan what to do when he comes back."

Owen spoke up, "You know him better. What do you think he's likely to do?"

Carl didn't want to conjecture, given Burt Hodges' unknown fate, but he needed to keep talking. "Maybe use us for hostages?" he ventured.

Owen thought a moment. "Depending on how desperate he is, it might make sense. And in that case, we're of value to him."

"Yeh. Why he didn't blast us to start with." What should they do? He tried to rub his chin in the way he usually did when the situation called for thinking, but couldn't move his hand. Aw, hell, he said miserably to himself.

The two lapsed into a dispirited silence.

Pat rose to her feet as the phone bounced to the floor. "I'm ready to leave now, Elliot," she said in an icy tone.

"Not yet, Pat," Elliot answered. "I have more I want to say. And I apologise for smashing your phone. I didn't mean to," he said, voice full of contrition. "It's just that you've been given a few pieces of information, wrong information, and you believe they point to me. You've obviously been misled by people who are trying to incriminate me."

"Have I?" she asked coldly.

"I'm as worried about Hank as you are. If he didn't set the fire himself, he must have gotten Burt to do it. Or anyone might have hired Burt. It's too horrible to think he'd cause a man to die like that."

"I cannot believe it of Hank, Elliot."

"I can't either. But what are we to think? He owed money, Pat. He begged me to help him out. He was aware of the Star management group that the charter school employs. Is that what you were referring to? Maybe he used that name for a get-rich scheme of some sort. He was close to being ruined, you know."

Pat sat back down. Elliot was beginning to be convincing. She wasn't at all sure that her mind wasn't confused, in no small part because of Elliot's disclosures about Jerry.

Elliot said, "The Chief told me the report hinted at Hank's problems. That was why, you remember, we didn't want it to get out."

"And yet, there was no mention of anything like that in the report."

"No? I wonder why the Chief thought there was," Elliot said, wrinkling his brow "Look, Pat. I'm mystified about Hank. We'll just have to go on until we find out. Why Detective Willard has been sniffing around again—oh, yes, he's been seen—I can't imagine, but I can guess: someone has tried to make me the fall guy."

Pat said, "If you are innocent of wrong-doing, Elliot, you should come forward to tell your side of the story. Covering up for Hank would be understandable. I wonder if we all wouldn't have done the same." And yet, her mind said, where in the world is Hank? There were just too many loose ends for her to think clearly. She looked at her watch. "I'm supposed to be at the game, so I think we'd better end this conversation now, before someone comes looking for me." She tried a wan smile after this statement.

"All right. I'll walk you to your car," he offered.

Paul had driven by the homes of both Pat and Elliot on his way to Jerry's. He'd seen no cars of the description he'd been given. As he turned on Main Street, he found it still blocked by the traffic cones put up for the parade. Not particularly wanting to advertise his presence in town to the local constabulary, he turned down an alley. And there he saw the BMW and Pat's sedan in the parking lot of The Pit.

He called Jerry. "Parking lot off the alley. Yes. I'm going to call for back-up from the County. No windows overlook where I am right now. See you here momentarily?"

When Jerry pulled into the alley adjacent to the parking lot of The Pit, he saw Pat's car parked next to Elliot's. The sight made his stomach lurch.

Paul met him as he got out. "As far as I can tell, there is no one else in the place."

Jerry could feel his heart begin to race. "What can I do? Pat means the world to me. I guess you already know that," he added, looking anxiously toward The Pit.

"We're waiting for the County boys now; then we'll move. But in the meantime, there are a few things to tell you. One is that the Chief of Police had a bit of a breakdown in the interview this afternoon. Told our man that when he balked at Elliot's wanting the report pulled off the record, he'd been threatened with blackmail over some poker winnings."

"Elliot read the report then. Why go to such lengths if he hadn't?" Jerry reasoned.

Paul nodded. "Oh, he'd read it all right. The Chief said he handed it to Elliot the minute he finished. Chief is scared. I think he's telling the truth. This is his home town; he's got a lot going here and doesn't want to jeopardize his reputation."

"Adds up, I guess," Jerry allowed.

Paul went on, "Second, someone with the name Elliot Lucas was booked on a Rhine cruise departing from Basel a few days after the start of Elliot's vacation date."

"So Pat was right. He did go there after all."

"He *went* there. Passport checked at the airport in Basel. But the cruise company said he never showed."

Jerry shook his head over that. "I can't see Elliot doing a stint mountain climbing. What do you do in Switzerland when you can't ski? Open a Swiss bank account..." Jerry started to say, then looked questioningly at Paul. "You don't think...?"

"That's what I did think. Or some kind of money laundering. Maybe a loan. It would be difficult to check. Swiss financial institutions are a different world. But the cruise no-show does make those things possible."

"Paul," Jerry asked, "what the hell are we up against with him?"

Paul was reluctant to tell Jerry what he was pretty sure Elliot's next moves would be. But Jerry had better be informed. "I think he's feeling cornered, and I think he's going to act. I'm afraid he sees Pat as a bargaining chip."

Oh, God, no, was Jerry's anguished thought.

A car pulled in and two officers emerged. Paul went to consult with them, then came back to Jerry. He said, "There isn't as much back-up as I would have liked, since the home game gets priority. But I think we can pull this off. Would you agree to walking boldly in and confronting him? You'd have me and two more at your back, but we'll stay out of sight. If it's you, he may get rattled enough to talk and give us the information we need to nail him," Paul suggested.

"I'll do anything to make sure Pat is safe," Jerry responded.

"Thank you, Jerry," Paul said, and went on, "I've already checked the two entrances off the parking lot and they're locked. We're going to gain access by the front door; our men know the place. The only illumination seems to be from the back, so we'll head that way."

They walked around to the front, so failed to see a van with its lights off pull into the alley.

It was half-time at the game and, against all expectations, the Colton Critters were winning. Sally Ann made her way down to the refreshment area to meet Jamie and Mel. Not finding them, she returned to her friends in the stands.

"No show?" asked Keith.

"I don't understand it. We were planning to get together before Mel had to go to her job. They were looking forward to meeting you and everything." Sally Ann had a way of appearing inconsolably sad when she met with obstacles. And an equal ability to register radiant happiness the moment she saw a way to rectify the problem. These two emotions crossed her face in the space of a few seconds, the radiant look prevailing. She said brightly, "I know where Mel works, so why don't I go down there before her shift starts?"

Keith asked, "Where's that?"

"It's called The Pit and it used to be an old Speakeasy. Like Cider Run was during Prohibition."

"Oh, right!" Keith said. "Owen told me about it. He planned for us to go there after the game."

Meanwhile, the Battle of the Bands, a favorite Cross County ritual, was starting up. This hugely entertaining tradition of rivalry had, as an integral part, an increasing crescendo of cheers, jeers and catcalls hurled across the field by the opposing fans. As the crowd warmed to its task, the music was effectively drowned out. Conversation became difficult.

"Problem is," Sally Ann said in close to a shout, "that Paul, wherever he went, took the car." The look of abject misery was threatening to appear on her pretty face again.

"Well," Lynn shouted back, "I can't just sit here any longer wondering what's happened to Owen. Let's take your car, Keith, and we'll all go."

"Did I come in this way?" Pat asked. They had wound through a labyrinth of connecting rooms and hallways, going down several short flights of stairs, and were now in a storage area. Boxes, crates, cartons and cleaning equipment lined the walls. Pat indicated a door opposite to the hall from which they entered. "I can't remember if this was the doorway. There are so many nooks and crannies in this place."

"That's a closet. But behind here is one that opens on a stairway going down to an entrance on the parking lot." He started to move a few boxes. "I wonder who covered it up? Not very smart of them," he complained. "I've gone this way often. Well, you've no doubt heard about the poker games."

Pat allowed herself a little laugh at this admission. "I guess everyone knows. And no one seems to care. Except for a few wives, that is. Tell me," she went on, as Elliot continued to move boxes, "was Hank ever a part of that group?"

"Pat," Elliot said in an exasperated tone, "get off Hank. I've told you what I know."

She'd heard footsteps somewhere in the building, and they seemed to be coming closer. Elliot, she was sure, was making too much noise to hear. Emboldened by the thought that staff had returned, she made one more stab at getting to the truth. "But Clarence was, wasn't he?"

Elliot, one hand on the now exposed doorknob, turned around to face her. In horror, Pat saw his other hand held a pistol. She stood frozen.

All at once, Jerry was in the room with them. "Yes, tell us, Elliot," he said acidly, "Was Clarence Halvorsen part of your group?"

Elliot pushed Pat in front of him. "Pat is leaving here with me. One move from you and I leave without her. Understand?"

He kicked the door open behind him and Jerry could see a stairway going down into darkness and realized, at the same time, that Elliot had a pistol thrust in Pat's back. What could he say to keep Elliot, obviously desperate and seemingly now volatile, from taking someone's life? Pat's! His Pat! Would Paul and the officers, who were within earshot, hold back? If they came barging in now, it might bring disaster. But surely they knew that.

He had to try. He softened his voice. "Elliot, I don't know how you've come to this pass, but let Pat go. If you want a hostage, take me," he offered.

Any doubts Pat had about Jerry evaporated instantaneously.

Elliot sneered. "I don't need you. I don't even need Pat. I've got two people ready and waiting. But as I said, Pat's leaving with me. So get back!" Elliot shouted, and Pat could feel the pistol dig into her ribs. She gave a little shriek.

Jerry tried again, "Nothing needs to come out, you know. School districts are famous for circling the wagons. We all want to protect Colton Area's reputation."

"Too late for that now," Elliot said savagely. "Oh, I saw Ed Deems go into your office. He knows everybody in the county and can't keep his mouth shut. Told you I was at his place, didn't he?"

"I swear to you, Elliot, Ed would never do anything that could malign the district."

Pat found her voice. "Elliot, all you've done is try to help Hank, and maybe it got carried too far. No one suspects you of anything. It's not worth it to risk everything because of petty fraud. We know you're not responsible for the fire or for Hank's disappearance."

"Be reasonable, Elliot," Jerry implored. "Put the gun away. We can deal with this."

"I can't take the chance," he said angrily. "No one can be trusted."

"At least let Pat go," Jerry tried one more time.

For answer Elliot pushed her roughly into the doorway and turned the gun on Jerry.

Chapter 43

Seth had been waiting for his dad so they could go to the game. He couldn't raise him on his phone and now was concerned enough to ride his bike out to the taxidermy. But Carl wasn't in his room and his truck wasn't there; instead, he saw the car that belonged to Coach. It was too late to call his friends for a ride. And his dad's tardiness bothered Seth, so much so that he got back on his bike to look for him. He must be with Coach, he told himself, and he probably took him somewhere he knows about. Let's see. Where might that be? The only thing he could come up with was the place down in the gully where his dad went to dig bait. Well, maybe they decided to go night fishing. Coach was a fisherman. Naw. Dad wouldn't do that. Or would he? Seth knew his dad was nuts enough for a zany antic like that.

Sure enough there was the truck, parked by the road cut. Seth took the battery headlight from his bike and set out down the slope. When he got to the bottom the lamp showed him a place where the grass was trampled down. Looking closer he saw brush piled up in the middle. Ah, hah! he thought. As I suspected. Dad's secret bait supply. But when he moved the brush, his light revealed a man-sized hole in the ground and, on closer inspection, a familiar-looking ladder.

"Holy Cow!" Seth shouted with rising excitement. "What have we got here?" Without a moment's hesitation, he clamored down, laughing, as Carl had when he first discovered the tunnel. "So this is what the Old Man has been up to!" he crowed. Everyone knew there was a mine tunnel around these parts. Well, his dad had found a way in. Not to be left behind, Seth started following the coal car tracks. He called now and then, but got no answer, figuring they had a long lead. In high good humor he quickened his pace.

Owen and Carl had been roused from their individual morbid and profitless speculations by what sounded like a commotion at the top of the stairway.

"What the..." Carl started to say, then stopped, and in a low voice said, "Swear I saw a light."

"Where?" Owen asked, peering anxiously into the blackness above.

"Along the tunnel. Comin' this way," he whispered. "Don't look like a helmet lamp nor a flashlight. Too big and bright. More like a...a... Hey! Boy!" he said in a pleased but barely raised voice. "It's 'bout time you got here."

"Dad! Where are you? Turn on your flash!" Seth responded. Then his light picked out the huddled figures by the support post. "Holy crap!" he exclaimed. "What's with you two?"

"Get us outta here," his father commanded him, "and keep your voice down. There's people up there, one of which has a gun."

"Holy crap!" Seth said again.

By the time they were freed, the door at the top of the stairway had opened and a light shone down. The three moved into the shadows.

Pat, staggered by Elliot's shove, pulled herself together. Slightly behind Elliot, she saw the menace facing Jerry. Her fear, like Owen's, had turned to anger and with anger came determination. *I cannot let this happen. I can distract him and Jerry will take his gun away.*

She took a step and Elliot became aware of her location. He kicked the door shut with a violence. It hit Pat, she lost her balance and fell, slipping down the stairway, grasping at the steps, with only a thin line of light from under the door giving the faintest illumination. Part way down in her fall, arm hurt and jacket sleeve torn, Pat managed to stop herself, and she lay huddled, catching her breath. I'm going to get up, she vowed. I'm going right back up there. Then she heard a whisper close by and saw a flashlight's beam.

"Mrs. Foster. It's Owen Griffith. Carl and Seth Morgan are with me. We'll help you down."

"Owen? Thank God! Jerry's in danger. I've got to do something!"

"Let me get you off these stairs. You're bleeding from a nasty gash on your arm that we'd better attend to first. Then we'll muster our troops."

Jerry gasped when he heard Pat tumble. I've got to get to her, he thought frantically. He tried to lunge at Elliot, but found that Paul was behind him and had grabbed him, holding him back.

In a calm voice Paul said, "Dr. Lucas, put the gun down on the floor. I have men with weapons trained on you. Put the gun down and we'll talk."

"We have nothing to talk about. I am walking out of here with two hostages. I'm the only one who knows where they are."

"Owen Griffith," said Jerry, tight-lipped.

"Clever of you, Dr. Strauss. Can you guess the other? He thinks he knows too much anyway."

Paul said, "I have a feeling we already know who he is, and he's been talking to us today."

"I doubt it and I'm tired of this," Elliot said irritably. He drew a bead on Jerry, and reopened the door behind him. "All I wanted was a legitimate business opportunity. But I've been thwarted at every turn. I'm not going to stand by and be accused because of somebody else's problems, of someone else's stupidity and carelessness."

Jerry said, "Put the gun down, Elliot. We are more than ready to give you a fair hearing." I've got to get to her, his head screamed.

"Fair?" he snorted. "No one has ever been fair to me. My ex cheated and took my kids. My partners reneged on deals, let me down and double-crossed me. I'm tired of this," he repeated. He took a step back. "I'm not worried," he said with a sneer. "Cross County keeps its secrets..."

Before he could finish this inexplicable fragment, an explosion of noise came from the direction of the door Elliot had called a closet. In its wake a sudden, blinding thunderbolt burst out, a thunderbolt shouting, "You! Lucas! You scum!" and hurtled itself into Elliot with a force that propelled him backwards through the doorway. The gun fell out of his hand and Elliot, with an outraged cry, plunged headfirst into the darkness below.

Chapter 44

"I never meant to kill him, Detective," said a sobbing Jamie. "I never killed nobody before."

They had gathered in a back room of the restaurant. Mel's arm was wound tightly around Jamie's shaking shoulders. Her cheek was next to his, wet with his tears.

"What's gonna happen to me?" he asked beseechingly.

Paul said, "You're a hero is what you are, Mr. Hodges. You probably saved several lives tonight. What's going to happen is a commendation. But we're going to keep it very, very quiet."

"Oh, God, I hope so. I don't never want it to come out," Jamie said fervently.

"We'll see that it won't," Paul promised.

"Heck, Jamie," said Carl. "You done the world a favor when you come bustin' through that service door. He woulda' finished us off too. Or tried leastways. Endin' up with a broken neck was his own damn fault."

Jerry very gently held Pat's hand, while her arm was being bandaged by one of the officers. A tee-shirt with bright red stains was given back to Seth. "You did a good job there, son, stopping the bleeding," the officer told him.

Sally Ann beamed on Jamie, and Owen shook his hand.

Jamie said, "Sorry we didn't get to meet up at the game. I was just too agitated to go."

"Well, I got tied up and never made it either," said Owen. Lynn groaned.

Keith complained to June, "Why is it I always miss the excitement?"

A week later on Saturday, Pat and Jerry headed to Martensdale on their way up to Connecticut. Autumn was still brilliant in Cross County. "But be forewarned," Jerry told Pat, "the leaves will be past their peak in New England."

"The only thing I care about is whether your mother will approve of me," Pat replied.

"She'll adore you," Jerry assured her. "Then she'll start arranging the wedding." He added, "I did ask you to marry me, didn't I?"

"I believe I was the one who asked you," Pat couldn't help saying.

"No matter," was Jerry's swift reply. "I accept."

They had survived a week of questions asked and some answered, with a picture starting to emerge. Starting, but not yet complete.

Since Jerry's first concern was the integrity of the school district, they were able, with Paul's help, to gloss over what had to be glossed over and make a smooth transition to Francine's becoming the new business manager.

Pat had taken Francine, as an administrator of the school district, to visit the home of the disabled children. Francine's sweet, slightly shy manner helped win over the parents. She arranged transportation, and the children were enrolled in special education programs in school.

Francine had also taken an in-depth look at the district's financial condition, now that she had the authority, and found they were in much better shape than Elliot had led them to believe. A proposal to rebuild a school on the Elk Creek site was going to be made to the board. "And we can withdraw the lawsuit, as the residents' association will finally be able to pursue buying the mobile home park," Pat told Jerry.

"It's a tribute to Francine that she, like others in the know, are entirely agreed to keep the unsavory elements of Elliot's tenure quiet," Jerry said.

The story in the *Colton Clarion* referred to "an unfortunate fatal accident to a valued member of the Colton Area School District staff" who had come upon a door, thought to have been barricaded, "which opened on a precipitous stairway going down to the area once used as a Speakeasy." Owners of The Pit, when interviewed, were "confounded about why the door was not blocked." Prior owners, the *Clarion* went on to say, had apparently "been in the habit of dumping obsolete restaurant equipment and furnishings" in the area. The present owners "want to assure the public that the situation will be remedied within a week," the trash removed and the door secured. Enough time, Jerry thought as he read it, for Paul to have a look around.

Paul stayed in Colton for several days to continue his investigation and he, Jerry and Pat met in Jerry's office daily, sharing what information they had, trying to put things together. Paul told them what he had learned, and also what he conjectured. "Elliot probably discovered that the area under The Pit could be useful," Paul started out. "He must have found Carl's entrance. Like the backdoor of a burrow, it could give him an escape route. I'm pretty sure the hostages would have been released if not needed. Carl wasn't so sure, as he'd been Elliot's eyes and ears for a while."

Pat asked. "Did you speculate about my role?"

"I think he planned to use you as a hostage, before Owen and Carl so conveniently came along."

Pat shivered, and Paul went on, "Carl was one of Elliot's spies. The information he was supposed to report on consisted of what Hank, and later Jerry, and you, Pat, were up to. Elliot was particularly sensitive to being cheated on, I think, from what he said about his ex. Carl said he was approached by Elliot to set fire to the school. He refused, and Elliot said he had others who would be happy to make 'a couple hunert bucks,' as Carl put it, to do the job."

"I guess it was Burt then," Pat said with a sigh.

Paul nodded, then went on, "And that brings us to some interrelated items. I believe Elliot was telling the truth, Pat, when he said that Hank had been padding expenses. It was never excessive, but it had been going on for some time. We checked with Elliot's predecessor, and he told us that was why he left, that he couldn't condone what Hank was doing. Elliot, however, went along with Hank quite willingly. But not because of any altruistic motive. There was going to be a quid pro quo. Elliot and his business partner wanted Elk Creek Elementary School closed, so they could buy the property for a housing development. Hank was to make this happen, to recommend it to the board. They also planned to buy and raze the adjacent trailer park, developing the whole as one parcel."

"It all fits," said Jerry. "Lord!"

"Well, you sniffed that one out with the 'star' connection, along with the scheme to get the near neighbors away. That must have been done early as a failsafe, should the need arise for a fire."

Jerry said, "Knowing Elliot, he would have covered all the contingencies in his meticulous way."

"And then," Pat put in, "when Hank changed his mind, in spite of Elliot, and decided to recommend the school board not close the school..."

Paul finished her sentence, "Elliot hired Burt."

"But Hank! What about Hank?" Pat asked, a worried look on her face.

"Here's where it gets sticky. It was known that Hank was gone for a few days right before the fire. We learned that in our first investigation. Now the question is, how was the district informed that he was out of town?"

"Let me see," Pat responded. "I remember Elliot told us that Hank said he'd be back in time for the board meeting."

"Well, I've been asking, and his secretary said she'd heard it from Elliot, and Francine said she had heard it from Elliot. Not from Hank before he left. Which was the usual practice."

Pat and Jerry were quiet. Holding our breath, Pat thought.

Paul continued, "My guess is that Hank and Elliot had an altercation about closing the school, which ended badly for Hank. After which Elliot let it be known that Hank was out of town." Paul sighed and said slowly, "I think we can assume Hank was killed at that time, either accidently or purposely."

They were silent for a few moments, taking in Paul's words.

"Although," Pat said sadly, "Hank could have committed suicide, perhaps even using Elliott's gun."

"And that's possible too," Paul agreed. "Remember, Elliot said he wouldn't take the blame because of someone else's problems. But I think Elliot drove Hank's car to the school and left it or had Burt drive it to the site. Hence the keys were found there."

"Oh, God," said Pat, tears starting to well up.

"Burt's death was probably an accident. Elliot referred to 'stupidity and carelessness.' But I think Hank's car was deliberately left to make it plausible that he might abandon it and disappear. Distraught. Filled with remorse. Whatever. Elliot didn't expect a body would be found in the school."

Paul paused a second or two, then went on, "The last thing Elliot started to say, that teaser, was 'Cross County keeps its secrets.' Well, if and when Cross County gives up the secret about Hank, Elliot's handgun could prove very important."

Jerry asked, "And Clarence? Did he meet with the same fate?"

"Carl gathered information for Clarence too. Clarence may have been a lush, but he was smart enough not to completely trust Elliot. Yes, Clarence." Paul looked serious. "If Elliot didn't know what happened to Clarence, he was probably very worried that Clarence would say something. If he did know, then it's uglier. That Elliot was apparently feeling such panic gives me hope that Clarence is alive."

Pat thought for a moment, and then said, "I don't think the panic was in regard to the whereabouts of Hank. I know Hank would have come forward long ago. Being in debt didn't alter the basic person he was, fudging expenses or not." Then she added in a softer tone, "Elliot. What a driven, troubled person you were."

"Still and all," Jerry admitted, "he did a very good job managing our financial affairs, and helping with the difficult problems that arise on the business side of a school district. Right up to the end, in fact, until he couldn't untangle his own messes. That he covered up for Hank was wrong, but it isn't that unusual for a business manager to be put in compromising positions. It would help explain the locked doors and his guarded attitude."

"That, along with a questionable real estate scheme," Paul reminded them. "Right now, we've no proof. Hank could have taken his own life; Elliot could be innocent of homicide."

"But not of arson," said Jerry.

At this point things seemed to be at a stalemate. Was there anything else, Paul asked, that Jerry or Pat could remember? Any little detail about Friday when everything came to a head?

"Only that I got sent on a wild goose chase," Jerry said with a groan.

Francine had discovered, crumpled up in Elliot's trash can, the note Pat had written giving the directions to the children's home. "Elliot simply tossed it," she told Jerry, "forgetting that on a home game night the custodians don't come in. It certainly wasn't the same as what he had me tell you, giving the whereabouts as being in the southern, not northern, end of the district."

Paul now looked at Jerry. "That cabin on Jacks Mountain Road," he said, "where you found yourself after being misled. I wonder: how would Elliot have known about that remote area of the county? To specifically direct you down there?

"I just remembered something," Jerry interjected suddenly. "My menacing friend with the shotgun made the statement, 'You ain't the first guy come up here in a fancy car.' Unfortunately, that's all he said. It just went by me at the time, but..."

Paul had risen to his feet and was making a hurried call. "Get some people up there right away," Pat and Jerry heard him say. "A black BMW. Late January, early February." When he was finished giving directions and instructions, he sat down and gave them one of his sad-eyed smiles. "Just maybe," he said. "Just maybe."

During the week, Jerry had spoken with his mother, asked if they could visit, and gotten an enthusiastic assent. He'd also arranged for them to stop at Cider Run to meet with Paul. There was always the possibility of Ruth being there. He decided Pat deserved to know about his past. He was wondering how best to broach it when, unwittingly, she beat him to it.

Towards the end of the week, with a relaxing of tensions, they were able to chat about other things. Pat had said, casually, "You know, Jerry, that first night when we were talking on your deck after dinner, you said something about being humbled for only the second time in your life. I didn't want to ask you then, but it was a rather dramatic statement."

"I haven't been evasive, Pat. We always got onto another subject, and filling in the gaps about my past was far less of the moment. But you're right; I've been meaning to dump my tiresome and lamentable history on you. Shall we? I'll try to keep it light."

She laughed. "No, not now. Just one thing. What was your other humbling experience?"

He took a deep breath. "The other time I felt humbled was twenty-two years ago when I held my newborn daughter."

"But that's lovely! And to be expected."

"Held her for the first and last time."

"Oh, Jerry, I am so sorry." She reached for his hand.

"It was the last time, but not because she didn't survive," he hastily clarified. "On the contrary, she has survived and thrived and graduated magna cum laud from an excellent college." He continued, "But I wasn't able to be part of her life, except financially. Her mother and I were not married and couldn't be. I was still married to my first wife."

It was a tale of a generation caught in the middle. His wife's parents had been in a concentration camp as children toward the end of World War II. Bergen-Belsen. After the war they emigrated, sponsored by a Jewish relief organization which the Strauss family endowed. Their daughter, close to the same age as Jerry, was born in the U.S. "It was always assumed we'd marry, so we did; we were practically raised together. After a few years, we knew it was a mistake. But as we were both starting careers, we just muddled on, not wanting to disappoint either of our parents. It was easier that way. Until I started working with Eric Arden. He encouraged me to get my Ph.D. and superintendent's credential." He also introduced Jerry to the woman who became the mother of his daughter.

"Ruth Arden," Pat murmured.

Jerry looked questioningly at her. "You knew...?"

"No. Elliot had some information from Celeste, and tried to use it. Go on, Jerry."

"Not much more to tell. My wife and I had been separated for years, but divorce seemed out of the question; she was sure her parents would have been devastated. We ultimately got a divorce after they'd passed away."

"And the baby?"

"Ruth developed preeclampsia, and the baby was delivered early by C-section. The baby was fine, but it was touch and go with Ruth for a while. We weren't sure she'd make it. We named the baby Ruth." Jerry took a moment to go on and Pat waited sympathetically. "The year before, Eric's wife had been pregnant herself with their third child. She miscarried. Ruth and I asked if they wanted to adopt little Ruthie, and they gratefully and lovingly took her. They raised her with their two daughters and, well, it couldn't have been better for her."

"Golly," said Pat. "Does your daughter know she's adopted? Have you met her? Do you know her?"

Jerry laughed, "Yes, golly, is right. She knows she's adopted. We decided to wait until she was out of college to tell her about her biological parents. I've seen her only from a distance. I went to graduations and performances. Eric has always kept me informed about her welfare. They are both doting parents."

"And her real mother?"

"She's the favorite aunt, and has been there while Ruthie was growing up."

Pat asked, not without some trepidation, "So you are still in contact with Ruth?"

"Is that what Elliot implied? No, and not for over ten years. Eric thinks it's time Ruthie met me. She's one smart cookie, and he's pretty sure she has figured out who her mother is. She doesn't know who her father is, though. Ruth and I need to talk about it, I know. Sometime. She and

I went our separate ways when I accepted my last position."
He made a distasteful face. "It came with a wealthy widow."

"Ah, the one with the gardener."

"And you're all caught up!" he exclaimed. "Celeste,
though," he went on more seriously, "sounds as if she knows
something. I wonder what?"

"Elliot said Celeste put two and two together when she
met you. Apparently, she's been around Eric's family."

"Two and two meaning?"

"Meaning, I guess, Ruthie takes after you."

"Poor kid."

"Jerry!"

Now, on the way to Martensdale, they talked about the
dinner party at Deems Barbecue they had planned for the
end of the month. It would be the twelve of them who had
ended up at The Pit that cataclysmic Friday evening. Pat
said, "It's going to be close to Halloween, so I can't wait to
see what Sally Ann will wear."

"You can ask her yourself in a few minutes. We're almost
there."

"Oh, no, Jerry," Pat exclaimed. "That would ruin the
surprise."

When they got out of the car in the parking lot at
Cider Run, Jerry took Pat over to look at the view of the
Appalachian ridgeline.

"It's beautiful and breathtaking," she said with an
appreciative sigh. "But, still, so almost tame, civilized even,
compared to Cross County, don't you think?"

"Maybe more manageable. Not that one couldn't still
run into an aggressive meth lab operator back in the hills."

"Willing to sell an early 19th century walnut game table
for $80," Pat said with shake of her head at Jerry's strange
misadventure.

"Speaking of which, shall I get it out of the Beast and we'll take it in? Owen said Hal's wife is eager to clean it up."

Before they reached the door of the shop, Paul came out, followed by Sally Ann. Jerry could see that Paul had something important he wanted to talk about, but Sally Ann's outfit got their immediate and full attention.

Sally Ann was togged out as "Rosie the Riveter," complete with a red polka-dot bandana tied in front around her hair, hair that was now a mass of dark brown curls. True to precedent, Sally Ann, excitedly welcoming Pat to the shop, was oblivious of the way she looked until Pat said, "And will you be doing some riveting?" indicating the outfit.

"Oh!" said Sally Ann, becoming aware of her overalls and work boots. "Come see my area! Veteran's Day is next month, so I've put in Home Front WWII. I have sheet music and everything!" And she swept Pat in the door.

Paul took Jerry aside and with an air of quiet satisfaction said, "Clarence has surfaced."

"I'll be damned!" exclaimed Jerry. "Where was he?"

"Holed up in a rehab facility over the border in West Virginia, under an assumed name, lying low. Scared out of his wits. Got him off the alcohol though, he said. He was even too scared to let his family know. The news that Elliot had been killed in an accident only got to him a day ago. We'll be interviewing him next week. I expect it will be very enlightening."

"How did you locate him?" Jerry asked.

"He contacted us. Said he had a lot to tell us. Carl was right, thinking Clarence didn't trust Elliot."

"I'll be damned," Jerry said again.

"I only talked with him briefly, but he said something that struck home. When he asked Elliot once what they would do if their scheme was interfered with, Elliot made a comment about Cross County keeping its secrets."

"Sounds familiar."

"And then went on to say, 'and the woods are deep in Cross County.' That's when Clarence decided to make himself scarce."

Jerry nodded, then looked questioningly at Paul, who obviously had more to say.

"Up near Jacks Mountain is where we found Hank. Took a while, but finally. One of those roads, not more than a trail. Off in heavy woods." He didn't want to keep Jerry in suspense, so went on at once, "Bullet in the back of the skull ..."

Jerry momentarily closed his eyes, picturing the deserted roads he'd driven up and their forbidding aspect. He felt a huge wave of horror and sadness, but also of relief. He'd tell Pat later, and she'd be relieved too, he knew.

"Thanks, Paul," he said, and they shook hands warmly.

Before Pat and Jerry left, they strolled over to have another gaze at the view, this time accompanied by Owen and Keith. While they were saying goodbye, a battered black pickup truck pulled in and parked. In its bed Owen could see a pinball machine, secured with a stout rope. "Hoo, boy!" he yelled and hurried to where Carl was standing with a small dented tin box.

Keith said, "By the way, Carl and I talked about it, and they have decided to donate the Parker to the Cross County Historical Society. That's where it belongs. He said his grandfather would 'like that fine.' If what he's got in that box there is what I think, Seth won't need funds from the sale of the gun."

Pat spoke up, "I'm so glad. My grandmother founded the historical society almost a hundred years ago."

As Keith went off to help Owen, Jerry commented, "You've given back to Cross County too, you know. Serving on the school board."

"Jerry," she said, fixing him with a searching look, "There's something I need to tell you. I've decided to make a run for the state legislature next year. I've been approached by the party's committee, and I've got backing and..." They walked to the car discussing the interesting possibilities ahead.

And we'll be together, thought Jerry. It's going to be better than all right with us. It's going to be wonderful.

Review Requested:
We'd like to know if you enjoyed the book. Please consider leaving a review on the platform from which you purchased the book.

CPSIA information can be obtained
at www.ICGtesting.com
Printed in the USA
BVHW071349170621
609230BV00001B/2